Honour the H⟨

still I live in hope to see
the holy ground once more

First Edition Design Publishing

Honour the Holy Ground
Copyright ©2014 James McKeon

ISBN 978-1622-876-27-3 PRINT
ISBN 978-1622-876-28-0 EBOOK

LCCN 2014940838

May 2014

Published and Distributed by
First Edition Design Publishing, Inc.
P.O. Box 20217, Sarasota, FL 34276-3217
www.firsteditiondesignpublishing.com

To
EOGHAN HARRIS
for his help and encouragement

Honour the Holy Ground

still I live in hope to see
the holy ground once more

James McKeon

Chapter One

Some of the congregation in the packed cathedral spilled out the back door and down the steps on to the gravelled yard. He stood at the back of the church alone. The window frame behind him rattled from the wind. He was tall, grey-haired and well-dressed; a conspicuous figure on the edge of the crowd. Memories flooded back; all the times he had served mass here as a nervous altar boy a lifetime ago; the weather-beaten bust of some old bishop still stood outside rusting in the corner of the yard; the marble pillars on either side of the iron gate where he'd once stood, freezing in his short pants, while his mother took his First Communion photograph.

The coffin shuffled up the aisle followed by mourners with their heads bowed. A veil of sadness hung over the congregation. They quietly blessed themselves murmuring hushed prayers. Slow bells tolled. The coffin was placed on the steps at the foot of the altar as the priest's voice echoed across the silence:

'Let us pray for the soul of our dearly beloved Steven Kennedy.'

The tall, grey-haired man shivered. Steven Kennedy, that was his name, too. He shared it with his nephew, the man in the coffin.

Steven Kennedy was born at home on 6 May 1940. It was a wet Monday. While war raged in Europe life in Ireland freewheeled along in blissful neutrality. The Kennedy family lived then at Railway Cottages, Kilbarry, Cork, in the south of the country. Their home overlooked the nearby train tracks. The baby was called Steven after his father. The parents were delighted but disappointed. The child was the fifth boy. They'd hoped for a girl. The cottage went with the father's job of linesman in the nearby train station. It was a miserable job. Cork city lay snug, tucked away, in a valley between two rivers. Often flooded, locals called it the Venice of Ireland. It was surrounded by hills; saucer-shaped, wet, loquacious and as intimate as any village.

Steven was a chubby little boy with a mop of curls and a face-full of freckles. Women constantly admired his curls. He hated them. Every time he sneaked into his mother's room and borrowed a scissors and cut one off, two seemed to grow. He was always on his own reading anything he could get his hands on; books on travel, space ships or brave explorers on a mission to the North Pole. His early life was filled with mythical heroes. These books fanned the flames of his imagination. By the time he could walk he'd developed an adventurous streak and often went rambling off on his own expedition with his mother worried about the danger of passing trains. She usually found him climbing anything, the higher the better, especially the ten-foot wall in front of the cottages. Hardly a day went by when she wouldn't be seen pleading with her little-boy-blue to come down for his dinner.

Looking back Steven vividly remembered standing by the kitchen door listening to the puff-puffing of the old steam trains farting and belching smoke like giant dragons as they clitter-clattered out of sight. The stale smell of the smoke still lingered in his nostrils. In his mind's eye he could still see his father, sucking a Woodbine, as he struggled over the wooden fence and waving goodbye before sliding down the earthen bank onto the edge of the railway tracks which ran behind their cottage. He watched him wait until a goods train, coughing and spluttering, laboured by and, with a noticeable limp, he hobbled across the tracks. Rheumatism, from years of wettings, had left its mark. This was his short cut to work every morning.

When Steven was three, he watched through the curtains of his bedroom window as a horse pulling a long cart drew up outside. The family were moving home. He had one last look at his wall. He knew even then he was going to miss it. Finally, the cart, laden down with tables, chairs, beds, rolls of lino, and packed tea-chests, and Steven perched on top, trundled down the hill, wound its way through the streets of Blackpool to the bottom of Fair Hill and up the bockety Well Lane until they arrived at Shamrock House, a farm house surrounded by an acre of nettles and sheds. The house was over a hundred years old, and looked it. Downstairs was one draughty room covered in red floor-tiles. There was an open fire always heaped high with logs. Nearby was a black hob. There was one other room downstairs. Although seriously damp there was a hint of grandeur about this room. It had a rickety table with a ping-pong net attached to it, and a small chandelier looking down on a worn carpet. A piano, which had seen better days, stood apologetically in the corner. Dozens of sheet music of old Irish melodies were stacked behind it covered in cobwebs; a spider's playground gathering dust. Outside, at the back of the house, stood a dilapidated toilet covered by sheets of corrugated tin. The inside toilet was a bucket on the upstairs landing.

Steven's grandfather lived in Shamrock House but since his wife died the family was uncomfortable with the idea of him living by himself. He was an old pro-British army veteran who had survived several battles from the Boer War to Khartoum and the First World War. He proudly drank his tea from a large chipped mug with a picture of the King of England embossed on it, and there were yellow photographs all over the house of him with army men in khaki shorts, posing under palm trees, with cricket bats and helmets, and jolly old fiddle sticks, and monkeys on their shoulders. During the burning of Cork City in the 1920 Troubles his allegiance to the Crown lessened a little. He tried to out the fire but British soldiers blew bullets up his arse and sent him scampering for his life.

Shamrock House and the surrounding area was an idyllic setting for a three-year-old boy; a jungle filled with mystery, oceans of muck, an apple tree, two pigs, an old mare named Napoleon and an Aladdin's cave of sheds. The Kennedys had the best of both worlds; the city was within walking distance yet the beauty of the countryside was at their doorstep; the undergrowth was teeming with rabbits, an occasional fox, and a lurking hawk could be seen circling the skies ready to swoop. When Steven's parents were out he sometimes struggled onto Napoleon's back and in his fantasy world saved damsels in distress and shot imaginary Indians with an imaginary gun. One day this old nag threw him into a forest of nettles. Not alone was he badly stung but he also broke his left leg. A twisting stream, the Glasheen, meandered along the edge of the quarry and sneaked behind the lane until it disappeared underground.

A cruel savagery lurked in the background which was deemed to be the norm: a captured cat would be thrown to a pack of dogs and onlookers cheered while it was torn to shreds; old dogs would be hung from nearby trees; and it wasn't confined to animals; a handicapped boy, convulsed in a fit, would continually bash his head against a wall until the frenzy subsided or he knocked himself unconscious. It frightened Steven to see the boy lying on the ground, froth on his mouth, his face covered in blood, at peace with the world, until the next fit. It also showed the cruelty of that time when it was accepted to see a horse being whipped unmercifully or a sealed bag of unwanted pups dumped in the stream. Yet, all through the summer, this innocuous stream was their Mecca. In their ignorance these boys knew nothing else. The stream was banked up with sods, and this was where everyone learned to swim. They didn't care about dead dogs, water rats or broken bottles.

This playground of Steven's youth conjured up a deluge of paradoxical memories: happiness, innocence, fleas, DDT and poverty. Well Lane was a dead-end; at the top was an old well covered with mud. Everyone was equal as they struggled to stay above the breadline. Steven's strongest memory growing up was utter poverty. He sometimes made a few pence by tackling up Napoleon to a cart and delivering bags of turf to some neighbours. The bags were bigger than himself and they were hosed down by the shady turf dealer to make them heavier. Yet, the lane was alive with colourful characters like Agoo Murphy who got his name from his pigeons. If one of them was reluctant to return to his loft he would imitate the pigeon's mating call by repeating 'agoo, agoo.' It worked every time but the name stuck.

Steven was the envy of his classmates as he rode to school on Napoleon. A nearby blacksmith looked after the old horse for him. He was a sturdy man with a club foot. He wore a leather apron; it glistened in the half-light, and Steven loved to watch him, drenched in sweat, lost in his work; the hiss of the sizzling steam when the steel shoe was placed in the water; the rhythmic beat of the hammer striking the anvil as he shaped the shoe to fit the hoof; the wheezing of the old bellows, the pungent smell while the red-hot shoe was being nailed on to the hoof.

Steven was completely ignorant when it came to the subject of sex. When he got an erection he didn't know what it was. He thought there was something wrong with him and he said three Hail Marys until it disappeared. His mother was full of old sayings to suit any situation. While serving dinner she'd say, *the fastest man gets the most.* If someone eat too much it was, *your eyes are bigger than your belly.* Her husband, Steven senior, was an easy-going man. He'd give you his last penny if he had it. This five foot seven colossus was built like the Mountains of Mourne, with huge bony hands and piercing blue eyes. He could pick up those heavy railway sleepers and throw them around like matchsticks. If Steven was on holidays from school he'd take him to work with him, the fifty-year-old man and the five year old boy. They'd walk the railway line together for miles, man-to-man, checking the tracks, all grown up. His father used to say he should always remember that, *in the face of trouble work the backbone, not the wishbone.* Steven didn't know what that meant. Although his father had a bad limp, he struggled to keep up with him. Sometimes the boy got tired and finished the journey home sitting straddled on his father's broad back.

Steven Kennedy, Senior, was from Ballina in the West of Ireland. He followed his father in to the Irish Railway. It was the done thing. He was transferred to Cork in the early thirties where he quickly settled down. His one great interest was boxing. He first noticed the two Murphy sisters at a boxing club dance. He danced them both regularly. Agnes was the prettier. Six months later he surprised everyone by announcing his engagement to Eleanor. They were married the following year and set up home in a cottage provided by his employer.

Eleanor Murphy was born in Shamrock House. In her teenage years she had little time for boyfriends. Her height seemed to put off boys; she was a tall brunette. When Stevie Kennedy came along she felt comfortable with him. Agnes emigrated to England, married a wealthy Yorkshire man and settled down in London. Her husband was killed in the bombing of London. After the war she sold the house and moved to Dublin where she bought an old hotel, invested in it and re-named it, the Emerald. She surprised everyone when she adopted a little girl, Molly. Her wealth may have influenced the adoption board to give a child to a widow. Agnes turned out to be a mystery woman.

Steven spent a lot of time at the seaside in Youghal with his father. Because of his job the train journey was free. He used to float on his back like a giant walrus with his son imagining he was sitting on a raft surrounded by sharks, escaping from a desert island. One day Steven tried to retrieve a ball from the sea. The tide was going out. He barely made it back and collapsed. Ever since, he feared the water.

Once in his life his father slapped him. He was going off to do some work and asked him to keep an eye on a sow who was expecting a litter of piglets. Steven got bored and started playing cowboys on the sow's back. He never saw his father coming in the side gate. He grabbed Steven, lifted him up high with his left hand, and gave him three slaps across the backside with his right hand. Nothing was said. He just led the sow away quietly. Steven limped to the sanctuary of the back shed where he sat alone crying in the darkness, not from the pain of the blows but from the fact that he'd let his father down.

He was never sure if his friends were genuine. He had an apple tree in the garden. Apples were always available to visitors. In Well Lane there was great faith in the Church and belief in God. When the feast of Corpus Christi came along the women would get buckets of water from the well and scrub every inch of the lane on their hands and knees in preparation for the passing procession. One day a girl in the lane got married. As she walked down to the church she stopped at her friend's house, borrowed her wedding ring, and carried on to the church for the ceremony. A flock of children trailed in her wake to the church gates. She got married, walked back with her husband, returned the ring to her friend, and had a knees-up in her little house. They were such practical times.

For the Kennedy family Friday was pay day. The children waited for their father to come home from work. Eventually he'd make his grand entrance, his face black from the dust of the job. He'd place a small box of chocolates on the table. As there were seven of them they all got two chocolates each. It was heaven. He then gave them their wages according to their ages. Steven's was six pence. He felt like a millionaire. Since his first visit to the movies he was hooked. He was a tiny four-year-old when he was sneaked in under the shawl of Lizzie Maloney from the top of the lane. He still remembered the film - *The Fighting Sullivans*. Now he was all grown up, ten years old, with his own money.

This *Lido* cinema was a glorified flea pit. It had no toilet. People went where they were and nobody cared. It cost three pence to get in but a jam jar was also accepted as payment. Glass was scarce in post-war Cork and the local jam factory paid the cinema three pence for each jar. The cinema was jammed every night.

There were wooden seats.

It was noisy.

It was filthy.

It was a wonderland to those children. They were bewitched, transported to the American Wild West, the jungles of darkest Africa or to the far-off North Pole. With their hearts in their mouths they could witness Tarzan wrestling with a deadly crocodile; the crocodile didn't stand a chance, the Durango Kid or Hopalong Cassidy could out-shoot a tribe of Cherokee Indians, or Captain Marvel take on the evil Emperor Ming as he tried to take over the galaxy. How the audience laughed at the antics of Laurel and Hardy and the Three Stooges. Those boys didn't just watch these films. They lived every second of them with passion, cheering if the hero won, warning him if he was in any danger and booing at the villain. For years Steven and his pals lived for Friday nights. He had Youghal for the summer but he had Friday night the whole year round.

Christmas was special, visiting church cribs, and snow; it always seemed to snow. Nothing was expected, anything was welcome. He knew Christmas had arrived when the tree appeared in the front room, just a plain tree his father had chopped down, stuck in a bucket of sand and plonked in the corner. A red candle was placed in the window and lit by the youngest in the family. Christmas was on its way. Steven felt a sense of wonder as he walked up Well Lane with each window overflowing with colour, in its own individual way, flittering in the blackness of the night.

The school was an old building. Education was basic. It could be rough at times, fights were common. Steven had a variety of teachers. Some were kind while others were brutal. One teacher held a weekly examination every Friday and he gave a prize to the winner. Steven won it most weeks. That teacher set the first seeds of learning in his soul. He even had his star pupil up in front of the class acting out scenes from Shakespeare. The school put on a production of *Julius Caesar*. Steven played *Brutus*. He also played the lead in *The Playboy of the Western World.* He was encouraged to write and one day he handed the teacher his first attempt at a poem.

'Boy with pliers, Electric wires, Blue flashes, Boy ashes.'

The teacher laughed out loud.

'It's not Shakespeare,' he said.

Steven was beginning to discover girls but he wasn't sure what to do with them. Every Sunday night there was a dance run by the nuns in the convent hall. His pals, Dave Cotter and Pat O'Callaghan went regularly and when they met Steven they bombarded him with tall stories of their sexual conquests and all the times they were French-kissing and doing 'it.' He really didn't know what 'it' was and wondered what he was missing. He decided to take the plunge. He trimmed his curls with a scissors and had one last look in the mirror; yes, he was ready for action. When he arrived they were out on the dance floor in a frenzy of rock and roll. A strong smell of alcohol hung like a cloud over Dave and Pat. Pat was shy like himself but Dave was a cock-eyed optimist. He'd chance anything. They had a flagon of cider stowed away for the occasion. Full of Dutch courage they were out for every dance. But lurking in the background was a frightening deterrent; a posse of nuns, each one armed with a twelve-inch ruler. They were determined that the sweating bodies remained the required one foot apart. This rule was set in cement. Any male breaking this rule was shown the door. At nine o'clock there was a fifteen-minute interval where a decade of the Rosary was recited. As the congregation prayed a thought struck Steven. As he looked over at Dave Cotter lost in prayer he wondered what his friend was really praying for. Knowing Dave, he was praying to God for French-kisses and 'it'. After the dance Steven made his way up Fair Hill alone. He sat on a wall near his home. He'd been at his first dance, disappointing. Life was strange. Dave and Pat were half-drunk and were out dancing and laughing all night. He was sober and eager yet every time he asked a girl to dance that night she refused him or walked away giving some excuse.

'No, I'm sweating, ask my sister.'

He couldn't make out what he was doing wrong. As he walked home the stars shivered in the black sky. They seemed to wink and mock him. That night he lay in bed, frail and vulnerable, his head filled with lonesome thoughts, until the tears came and sent him to sleep.

Early that summer Steven felt that all was not well with his parents. His father was now only able to work part-time because of the rheumatism in

his leg. Steven was lying on the bed listening to the commentary of a match on the radio. He'd noticed it for the past month, the whispered conversations from his parents' bedroom and whenever he entered the kitchen they immediately indulged in mundane small talk. There was a knock on his door.

It was his mother.

'Are you there, Steven?'

He turned off the radio as she entered the room followed by his father, the remains of a dying Woodbine stuck to his lower lip. It struck Steven how different they were, she was a tall, serious woman, the opposite of her husband who was of broader build and light-hearted by nature. They both sat on the bed facing him.

'Steven, we have something to tell you,' she said.

His heart skipped a beat. He waited for the bad news.

'Would you like to live in Dublin; in the big smoke?' his father said. The Woodbine bobbed up and down as he spoke. His wife sighed and looked at him, a gentle rebuke in her eyes.

'Son, for the past six months we've been finding it hard to make ends meet. The seven of you are growing by the day and you can't half eat. I'm not complaining. It would be worse if you were sick.'

She paused again, clasping both hands together and continued.

'We feel it would be better if you went and lived with your aunt in Dublin for a while.'

'Your Aunt Agnes asked especially for you,' his father said. 'I know she's a bit eccentric but behind it all she's mad about you.'

His mother glanced at her husband. Agnes was her sister.

'Your father's right,' she said. 'She's expecting you next Saturday. So then, what do you think, son?'

'It's all a bit sudden.'

'You'll be like a toff,' his father said. 'Look at the big matches you'll see in Dalymount and Croke Park, and all the shows in the Theatre Royal.'

His father's enthusiasm always amused Steven. Their job done, they left him to dwell on their conversation. Steven lay back on the bed bandaged in his own thoughts. In the few times he'd met his Aunt Agnes they didn't get on. Dublin was no stranger to him. He'd travelled up to matches with his father a few times. There was no work in Cork, just a few dead-end jobs. Like most of Ireland it was caught up in the post-war depression of the mid-fifties. He got one week's work in the railway as a trainee linesman. Every day he walked for miles in all kinds of weather. It was boring. The wages were poor. He'd also worked for a few weeks as a messenger boy in a grocery shop on the North Main Street. It was a soul-destroying job. He spent hours roaming the posh hills of far-off

Montenotte trying to find houses so that he could stuff a half-pound of sausages through the letter-box.

A shaft of sunlight, overflowing with countless dust particles, blazed in through his bedroom window. He could hear the squeals from the football match taking place below him. The dusty pitch was now like a desert storm; a rough patch tattooed by the sun. His bedroom door opened and young sister, Marie, stuck her head in. She was small and pretty with a mop of brown curls. She was his favourite. He lifted her up and she hugged him tightly. Marie was very special and very spoiled. To the delight of his parents she arrived after five boys.

'Are you going away, Steven?'

'Only for a little while, buttercup. I'm not going very far.

She tightened her grip around his neck and started to sob to herself.

'I'm surprised at you; all these tears at your age,' he said.

'Why do you have to go to Dublin?'

'I'll explain when you're bigger.'

'Can I come with you?' she said.

He sat her on his lap.

'You're a big girl now and you must look after your mam.'

'I heard mam say that Auntie Agnes has bags of money. Will you come back with loads of money and bring me to the pictures and the circus and buy me sweets and toffee apples?'

He'd always felt that Marie should be on stage. She was a natural.

It was Saturday morning. He was alone with his parents; his father limping around the kitchen, puffing on his Woodbine, and his mother fussing over everything and nothing. She kept looking at the clock. It was time to go. Steven went to the bedroom to collect his case. He had one last look around the room: the patched-up quilt, the worn lino on the wooden floor, the yellow ceiling paper falling down in the corner by the wardrobe, the dull, green wallpaper which seemed to be there forever, the small, cracked mirror on the back of the door, the net curtains across the window, and the picture of the Sacred Heart hanging from a rusty nail on the wall facing the bed, with the ever-flickering red light which seemed to be staring back and winking goodbye to him. He felt his father's hand on his shoulder.

'If you miss the train, son, your mother will have a seizure.'

He walked to the station flanked by his parents. Not much was said. He boarded the Cork to Dublin train, placed his case on the rack, and leaned out the carriage door to say awkward goodbyes. His father shook his hand and nearly crushed it. His mother kissed him on the cheek. For the first time he noticed the strands of grey in her hair. A uniformed railway man waved his green flag at the engine driver. The train hissed, spluttered up black phlegm, and coughed into life. The acrid smell of smoke was everywhere as the train picked up speed. He gave one final wave and pulled up the window to keep out the smoke. At last he was alone, a stranger in a carriage of strangers. For some time he hardly looked up from his feet but, after a while, he settled down and began to relax. His fellow passengers were a priest who was reading a newspaper, an old lady who knitted non-stop, and a farmer who looked out the window at the fields. The train stopped at Mallow and a big, hefty woman came into their carriage, sat down, and nearly flattened Steven. He was pinned to the corner. After a while she produced a greasy crubeen from her bag, removed her teeth, and started munching away with utter pleasure. When she finished she licked her lips. The bones went back into her handbag and the teeth went back into her mouth and she leaned back like a contented cat. Steven could hear and smell a series of long hissing farts. He was trapped. Luckily the window was open. After going through Thurles the clickety-clack of the wheels on the tracks helped him doze off for over an hour. The heat of the sun through the glass eventually woke him up. The heavy woman was gone so he could relax a little but he was sweating. His face was hot. He realised that the train had already slowed down. The priest, who had been engrossed in the crossword since they'd passed Kildare, began to fold his newspaper. The lady stopped knitting and stuffed the wool into her canvas hold-all. She stood up and stretched.

'We're here, the big smoke,' she said to no one.

Steven took his case down from the rack and yawned. The train snaked its way between the backs of a long line of smoke-stained houses, disused warehouses, and an array of discarded old carriages, rotting and rusty, which reminded him of deserted cattle carcasses he'd seen in some long-forgotten western. Groups of young boys, who were playing in the back gardens, waved to the passengers. He could see tall buildings in the distance. The train weaved through a labyrinth of tracks and pulled in to Kingsbridge Station and shuddered to a halt. He stepped onto the platform only to be swallowed up in a sea of frantic activity. He was nearly knocked off his feet as he made his way towards the exit. Porters rushed to and fro, laden down with baggage, and a queue of empty buses, their engines revving, waited at the front gate. He decided to stand under the clock trying to make himself conspicuous. After a few moments he saw his aunt coming towards him. She was wearing a full-length, fur coat. It struck him that this was unusual on such a fine day. Her daughter, Molly, was trailing in her wake. Agnes shook his hand and looked him up and down.

'Come on. There's a taxi waiting.'

He followed her to the black cab parked outside the main gate and sat in the back seat with Molly. Her red hair was tied up at the back in a ponytail. She was seventeen, a year older than him. As the cab eased through the traffic he realised that it had been four years since he'd seen Agnes. She was much heavier, her hair was shorter and she wore more jewellery than he remembered: pearl earrings, a gold watch and necklace, and several rings which glistened in the sunlight. They passed by the Guinness barges and the Four Courts and made their way down the quays to the city centre. He chatted cheerfully with Molly. Her blue eyes sparkled. They had always got on well. She sat close to him and he was conscious of the warmth of her thigh against his. The cab turned off Pearse Street and into Westland Row. Agnes sat in the front seat stroking her pet corgi, Binky. Steven took an instant dislike to Binky.

'Pull in here, driver,' Agnes said.

The driver stopped outside the Emerald Hotel across the road from the train station. The Emerald was a small hotel, twenty-seven bedrooms, Its clientele were from the West of Ireland because of the nearby terminus from Connaught. Agnes was a tough taskmaster, a different personality to Steven's mother. She hired the best chefs and waiters, paid good wages and demanded the best. Molly showed him to his room. She sat on the bed and talked while he unpacked. She had just started college and had a flat near the university but she stayed in her old room some weekends to help out in the hotel especially when there was a big match in town. Steven was jealous; her own boss in her own house, able to come and go when she liked. He wondered if it would suit him. He was brought up in a packed house filled with noise and no secrets. It didn't take him long to find out that his stay in Dublin was not going to be a holiday.

At nine o'clock on Monday morning Agnes summoned Steven to her office. Binky sat in the corner watching every move. It was a small room filled with smoke. Agnes was sitting behind a desk smoking a cigar and writing in a ledger. She stopped writing, stubbed out her cigar, and spoke with a hoarse voice:

'You met Jim and Donal last night; the three of you work as a team. You'll meet the rest of the staff later. Your hours are eight to eight Monday to Saturday with a break between two and six every day. You'll work wherever you are required; waiting in the restaurant or washing up in the kitchen. You'll receive two pounds a week. A week's training starts from now.'

She picked up the phone.

'Tell Peg I want her in my office right now.'

She lit another cigar, stood up, and walked around him like an officer inspecting a recruit. She was broad-shouldered and of average height. An attractive woman entered the office. She had a friendly face and a warm smile.

'You wanted me?' she said.

'This is my nephew, Steven. I want you to introduce him to Lillie. Then take him out and get a new shirt and a pair of shoes. Sandals don't look well on a waiter. By the way, Steven, at seven-thirty every morning bring me a pot of coffee to my bedroom.'

From the start he hit it off with Peg Coogan. She was friendly and helpful to everyone. He enquired about Molly but she had gone back to her flat. That first day flew by, at times he was rushed off his feet, but the day was over before he knew it. He was just about to go upstairs to his room when Agnes appeared with Binky on a lead.

'One small favour,' she said. 'Walk him around the block, up past College Green, and back around Pearse Street? The poor thing is in all day.'

He set off up Westland Row. Suddenly Binky bit the back of his leg. He let out a yell and gave the dog a kick up the backside. Binky let out a bigger yelp and tried to bite him again. He dodged him this time and continued to limp around College Green. When they finally arrived back the hotel he released Binky from the lead and the dog scampered towards Agnes' bedroom. Steven put a plaster on his leg and went upstairs. Jim O'Reilly and Donal Purcell laughed when he told them about the dog. They too had their problems with Binky. They were both from the West of Ireland; Jim, aged fifteen, from Mayo, was short and slim with brown curly hair; Donal, nearly eighteen, from Spiddal in Galway, was tall and handsome with black hair. He stood by the mirror combing his hair and straightening his tie. It was an attic room with a skylight, three single beds and a wardrobe. The words of the song 'Stardust' were hanging on the wall. Donal went off dancing and left the two boys sitting on their beds. Jim, who had a similar background to Steven, was working at the Emerald for twelve months but Donal was there three years. Jim invited him to go to the cinema but he decided to have an early night. Jim was from the village of Cong and he saw the *The Quiet Man* being filmed there. Several of the locals had bit parts. One day, he spoke to John Wayne and Maureen O'Hara. They were buying a newspaper in a shop. All the men followed Maureen O'Hara around the village. He remembered her red hair blowing in the wind. As Steven lay in bed all the clanking and puffing and wheezing of the nearby trains reminded him of home. He was here only two days and he missed his parents, Marie and the mangel field. He wondered would he ever see home again?

The clanging of the alarm clock woke him at seven o'clock. It took him a few seconds to find his bearings in the darkness. He'd put the clock on the far-off wardrobe so he'd have to get out of bed to stop it. The noise had no effect on his two snoring friends. He made his way down the stairs to the kitchen. It took a while for his eyes to get used to the brightness of the kitchen. A plump woman dressed in white was busy over a steaming pan.

'I'm Cookie McGann. You can call me Betty. You must be Steven. Peg told me about you.'

She handed him a tray.

'Coffee for the boss.'

He took the tray, went carefully back up the stairs, and knocked on her door. Agnes was sitting up in bed with Peg lying beside her. A growling Binky stuck his head out under the clothes at the foot of the bed. Peg quickly took the tray, yawned and thanked him. He closed the door and went back to his bedroom. He saw nothing wrong with seeing two women in the one bed. He shared his bed with his two brothers, and he remembered the O'Mahoneys in Well Lane who had eighteen children. They hadn't a bed; six of the girls shared a mattress on the ground in one room, and nobody thought there was anything wrong with that. It took him almost a year to realise there was a relationship between Peg and his aunt. He soon found that Agnes had one more quirk; she kept a weighing - scales in the kitchen and insisted that he weighed himself before and after his dinner every day.

He got more and more used to the work and a pattern was developing. For his four-hour break he'd put on a T-shirt and sandals and walk up to Stephen's Green. At first he watched the local teenagers playing football but he was delighted when he was asked him to join in. On Friday he had his first run-in with Agnes. He was due in the kitchen with Betty at six o'clock. He arrived ready for work at ten to six in his T-shirt and sandals. Not realising that after running around the park for two hours his face and feet were covered in dust and there were sweat marks on his T-shirt. Agnes was not happy.

She roared at him.

'Where the hell do you think you are? Get up to the bathroom quick and wash yourself, and take off those sandals and that stinking T-shirt. You're like a long string of misery. This isn't some dive in the wilds of County Cork. This is a hotel in the city of Dublin.'

This dispute may have been their first but it wouldn't be their last. Like a time-bomb all the ingredients were there; a dogged authoritarian and a young country boy. When he finished work he escaped to his bedroom. A quiet knock interrupted him and Molly stuck her head in the door.

'Are you decent? A little bird told me you've been fighting with my poor mother again.'

Steven shrugged his shoulders.

'Do you fancy a walk around the Green? This time without Binky or I'll bring you somewhere I know you'll like,' she said.

'Anything would be better than hanging around here getting the height of abuse for scratching my arse the wrong way or looking crooked at your mother.'

Molly knew that Peggy was a special friend. Agnes was a strict woman but she'd been a generous mother. She took Steven's hand and led him down the length of Pearse Street, through O'Connell Street past the GPO until they arrived at a grey building. He saw the sign over the door - Gate Theatre. He had read about MacLiammóir and Edwards' theatre, the opposite to the Abbey's reputation for Irish plays. Molly spent most of her time here when she wasn't in college. Backstage was a madhouse of noise with several young people hammering and sawing and painting the flat sheets of a stage set. Molly introduced him to everyone and she explained that this was for their next production. He was invited to come along and help whenever he wished. As they walked back to the Emerald Molly linked him. It felt so natural. He saw her to her bedroom. As he left she kissed him on the cheek. The door suddenly opened and Agnes stood there with a face like thunder. Molly protested.

'Mum, this is my room. Please, at least knock.'

'Stay away from him,' Agnes said.

'If you want to blame anyone then blame me,' Molly said.

'You, get out,' Agnes said, pointing at Steven.

He left quickly and as he hurried down the stairs he could hear the noise of raised voices. Alone in his room he decided to write his first letter home. There wasn't a lot of news so he kept it short and finished by telling of his row with Agnes. He included a postal order for a pound to his mother and a note for Marie and went to the office to find out the location of the nearest post box. His aunt asked him for the letter. She tore it open, read it out loud, and handed it back to him.

'I insist on reading every letter before you post it.'

'That's not fair.'

'Take it or leave it. Two small changes and then you can post it. You mentioned our row. Delete that, and change the start to 'Dear dad and mam, not Dear mam and dad. When you do that give me the letter and I'll post it. one more thing; stay away from Molly. She's out of bounds'

She handed back the letter and he went to his bedroom to rewrite it. He couldn't understand why she made him change the start. Did she think his father had married beneath himself? Had she something against her sister? He gave her back the letter. She read it and posted it. He was aware that Molly was nowhere to be seen.

Chapter Two

Looking back, Steven could now see clearly where his stars had dimmed and where they had blazed. Many dims, few blazes. He tried to hide it but he was still nervous in the company of girls. Like the night when Donal had tried to blood him sexually when he was not ready, was still a virgin. Like most Irishmen of his time he was still devoted to another virgin, the Blessed Virgin, Mother of Perpetual Succour, to which his mother made novenas and prayed for his soul, and the souls of her family.

That night in the *Monument* café off Burgh Quay, two girls had walked in and sat tentatively at the next table, clearly not accustomed to what passed for café society in Dublin, or to its prices. They whispered over the menus, digging in their purses, dredging for silver.

Donal winked at the older one, who had smeared Woolworths' cheapest lipstick too heavily because the stains were visible on her teeth when she smiled back shyly.

'What do you think, Steven?'

'About what?'

'Are you up for it?'

'Up for what?'

Donal shook his head in despair.

'For Christ sake, Steven, where did you come from - Outer Mongolia? Are you game for a jump, a ride, sexual fucking intercourse?'

Steven didn't know what to say. He wanted to run out the door. But then having found the meagre menu still too dear for them the girls had saved him by leaving with heads low. Donal watched them go, gave Steven another glare and got up.

'I'm going back to the hotel.'

Donal strode to the door leaving Steven to catch up. They turned up their collars. It was cold outside; too cold for the scantily dressed girl leaning against the wall of Burgh Quay below O'Connell Bridge. But shivering she still winked at Donal. He stopped and smiled without warmth.

'Hello, sweetheart. How are things?'

'Could be better. Are you interested?'

'Not right now; some other time.'

'What about your friend here. I'm very reasonable,' she said.

'You'd be the death of him,' Donal said.

Without another word he turned his back on her and hurried Steven along towards D'Olier Street. Steven looked back, then gave him what he hoped would look like a man of the world dig in the arm.

'She's a nice girl. Is she a friend of yours?'

'Never saw her before.'

'She seemed to know you.'

'She's friendly with everyone. She's a brasser. She sells sex. Women pay me for a ride. Come on Rudolf fucking Valentino? We're late.'

Agnes continued to rule with an iron fist. As the weeks went by there was no let-up. She left Steven get away with nothing. This Sunday he was rushing off to a football match. On his way out he decided to use the toilet; it was a long walk to Croke Park. As he left the toilet Agnes passed by, had a quick look in, and bellowed after him.

'Steven, come back here at once.'

She pointed in the bowl with one hand. She grabbed his hair with the other, stuffed it down the bowl, and flushed the toilet.

'Always flush the toilet after using it.'

He stood there embarrassed, not knowing what to do. In his hurry he'd forgotten. She strode off back to her office. He made his way to his bedroom to dry his hair and eyes. There was a light knock on the door. Molly stuck her head in. Her eyes were full of mischief.

'Meet me around the corner in two minutes.'

He tidied himself up, had a quick look in the mirror, and sneaked out the back door. She was there waiting. She linked his arm and they scurried off. She explained that Agnes was watching her like a hawk. Steven admitted that he felt the same. They turned off Harcourt Street where Molly opened the door to the side entrance of a house. She led him up the stairs. It was a converted attic with varnished beams across the ceiling; a cozy room with two single beds, a gas cooker and a radio. She showed him around

'What do you think?'

'It's lovely. It must be strange living by yourself.'

'I share it with Rita, a friend from college.'

'There were five of us in one room,' he laughed.

She liked it when he laughed. They had tea and toast and marmalade and he told her all about Shamrock House and Railway Cottages and she laughed when he told her about the noise from the trains. She turned on the radio and Fats Domino singing 'Blueberry Hill' filled the room. She took his hand and asked him to dance. They shuffled around the small room as one, an unlikely couple, the tall country boy and the petite city girl. When the song finished she kissed him.

'Agnes will have a search party out looking for me,' he said.

They kissed again and she watched him disappear into the night. He was light-headed with happiness as he hurried back to the hotel and felt as if he could put his hand up and play with the stars.

Steven enjoyed his nights in with Jim and Donal, and the privacy of their bedroom; three men against the establishment, in their own little world. Some nights they'd talk about where they came from, where they were going and where they'd be in ten years' time. Jim had simple expectations. He loved the western films especially John Wayne. All he wanted was to play football for Galway and be married to a nice girl in a nice house. When pressed, Steven said he dreamed of being in a play in Broadway. In his spare time he'd like to climb Mount Everest, conquer the North Pole and sail the seven seas.

Donal couldn't contain himself.

'Corkie here wants to sail the seven seas. He'd get sea-sick if he crossed O'Connell Bridge.'

Steven admitted that Donal was right. When pressed about his own aspirations Donal paused for a moment, his mind miles away.

'In ten years' time I'll be married to a middle-aged Yank, a millionairess, dripping in dollars, living in a mansion in Miami. I'll service her twice a day to keep her happy and spend my time on the yacht sipping champagne with a dozen young maidens at my beck and call.'

They'd all laugh, have a cup of tea and play cards but Steven enjoyed the talk about their silly dreams, girls and sex. Donal was a self-appointed expert on all these adult subjects. One night things got out of hand. When Donal came in there was a smell of alcohol from his breath. He was laughing at everything they said. He pulled out an old copy of *Titbits* from his inside pocket. His cousin posted it on to him from London. Donal made sure the door was locked. When he turned over to page three it was the first time Steven laid eyes on a topless female. They studied it from different angles. Donal even turned it upside down.

'What a pair of knockers? They're massive.'

A wide-eyed Jim put on his glasses and had a closer look.

'They remind me of Christmas, big balloons and plum pudding.'

Donal put his finger to his lips in a gesture for silence and took out a bottle of sherry from under his bed. He filled the three cups on the table, made a toast to the women of Ireland, drank the sherry, and refilled his cup. He handed a cup to each of them.

'Here's to the fair sex; ride 'em, cowboy; down the hatch.'

They sipped apprehensively as Donal had another and filled their cups again. It was sweet and strong. It reminded Steven of his mother's perfume. Donal spent most of the night boasting about his conquests; one-night-stands, bored housewives who longed for a little love, naïve girls who travelled to Dublin looking for a husband. Donal insisted that he was providing a national service. He finished the bottle and threw his arms around Jim.

'What about you, red Romeo? I bet you're a bit of a lad in Mayo.'

'I come from a place called Cong. I've never been out with a girl.'

Donal found this hilarious.

'A fifteen year old virgin; when I was fifteen I had a dozen notches on my weapon. They used to call me the Spiddal stallion. And what about you, Corkie?'

Steven wouldn't let Donal get the better of him.

'Women, where I come from, they're a dime a dozen.'

'I'd say you were never out with a woman in your life.'

'I stopped counting after twenty-one.'

Donal was taking the bait.

'You wouldn't know your thumb from your langer.'

Steven was enjoying this.

'I'd say you're full of old piss and wind. I don't know could you rise to the occasion at all?'

Donal's face flushed. He stood up on two shaky legs, opened his trousers and took out his erect penis with his hand.

'I'll give you "rise to the occasion.' Would you like to get a slap of that across the back of your fucking neck?'

Steven and Jim sprang from their beds and ran out the door. They hid in the empty kitchen for over an hour. When they returned to the bedroom Donal was lying on his bed snoring. Next morning Steven was working in the kitchen. He'd have hated doing waiter service with Donal. They met during their break at two o'clock. Steven was the first to apologise for questioning Donal's manhood and Donal reciprocated by promising to keep his lip and his zip closed.

Chapter Three

Steven had grown very fond of Peg. He was jealous when he saw her in bed with Agnes every morning. Some nights when Jim and Donal were out she'd pop upstairs for a chat. Peggy was in her late thirties from Castlebar and had worked in the hotel twelve years. She knew he was homesick. Agnes had been hard on him but she wouldn't have a bad word said against her. When he sneaked off to Stephen's Green Peg would secretly let him out the back door. This was their little secret. When Agnes was giving him a dressing down Peg would step in and take her elsewhere with some made-up excuse.

Agnes played poker with her well-off women friends on Sunday afternoons. These card games took place in her guest room which had red carpet and a golden chandelier. If the weather was wet he was sometimes allowed watch from a far-off corner. They drank wine and Agnes smoked her cigar but what really caught his eye was the amount of money they played for, huge bundles of notes, and it didn't seem to matter if they won or lost. Binky sat under the table on guard duty. The one aspect of these games which annoyed him was the derogatory way they treated Lillie the waitress. Agnes continually referred to her as 'tits.' He didn't understand this but every time she said it there was a chorus of laughter from the women.

It was Christmas before he knew it, his first Christmas away from home. He was lonely. To make it worse, the hotel closed for two days and Donal and Jim went home for a short holiday. Peg surprised him, sticking her head in the door and telling him he was wanted on the phone. He rushed down, his heart in his mouth, but it was his mother just wishing him a happy Christmas. She was phoning from Uncle Tim's shop in Shandon Street and Steven really got homesick when he heard the nearby steeple bells ring out. The bad weather kept him in and he passed the time by reading about faraway places and listening to the little radio in his bedroom. Sometimes he just lay on the bed and in his mind's eye he could see the darkness of Well Lane, each glittering window, a barking dog, a passing drunk staggering by, singing to himself, the Sheehan house on the left by the old well, the sharp turn past the mangel field on the right, through the old gate to Shamrock House, up the muddy path and past the apple tree, the big red candle flickering in the window and the laughter, the waves of laughter. He could feel it; he could almost hear it and as he lay there in the darkness quiet tears petered down his face and the silence hung like a shroud in the bedroom.

Aunt Agnes bought him a new pair of Wellington boots and a raincoat for Christmas so he wouldn't get wet on his walks with Binky. Peg gave him a book of short stories. Lillie brought him in to the Capitol cinema to see *The Ten Commandments* on St Stephen's Day. Although he was engrossed in the grandeur of the film his mind kept dwelling back to Well Lane. His pals would have been finished their singing by now and he could se them counting the takings. Would it be the Savoy or Ritz in town or would it be the runners-up prize of the nearby Lido? Lillie's elbow nudged him back to reality. She put her arm around him and kissed him on the cheek. She was lonely too. She missed Sligo. The darkness covered his red face. His body enjoyed her closeness and he noticed for the first time her heaving breasts. He couldn't concentrate on the rest of the film as he began to wonder if his Aunt Agnes' description of her meant what he thought it meant.

He never thought he'd see the day when he'd be glad to see Donal O'Reilly but it cheered him up when he breezed in the bedroom door late that night. He wore a woollen jumper with pink reindeers on the front. Steven stared at it and couldn't keep in the laughing.

'Did you get sunglasses with that?'

'The ma got it for me for Christmas,' Donal said. 'Well, how's your love life?'

'I went to the pictures with Lillie today.'

'Serious. Jesus, she has a massive pair of...'

'I know,' Steven said. 'I suppose you left half the female population of Spiddal crying at the bus station?'

'Only a dozen saw me off. I must be losing it.'

Donal put his hand inside his jacket pocket, took out a package wrapped in Christmas paper, and gave it to him. It was a present from Galway via Soho. He flicked it open. In the centre there was a full-length nude woman in a suggestive pose. He noticed several smudge marks on the pages. Donal insisted that he felt it necessary to act as a stand-in customs officer and research the product to ensure that the present was up to scratch. Donal lifted the lino on the floor under the bed and hid it. He had a feeling Agnes checked the room when they were out. An hour later Jim arrived from Mayo and the three of them talked and swopped stories late into the night.

Steven regularly went to the Gate and helped out backstage. He got on well with Mr. Edwards and MacLiammoir, the founders of the theatre. Molly had been telling them about him. He couldn't be kept away from Stephen's Green. When Molly had no lecture she'd meet him there in a quiet corner. Agnes was getting suspicious when he wore his shoes and good shirt going to the Green. She regularly banned him. When this happened he'd escape to the back yard in his sandals and he'd kick the ball off the wall for hours on end. This got him into trouble with Agnes. She caught him one day and frogmarched him to the bathroom where she pulled off his sandals without opening them, grabbed his ankles, one by one, lifted them up high, stuck them in the sink, and washed his feet.

'When I say no football I mean no football.'

For months now he felt Agnes was waiting to pounce. Some nights he wondered and worried about his mother. How could she be so different from her sister? He felt like a prisoner. He couldn't tell his mother by post. He was tempted to send a secret letter but he was afraid of being sent back home, an unwanted burden. The one consolation was Molly. Her encouragement kept him sane. And life would have been unbearable without Peg. She hovered in the background helping him, protecting him, watching over him like an older sister. She seemed to understand everything and could almost read his mind. One night after she'd read a story to him they talked for a while. Just as she was leaving he stopped her.

'Peg, do you know when I'm big, when I'm a man, if I ever have a serious girlfriend, I hope she'll be exactly like you.'

Peg stopped in her tracks and tears rolled down her cheeks. She looked at him and hurried out the door. He lay there confused, wondering what he'd said to upset her. He remained on a collision course with Agnes. She called him a stubborn little Cork pest. But Peg was his saviour, his guardian angel.

Before he knew it was his seventeenth birthday. Cookie McGann made him a red and white cake, the Cork colours. Lillie bought him a bottle of after-shave lotion. He even got a card from Marie, Agnes bought him a pair of black, leather shoes and Peg gave him his first watch. He felt all grown up and kept looking at his hand all day, but the best was yet to come. He was in his bedroom, trying on his shoes, when Peg told him he was wanted in the office. He couldn't think of anything he'd done wrong as he knocked on the door and entered. He couldn't believe it; there was his father all dressed up in a suit and that eternal Woodbine in his mouth.

'Dad, what are you doing up here?'

'Is that a Dublin accent you have there? I said I'd get the early train up to wish you a happy birthday. How are you?'

He caught his aunt's eye.

'I'm fine. I have lots of new friends. They'll be playing football now in Stephen's Green. I could introduce you.'

He noticed the look of disapproval in Agnes' face.

'You get ready. I'll be with you in a minute.' his father said.

Steven ran to his bedroom, put on his sandals, and when he returned his father and Agnes were at the front door, heads in a cloud of smoke, chalk and cheese, in animated conversation. He was worried why his father had appeared in Dublin. Was there something wrong at home? His leg was as bad as ever as they talked and laughed and limped all the way up to the Green. A group of young boys were caught up in a noisy game of football. Further away some older boys were playing cricket.

'You're looking well, son. You've put on a bit of weight.'

'Agnes weighs me before and after every meal.'

'She can be eccentric,' his father said.

He gave his son an envelope and wished him a happy birthday. It contained a wooden half-moon pendant, one side round, the other jagged, on a silver chain.

'It's not much. My father gave it to me when I was your age.'

Steven placed it around his neck. He sat in silence for a while.

'Is everything alright at home, dad?'

His father finished his cigarette. He had one last lingering pull on it.

'Things have been worse and things have been better.'

There was another long silence.

'How long will I be here?' Steven said. 'Am I ever going to go home?'

'I wish I could tell you but I don't know.'

'I don't get on with Auntie Agnes. Did she tell you?'

His father lit another Woodbine.

'She's a tough woman. She was always different. Try and hang in there.'

His father explained that they were getting by. He now had a watchman's job in a factory on the Commons Road. Pat was going to London to work and Brian had joined the post office.

'Dad, I have a steady girlfriend.'

His father's face lit up.

'Is she a Dublin girl? When can I meet her?'

'You met her. Her name is Molly.'

'Is that Agnes' little girl? Does Agnes know?'

'She's suspicious,' his son said. 'She's warned me off several times.'

'For once I agree with her,' he said. 'You have enough on your mind.'

Even with all his brave talk of friends and Molly and the Gate the father could see the sadness in his son's eyes. As the boy was on duty at six they had to hurry back to the hotel, and his father had a train to catch. It was time to go; the taxi was waiting. Suddenly he grabbed his father in a flood of tears.

'Can I go back home with you, dad?' he begged. 'I won't be in anyone's way. I promise; I'll get a job. I'll do anything. I'll get two jobs.'

His father shushed him into silence.

'It won't be long more. We'd be lost without your money. You'll be back home soon. Your mam misses you and she sends her love'

He turned quickly and was gone, limping out the door. Steven made his way slowly up the stairs to his bedroom. He found a red package sticking out beneath the pillow. He opened it to find a book on the history of Cork theatre. On the inside page was a card in the shape of a heart with a scribbled message: *A little bit of Cork on this special day. Tons of love. Molly*

Chapter Four

Los Angeles was in the middle of a heat-wave. It was late Saturday night. Two men stood outside the large oak door. They looked at each other but never spoke. Both of them hated this part of their job. The doorbell rang. Jeff Bradley was at home alone looking at television. He had a strange sense of foreboding as he opened the door. The two men stood there, tall in dark clothing. Nothing was said. They showed him their badges. He asked if they would like to come in. They avoided eye contact. The older of the two asked Jeff to sit down.

'Mister Bradley?'

'Yes.'

'I have bad news for you. Your son, Jeffrey, has been involved in a car accident. I'm sorry but I'm afraid he's dead.'

Jeff Bradley was president of Bradley Advertising. He was one of the wealthiest men in California. He had everything; a successful business, a beautiful home in Santa Monica, apartments in New York and London, a devoted wife and two daughters at Stanford University. He sat alone in his darkened room crying. In his hand was a framed photograph of his late son, Jeffrey. The boy had crashed in his father's car. They said it was a freak accident. An oncoming lorry skidded across the road. Three weeks had passed and Jeff still hadn't come to terms with his only son's death. He was still bitter, frustrated and angry; angry at the world, at God and at himself. A half-empty bottle of scotch stood on the nearby table and glared back at him. He looked at his watch. It was almost 9.30 am. It had been another sleepless night. All the plans for his son to follow in his footsteps and take over the business were shattered, snuffed out in a split second. Life was perfect, too perfect. Jeff found it difficult to cope and still couldn't forgive himself for loaning the car to his son. He ran his fingers through his hair and emptied his glass in one gulp before slamming it on the table with a vengeance.

'Why? Why? Why?'

The room door quietly opened. It was his wife, Susan. She switched on the light, drew back the curtains, and sat next to him on the sofa. She took the photograph from him and put it face down on the coffee table.

'Jeff, come on down and have some breakfast.'

'I don't want any.'

She took his hand in hers and said nothing for a moment.

'If only I...,' his voice trailed off.

'We can do nothing about it. He was my son, too,' she whispered.

He noticed the red around her eyes.

'I'm sorry, Susan. I have been selfish, haven't I.'

He got up and paced around the room while his wife looked on. He stopped suddenly, as if he'd come to a decision, picked up the phone and dialled a number.

'Martha, give me Richard, please...Hi, Jeff here. How's the Maginley account?... Good. Look, Richard, I owe you big-time. Do you fancy a bite to eat? See you at noon. We have a lot to talk about. The usual place...I'm fine, thanks.'

He disappeared through the bathroom door. After a long shower he felt better. The pounding jet of warm water cleared his head and seemed to wash away the pain. As he shaved he closely examined his face. It had got thinner. The lines under his eyes were more noticeable and his hair was now much greyer around the temples. He glanced at his naked body in the full-length mirror. It was firm and slim, tanned from the California sun, in good shape for a fifty-eight year old. The agency had its own gymnasium and employees were encouraged to use it. Jeff was a great believe that a healthy body meant a healthy mind. He worked out twice a week and tried to get in a round of golf with a potential client whenever possible. The relaxed atmosphere of a golf course often helped to clinch a business deal. While dressing he mentally reprimanded himself for having wallowed in self-pity. It made him realise yet again that Susan was the rock in their marriage. He promised to make it up to her. As he entered the kitchen he could smell the bacon and eggs. Susan put down the newspaper and poured his coffee. She loved watching her husband as he ate.

'What time will you be home?' she asked.

'I must meet a few people, including Richard, and I'd like to nail down the timber company account. Hopefully, before seven.'

Several beeps of a car horn could be heard from outside.

'That's Charlie. I gave him a buzz,' she said.

'I'll be off then. Any plans now for the day,' he said.

'I'll pick a few flowers and drive out to the grave.'

Charlie Grainger was practically one of the family. He was a big, friendly black Texan. Although he never spoke about it he'd distinguished himself in the Korean War. He was with the Bradleys for four years now, initially as a gardener but he could turn his hand to anything. Driving was one of his loves. He'd never married and lived happily in the two-bedroom cottage on the Bradley estate.

The dark green Mercedes was half-way into their journey to downtown Los Angeles. Although he enjoyed working around the flowers in the garden Charlie preferred driving into the city for two reasons: one, his day went quickly by and, secondly, he had his eye on a girl who worked in the library and it gave him a chance to work up the courage to ask her out. Although he had witnessed many atrocities in the war Charlie was still shocked by Jeffrey's death. He'd witnessed slaughter, survived hell and worse, in Korea and came out the other side all in one piece. Then Jeffrey, a fine young man with the world at his feet, had his life snuffed out in a freak accident. Charlie gave him secret driving lessons when his parents were away. They went to baseball games together and had shooting practice in the make-shift court behind Charlie's cottage.

The Mercedes turned in to Sunset Boulevard. They were nearly there. Charlie knew Jeff only too well; his mood swings, when he wanted quietness to mull over a business problem, or when he wished to discuss something using Charlie as a sounding board. A glance in the rear-view mirror told him that his boss looked like a man who had a lot on his mind.

'That's fine here, Charlie. The walk will do me good. Give me a shout about six,' he said, striding down the Boulevard to his favourite café, *Oscar's*

Jeff Bradley sat in the corner by the window and watched the world go by in a blur of impatient colour. His business adversaries had always considered him a lucky man. Everything he touched, every venture, seemed to turn to dollars. He was born in Bakersfield, Southern California, an only child to well-off, Catholic parents. He was a determined student and he left Berkeley University with an excellent Master in Business Administration degree and went back home for a year to work in his father's insurance business. This gave him valuable work experience especially when dealing with people but it was not for him. He went back to Berkeley and joined an advertising agency. For the next five years he was embroiled in the helter-skelter of the advertising world and revelled in its cutthroat unpredictability. He loved his job. The struggle to meet deadlines sent the adrenaline pounding. He shot up the ladder of success but it was an old-world company and wary of change. They found that this brilliant young businessman was going too far and too fast for comfort. He made a lot of money for the firm but at the end of his fifth year the relationship between the eager youngster and his superiors had grown increasingly static. Reluctantly they agreed that it would be best if the parted company.

Jeff Bradley took the plunge. With the help of his parents he started his own advertising company. It was small but inventive. It was different and exciting. At times he shocked post-war America with his brash ideas. For ten years success followed success. The press called him the golden boy and labelled him California's most eligible bachelor. His enemies called him 'Midas' behind his back. He had a few brief romantic liaisons but he hadn't time for a serious relationship. Both of his parents had died; he lived alone in an empty house and, at times, he longed for the happiness of the family environment of his own youth.

Then it happened.

Then he saw her.

He was guest speaker at a boring awards night. She was sitting alone in a corner like nobody's child. She caught him looking at her and smiled. He later made discreet enquiries about her. She was Susan Kelly with an Irish background. He laughed when he discovered that she was a secretary with his main rival in the advertising world. He was head-over-heels in love at thirty-four years of age. His mother would have liked that. He whisked her off her feet. Four months later they were married in a quiet ceremony at Lancaster Sacred Heart church. The marriage was blessed with two baby girls in three years, Louise and Mary, both blonde, both beautiful. There was only one thing missing in his life. He longed for a son. Then one night he arrived home from work. Susan filled two glasses of wine. She handed him a glass and raised her own.

'Congratulations, Mister Bradley. I'm pregnant.'

Jeffrey Bradley was born in the lap of luxury in a private nursing home in Santa Monica. The baby was called Jeffrey after his father. The parents had two daughters and they'd longed for a boy. The child's mother laughed when her husband promised that he wouldn't spoil his son. She insisted that he be treated exactly like his two sisters, nothing special. She found herself being deliberately strict with him to make sure he wasn't spoiled. But Jeffrey wound his father round his little finger. They went to basketball games together, always the best seats. Jeff would arrange a meeting with the star players after the game. They went camping in the mountains, fishing and climbing, father and son, man to man. When he was on holidays Jeff would bring the youngster to work with him and allow him to soak up the mechanics of the agency. He would sit in on meetings with the creative team. The boy was fascinated at how a concept was hatched, developed and finalised. Someday he'd take over the business. Susan Bradley was proud of her three children. She couldn't be happier as she fussed over them like a mother hen. Louise and Marie were inseparable and Jeffry was tall and blond with a mop of curls and an adventurous streak.

Susan's parents were from the Coombe in Dublin. They were caught up in the late 1920's slump in Ireland. Dublin was still suffering from the battering the city took during the 1916 Rising and the aftermath of the Civil War. Her father was a window cleaner with no windows to clean. Most people left for Liverpool or London. The Kelly family took the plunge. It was brave decision with four children; California, the land of milk and honey. The journey by sea was dreadful; they were sick all the way. At first the heat nearly killed them but they settled down and they fell in love with California and the American way of life.

Jeffrey Bradley followed in his father's footsteps by enrolling in the Haas School of Business at Berkeley. He settled in quickly and loved the freedom of college life. In no time he looked forward to his first weekend with his family. His mother was anxious to hear all her son's college gossip. They were always close. As he was back home Jeffrey decided to check up on an old girlfriend. His father loaned him his car.

Richard Steinman strode into *Oscar's* cafe. He was a thickset man, in his late forties, bald with heavy glasses. He rarely smiled. His one weakness was fishing. He spent many a weekend with Jeff fishing Lake Irvine in Orange County. Even then he constantly talked shop. To him business was a serious business and he liked to get things done yesterday. Richard was Jeff's right-hand man. When it came to advertising he was a genius. He shook hands and sat down, glad to see his old friend again. They hadn't met since the funeral.

'Hello, Jeff. Great to see you back. Sorry about...'

'Life can be a bastard, but we'll have to get on with it. What's happening. Any problems?'

'No, we're nicely ticking over. We can pick and choose our customers. I'd like to talk about the possibility of expanding.'

Jeff had also been thinking along these lines. Both men ordered a salad and talked shop while they ate; the opening of another company in San Francisco or San Diego was high on the agenda. Business was booming. Money was available. They finished up and walked the short distance to work. Jeff felt good to be back in harness. At five he asked the staff to gather in the outer office.

'You are not just my workmates. I am proud to call you my friends. I want to let you in on a little secret. The company may be opening up elsewhere.'

There was a notable murmur all round. Jeff continued.

'If and when we move it will mean several promotions. This may take a year when I'll be stepping down and Richard will be taking over. By the way, you'll all find a bonus in your pay-packets this week. Thanks.'

Chapter Five

It was the hottest June in Dublin for decades. One Saturday Steven was eager to visit the beach in Dollymount Strand during his break. He had no swimming shorts but Agnes quickly solved that problem. She dug up her old one-piece outfit, stowed away in the bowels of her wardrobe. It was mouldy. When he appeared in this costume everyone went into convulsions of laughter. It was made up of dozens of little elastic squares but Agnes rolled down the top and tucked it inside the lower section to make it look like a man's shorts. It was very bulky around his midriff. Off he strolled up Pearse Street and on his way to the beach. The strand was crowded but he found a quiet corner where he enjoyed the sun. All was well until he had a dip in the sea. Disaster struck. It was a struggle to hold the wet, bulky costume up. He could hardly walk and when it was time to go he flopped all the way back to the hotel. He fought a losing battle; it was like a tractor tyre around his middle. It kept slipping down and he had to stop and heave it back up again. He squelched along leaving a water trail behind him. There was now a crowd of children following behind him. He tried to run but he was slipping in his bare feet. He couldn't escape with the weight of the costume. At last he came to Westland Row and dived in the side door of the Emerald. He quickly changed into his clothes. Agnes came in and told him to take the dog for a walk. That was the last straw.

She couldn't believe it when he refused.

'I said take Binky for a walk.'

'And I said "no".'

She slapped him across the face, told him that the dog was waiting in her bedroom, and walked out leaving the door wide open.

All through that summer he felt trapped between the tension with Agnes and his fear of doing anything that would affect his parents' situation. His father had lost his watchman's job. He was unable to walk the mile to the Commons Road factory. Peg assured Steven that things always worked themselves out. He was seeing more of Molly; all cloak and dagger and secret rendezvous. They met in the Green, under Nelson's Pillar, and in her flat but mainly at the Gate. With her encouragement, he auditioned for *Cherry Orchard.* He got the part of *Pyotr*, the student in the Chekhov play, and received good reviews for the fortnight's run. By now he had told Donal and Jim about his romance. They liked Molly and enjoyed working with her. Donal pestered Steven. He had one thing on his mind - their sex life.

How far had he gone?

When and where?

How many times?

Donal and Jim were up to all kinds of antics arranging dates and excuses for the couple. Agnes never trusted any of them. The Gate's next project was an Easter production of *The Wild Duck* by Ibsen. Steven played the part of *Gregers* and again the reviews were fine. But, now there were nightly whispers about an oncoming controversial production in the Gate. It was the talk of Dublin.

Steven had a quiet celebration for his eighteenth birthday. He worried about his future. Where was his relationship with Molly going? Her background was still a blank. She couldn't trace her parents. She did find out that she was born in England. Everything else about her was a mystery. She was busy with exams but dropped by and gave him a present of a Cladagh ring. He couldn't wear it. Agnes would not approve. She was a tough woman. She preferred the dog to him. Donal woke in the bed next to him noisily snorting and coughing.

He slapped Steven on the back.

'Congrats and all that shite. At last you're a man. It's official. You can vote and drink and fart and ride all round you, not that you don't already.'

Donal winked and yawned and farted and went back to sleep.

Hilton Edwards sat at his desk and watched Michael MacLiammoir pacing up and down their office at the back of the Gate Theatre.

'To hell with the begrudgers, Michael. Let's do it for the month of August. Dublin will be teeming with tourists. The Yanks will love it.'

'But that's Abbey stuff, Hilton. We started the Gate to get away from the Abbey. Now you want to do *The Playboy of the Western World*. Half the country would be talking about us.'

Hilton smiled at his partner.

'It would be worse if they weren't talking about us. I'd love to knock the cobwebs off the playboy.'

Michael had a mischievous look on his face.

'We were always different.'

'I've always liked Synge, Hilton. His dialogue has great colour; *She's about on the cnuceen seeking the nanny goats the way she'd have a sup of goat's milk for to colour my tea.* Now there's a great line, pure poetry. It flows off the tongue.'.

'Michael, my dear boy, why do I feel you're up to something. Your two eyes are dancing an Irish jig in your head.'

.Hilton took a sheet of paper from his pocket.

'I've cast it with our own people. The only problem is the Playboy. He's vital and I don't want to go outside the theatre to cast him.'

Michael studied the list.

'None of these will let us down. Why not Steve Kennedy? I believe he's played the part before. I have a feeling he'd make a great Playboy.' .

'There's a big difference between doing the Playboy in the Gate Theatre in Dublin and a convent hall in Cork,' Hilton said.

'At least give the boy an audition,' Michael said.

The two friends looked at each other and they burst out laughing like two happy schoolboys. Hilton was enjoying this.

'I want Dublin's shiterati to get a smack in the gob when we announce this. We are going to be slaughtered by the media for our choice of play. Do a reading with Steven. If you feel he's ok give him and Pegeen Mike an early script to work on.'

As the two men left the office Michael put his hand on his partner's shoulder.

'Hilton, my dear boy, why do I have the distinct feeling that you like to stir the you-know-what?'

The following night Steven and Molly were called in to the office of the Gate. MacLiammoir asked both to sit down and handed Steven a script.

'Our next production will be *The Playboy of the Western World.*

Steven was surprised.

'But, sir, I thought the Gate didn't...,'

Michael raised his hand in silence.

'I'd like you to read the Playboy from the top of page twelve. Molly, will you read Pegeen Mike like a good girl? Off you go in your own time.'

Steven opened the script and cleared his throat. They read that scene until Michael stopped them.

'Well done, young man, you almost have the character. I must talk to Hilton but I recommend you for the part of the Playboy. It's a major challenge.'

'I always liked a challenge, sir. When do I start?'

'We hope to run for the month of August. When it comes to theatre Dublin is a bitch. Molly, could help Steven with his lines and I'd like you to do the part of Sara Tansey. Hilton is directing and I'm playing Old Mahon, your father.'

Steven usually walked her to the bus stop and they went their separate ways but he insisted on seeing her to her flat. Her friend, Rita, was gone home for a few days. Steven looked worried.

'Am I taking on too much, Molly?'

'You did it before. You'll be fine.'

'I did, in the oratory hall, directed by Sister Majella. She was a demon. After her the Gate should be a doddle.'

'Steven, you can stay the night if you want to.'

'I'd like nothing better but your mother will be waiting at the door with a shotgun. I'd like to stay some night when the time is right.'

She held him close for a moment before he disappeared down the stairs. She lay awake for hours. She had never met anyone like Steven. He'd never been rude or made a pass at her. Some nights she wished he did. Her mind dwelled on what it would be like to have sex with him. She smiled at the situation in college where she was bombarded with sexual invitations and lewd remarks on a daily basis. She laughed at the irony that the one person she longed to touch her, hold her, sleep with her, was also alone in his bed. She wondered what he meant when he said, 'when the time is right.'

The following month was gruelling. Every chance Steven got he rehearsed with Pegeen Mike behind closed doors. Molly looked on as MacLiammoir read all the other parts and Hilton directed them. At times he showed touches of genius. He had a real turf fire and added specially written Irish music to heighten the drama and to freshen the play. He didn't rush Steven into the part but he allowed it to grow on him. By now he was Christy Mahon. He found himself mumbling lines as he worked in the kitchen and people gave him funny looks as he walked around Dublin talking to himself. There was great excitement at the dress rehearsal. Hilton invited a friendly audience for the performance to add some realism to the occasion. It got a deserved standing ovation but Steven knew he'd made several mistakes. When the audience had left and the theatre was empty Hilton summoned the cast and crew on to the stage. They shuffled in and sat, scattered in silent apprehension. Hilton commented on the merits of each individual performance. There were some hiccups but that's what rehearsals are for. He reminded them that he would be worried if the rehearsal was perfect.

'Just remember who you are and what you are doing at all times. Tomorrow night the fun begins.'

There was a round of applause and everyone left the stage in a babble of conversation. After changing and hanging up his costume Steven walked Molly to the bus stop. They decided to have an early night. Steven was tired and went straight to bed.

He lay there in the darkness exhausted. It had been hectic week. Everybody helped him. Jim stepped in and took over the task of walking Binky. Peg kept him going and Molly lived in his shadow. Agnes had mixed feelings about all the commotion. She was irritated with photographers snapping Steven as he waited on tables. There was a huge media interest in Steven.

Where did he come from?

What was his background?

The press pestered him for interviews and his photograph was all over the papers. He dozed off to sleep knowing full well that if he didn't come up to scratch on opening night these very same papers would slaughter him.

The following night he arrived at the theatre two hours early. There was a card from his parents and Marie and a huge card in the shape of a shamrock from Dave Cronin, Tom Murphy and Pat O'Callaghan. He laughed when he saw it signed *The Well Lane Mafia*. He got ready and read the script concentrating on his own lines. Before he knew it there was a ten minute call. Everyone was tense. Everyone was excited; a cloud of expectation tinged with fear hung over backstage. The murmur of the audience sliced through the tension. Hilton and Michael hugged each other and both shook Steven's hand. Nothing was said. It was time. Steven took a deep breath. When the lights came up on the set, a country pub with old barrels as seats and a fire spitting smoke, there was a thunderous round of applause. Pegeen Mike sat at the table writing a letter. The sound of soft violins crept around the theatre humming a gentle tune followed by dramatic rumblings of a bodhrán. The audience's reaction was instant. The hair stood on the back of Molly's neck as she waited in the corner backstage watching Steven. She wouldn't be on stage until the second act. She stayed away from him. He had enough to think about; who he was and what he was doing. She couldn't keep her eyes off him. She was fascinated, hypnotised. Normally he stood tall and walked with a long stride from all the years of walking up and down Fair Hill but he seemed to change before her eyes. He slowly became Christy Mahon, hunched down, a bedraggled young traveller with short apologetic steps. She hardly knew him. She felt for him and prayed for him and loved him. MacLiammoir's exploded on to the stage. There was an audible gasp of expectation. Head covered in blood and bandages, Old Mahon's confrontation with his wayward son was a riveting scene; the learner and the master crossing theatrical swords but Steven gave as good as he got. The cast and crew were engrossed in their own job. Before they knew it Pegeen Mike was pulling her shawl over her head and lamenting the immortal words:

'I've lost him surely. I've lost the only Playboy of the Western World.'

It was over.

There was a brief, deafening silence, a nervous, collective holding of breath. Then the audience got to their feet unified in appreciation. The cast stood as one, arms linked in a line. Steven was centre-stage flanked by Pegeen Mike and Michael MacLiammoir. He felt light-headed, drained, and relieved. He was surrounded by friends yet he felt alone and home sick. He escaped the later razzmatazz and quietly walked Molly to the bus stop. He reminded her how well she did; with her sparkling blue eyes and her red hair she was a perfect Sara Tansey.

Next morning he was detailed to work in the kitchen. He was glad of the privacy. Peg called in to show him the newspaper reaction. The Independent praised the Gate for their bravery and Hilton Edwards for his exciting direction. The Irish Times was glowing in its praise and picked out Steven as giving, *the Playboy a new lease of life with a fresh and raw performance.* He cut out the reviews to show to his parents. Donal, who was on waiting duty upstairs that day, stuck his head in the kitchen door and went down on one knee with a cigarette box in his hand.

'Please, sir, I'm only a humble servant.

Could I have your autograph?'

Just as quickly he disappeared laughing. Steven and Molly had no time to themselves. He had work and she had college and, at night, they barely had time to say hello.

At the Gate Hilton was like a general preparing his army; always lurking in the background quietly watching, coaxing, observing the mood of the actors, keeping an eye on his team, ready to stifle any sign of over confidence. Every night before the show he took Steven aside and reminded him to take nothing for granted and to treat every night like the opening night. It was a relief to be off on Sundays. Steven and Molly made it their special day. They'd go to the cinema, visit a café, stroll up to the zoo or just sit in the corner of the Green. He wore his Claddagh ring when he was with her. They talked about their future. She had one more year in college. What would she do then? What would they do then?

For Jeff Bradley it had been an emotional day, his last day as a working man. Bradley Advertising had been his baby, his pride, his joy and, after thirty-five years, it was to give up the habit of a lifetime. He was 59 years old; time to go. He'd promised Susan; one more year. For the last few weeks Richard was practically running the business. They'd made meticulous plans for this day. The two of them had looked at possible locations especially Sacramento and San Francisco but Richard's advice was New York. The money was there. New York was back on its feet. When it came to the dollar Manhattan was the centre of the universe. Jeff surprised Susan when he arrived home that night.

'Do you fancy a trip around the world, Susan? We could hit Broadway and catch *West Side Story,* then hop over to see *My Fair Lady* in the West End and maybe call in to see your cousins in Ireland and kiss the Blarney Stone. You're going to be so fed up with seeing your husband's ugly mug every minute of every day you'll wish to God he'd go straight back to work. Start packing your bags, woman.'

'But if Mary and Louise call who'll look after them? And what about the house?'

'They are two young women well able to look after themselves and Charlie will keep an eye on the house.'

'I have nothing to wear,' she said.

Susan had two wall-to-wall wardrobes packed with clothes, half of them new and never worn.

'We'll get the midday flight to New York tomorrow,' he said. 'I must check something first, then I'm all yours.'

New York was buzzing. Jeff wanted to walk the streets, smell the smells, the Bronx, Chinatown, Fifth Avenue, Times Square, and hear the noise that was New York. He had an appointment with the owner of a disused factory on Seventh Avenue not far from Central Park. He'd inspected the site before with Richard. They were ready to move. The owner badly needed money and Jeff was in a position to pay him cash in 24 hours. It was given a structural all-clear. The contract was signed. Jeff rang Richard with the news and set off to meet Susan at the apartment. The holiday began. They ate too much, drank too much wine and did the tourist trail; Broadway, Empire State Building, Statue of Liberty. After ten days they were exhausted from New York and decided they could recover in the more sedate surroundings of London. It was Susan's first visit. They went on a barge down the Thames, a picnic in Hyde Park and a stroll down Oxford Street. To Susan a visit to Harrods was a must. She felt like a little girl in a chocolate factory. After a week they flew to Shannon Airport. Jeff hired a car and they drove to Killarney to see the lakes. He parked the car and they walked around the town. The easy-going attitude was like a different planet to New York. They stopped at a pub for a coffee. It was as if they stepped back in to the last century.

A turf fire.

Ceili music.

Irish dancing.

No radio.

No television.

There was just singing and plenty of talk. They stopped a passing jarvey and climbed aboard his horse and cart and took a tour of the Lakes of Killarney. Jeff couldn't believe it: no traffic, no people, no noise, just the shimmering lakes set against the eerie silence of the dark mountains.

The next day they drove to Cork to kiss the Blarney Stone. After struggling up the countless steps to the top of the castle they were held practically upside down to kiss the famous stone. Tradition stated that this gave them the gift of the gab. Next stop was Dublin, the capital of Ireland. This was Susan's first time back to her home town. Jeff hoped to see a play in the Abbey Theatre. They booked into the Gresham Hotel. Next morning they walked across O'Connell Street to the GPO where the rebels had fought a losing battle against the might of the British army before being shelled into submission. Then they made their way to Trinity College to see the Book of Kells. They could almost feel the ghosts of Bram Stoker, Oliver Goldsmith, Jonathon Swift, Samuel Beckett, Robert Emmet and Oscar Wilde, all of whom had once been students here. At last they arrived at the Coombe. Susan wondered if anyone would remember her family. It seemed different now from all her childhood memories. They had lunch in a nearby café called *The Shillelagh* and headed off to the Abbey Theatre. Sadly, the building had been destroyed by fire a few years previously. He'd been looking forward to seeing a play there. Their last port of call was the Gate Theatre. When he turned the corner of Parnell Street across from the Gate he could hardly believe his eyes. They were showing a play he was so familiar with, *The Playboy of the Western World*. This play had made headlines all over the world. There were riots on opening night in the Abbey Theatre. On its first appearance in New York vegetables and stink bombs were thrown at the cast. During the Philadelphia performance the company was arrested and charged with putting on an immoral play. He was delighted to get two tickets for the Thursday night performance.

Every night Steven prepared for the show the same way. He liked to arrive at the theatre early and put on his costume. This helped him get into character. Then he'd find a quiet corner where he would go over his lines. The month had flown; three nights to go. What was he going to do when it finished on Saturday? Hilton gave him a thumbs-up. The rustle of the audience could be heard outside. Suddenly there was a death-like silence. The violins were electrifying; they split the air like a medieval war-cry. There was a knot in his stomach. The sound of the bodhráns thundered to a crescendo. Steven blessed himself. This was it.

Susan and Jeff had seats just a few rows from the front. There was a buzz of conversation in the theatre. It was packed. The Gresham Hotel was only ten minutes away but they'd left early. They wanted to visit a pub on the way. Jeff sampled his first pint of Guinness surrounded by smoke, heated conversations, all going on at the one time, two men playing darts, and a pensioner in the corner singing 'Molly Malone' off key. Jeff loved it. Why hadn't they something like this in California?

As the soft lights brought the stage to life Susan and Jeff were mesmerised. They settled back in anticipation but when Steven made his entrance they froze in their seats. They were transfixed as if they'd seen a ghost. Susan stifled a scream and clung on to Jeff. The colour disappeared from her face. The actor playing Christy Mahon just feet away from her was a twin of her dead son. They held out until the interval and made for the street outside for fresh air. Jeff opened the crumpled programme to see the actor was Steven Kennedy, nineteen years of age, the same age as his son.

'I can't go back in,' Susan said.

Jeff put his arm gently around his wife.

'I've never seen anything like it. I could do with a drink.'

They went back to their hotel bar. Jeff ordered a large whiskey. Susan, who rarely drank, asked for a gin. They stayed on in the bar until closing. Bed and sleep was the last thing on their minds. The next morning they were still uncertain. Eventually they decided to see the play again and this time they would stay until the end. Jeff wanted a walk to clear his head. The fresh breeze along the bank of the Liffey was welcome. When they arrived at the Gate Theatre box-office they found Friday night was sold out but they managed to get tickets for the last performance on Saturday night.

Steven and Molly met at six pm on Saturday at the Pillar Café around the corner from the theatre. Molly took his hand

'I hardly saw you for the last month, except on stage.'

'I didn't know whether I was coming or going.'

'I thought you were gone off me.'

'Molly, from tomorrow on you'll have to beat me off with a stick.'

'We'll see about that.'

At the theatre Hilton reminded everyone not to relax until the final curtain. It was another riveting night. Jeff and Susan had eyes for only one person. Jeff made an instant decision. It was time to take the bull by the horns. After the show there was a party backstage. Guinness was flowing. Steven got a message that he was wanted at the stage door. He hurried out, dreading that it was bad news. He was surprised to find it was two strangers. Jeff asked him to meet them in the Gresham Hotel the following morning. There was something about the couple and Steven agreed to see them at eleven am. Steven and Molly left the party to a howl of good-natured banter and caught a bus to her apartment. He insisted on seeing her home. She was a chatter-box. He was very quiet. She had seen him like this before and she knew there was something bothering him. Was he leaving the Emerald? Was he going back to Cork? When they got to her apartment he didn't say much. She knew there was something on his mind. He sat her on the bed and told her he had something very important to tell her. Now she was worried. Was he breaking it off. He looked so serious.

'I'm not great at talking, Molly. I've seen many beautiful things; the August sun going down in a red haze near the bog at Glasheen Stream, the full moon perched over the snow-covered Fair Hill at Christmas, clutches of early daffodils dancing in the April wind in the woods behind the house, but I've never seen anything or anyone as beautiful as you. Molly, will you marry me?'

He took a ring out of his pocket. She burst into tears and threw her arms around his neck, kissing him all over his face. She held him at arm's length, laughing, drying her tears, and shaking her head.

'Steven Kennedy, for fuck sake, I know you're not great at talking, but, sweet Jesus, you frightened the life out of me. Of course I'll marry you.'

His hand shook as he put the ring, with two small diamonds, on her finger. It was slightly loose.

'I've been saving for months.'

'What about my mum?'

'We'll face her together. She'll have to know sooner or later, and I'll write and tell my parents tomorrow.'

She asked him to stay but he knew Agnes would be waiting. They made their plans for Sunday. He kissed her and told her that maybe the time was right tomorrow night. At the door he held her hand.

'Life wouldn't be worth living without you.'

He was gone. She looked forward to tomorrow night. She kept twisting the loose ring on her finger and repeating 'Mrs Molly Kennedy' over and over again until sleep found her. She liked the sound of it.

Steven made his way through the foyer of the Gresham Hotel on Sunday morning. He spotted Susan and Jeff sitting at a table for three. Jeff stood and asked him to join them. After some small-talk Jeff cleared his throat.

'I have some explaining to do. Last year our son, Jeffrey, was killed in an accident. Last night was our second time seeing the play. We couldn't believe it the first time.'

'You couldn't believe what?'

Susan gave him a photo of Jeffrey. It was like looking at himself.

'That's why we asked you to meet us here this morning. It's like looking at my own son.'

Steven didn't know what to think.

Was this for real?

Was the photograph real?

Were these people real?

Jeff explained all about Los Angeles and their family. There was something Steven liked about them, genuine, decent people. He told them about his Cork background, his time in Dublin, and the Gate. Susan sat there in silence, lost in her thoughts. She wondered if God, in a roundabout way, was giving her son back to her.

'I'm sorry, Steven,' Jeff said. 'We crash into your life with this strange story. We can't believe it, but it must be a bigger shock to you. I'll come straight to the point. You have an open invitation to come to Los Angeles. Our home is your home, a pool, your own bedroom, a job.'

Steven was doing his best to take all this in.

'I'll have to think about it. My mother depends on me. My dad is out of work. She relies on the two pounds I send her.'

Jeff was conscious of putting pressure on Steven. There was a danger of frightening him away.

'Don't worry about your mother. Would fifty dollars a week keep her going? Just say the word. You know where we are.'

He handed Steven his card and shook his hand. Susan gave him a hug. He blushed, thanked them and made his way out on to O'Connell Street. His mind was miles away. Los Angeles, Hollywood, a new job, a pool, a big change from what he was used to, surviving in a room-full of brothers. What would Molly think?

As Steven turned in the front door of the Emerald Peg hurried towards him. She looked anxious and quickly showed him to his bedroom and asked him to sit down.

'I'm sorry, Steven. We got word an hour ago that your father has died. Your mother rang. You're to get the next train to Cork. You grab a few things in your hold-all. I'll have a taxi here in five minutes.'

Steven sat alone in the carriage of the train to Cork. He seemed to spend so much of his time on trains. All his life he dreaded the thought of his father's death. The last time he'd seen him he was his usual self; all guff and bluster and laughter. In the last letter from his mother she said the doctor had examined him and as he left the house he looked at her and shook his head. He'd deteriorated in recent weeks and spent most of the day propped up in the armchair like Lord Gough on his throne looking out the kitchen window. He never left the house except on Sunday when he limped to mass in the cathedral. Steven found it hard to accept that his father was gone.

When he arrived in Cork he decided to go to the funeral home first before going home. He wanted to be alone with him. His father was laid out in the coffin, pale, no Woodbine in his mouth. Steven hardly knew him. He looked strange in a shirt and tie. Steven broke down in tears as he bent over to kiss him. He thought he'd live forever, this five-foot-seven giant, always smiling, with fists like shovels and shoulders as broad as a barn door. How could he die? Steven felt guilty for not doing all the things he should have done. He left and crossed to the other side of Shandon Street. It was quieter and darker there as he made his way home with his head down trying to avoid everyone.

Shamrock House was full of mourners. His heart went out to his mother. Her eyes were red. Her face was drawn. They escaped to the back room. Words didn't come easily for Steven.

'Was he bad?'

'You know the way he was, all talk as usual, never in bad form. He was worse than any of us thought. At about eight o'clock this morning he stopped breathing. He was gone in a minute.'

That night the removal was the worst. There was a huge crowd at the funeral home by the North Gate Bridge. Marie knelt next to Steven and held his hand. His head was bowed and he could be heard sobbing over the drone of the Rosary. When the lid was put on the coffin Steven panicked. He realised that he'd never see his father's face again.

Next day he struggled through the funeral mass. There were no more tears. He was still angry during the ceremony. He hated the spraying of holy water and incense over the coffin in what he felt was a load of hocus-pocus. As he helped to carry the coffin down the aisle he laboured under his father's weight and his mind wandered back to all the times his father's leg must have hurt when he carried him on his shoulders up Fair Hill, along the strand in Youghal, and all those miles back home after walking the railway line. Steven felt bitter at the cemetery as he huddled in the rain by the graveside, looking on in a trance and mumbling the prayers apathetically. It was the same later in the pub. He sat in the corner drinking too much. He was angry as he watched his friends laughing and joking.

How dare they laugh at his father's funeral.

Did they realise who was dead?

The kindest man that ever walked the streets of Cork.

Did they know about all the times he'd given him his last penny?

Steven was bitter. He fucked God, fucked St Peter, Mary and all the saints in heaven. But, most of all, he fucked Woodbines. They killed his dad. Later, when he was able to look at things more sensibly he realised how unfair he'd been to his friends. He apologised to them all. What if they were singing and laughing after his father's funeral. Didn't they give him a great send-off, a celebration. He'd have liked that.

He was still forever in Steven's thoughts. Each memory triggered off another; when he was young at a bowling match this man was annoying his father. Steven remembered it went on for a while. His father, an easy-going man, surprised everyone by throwing a punch and knocking the man unconscious. Then for the next five minutes he knelt over the prostrate body telling the man he was sorry. Once, he was selling a donkey to a farmer for ten shillings. The donkey could hardly walk. As they made their way up the drive to the farm house he lifted up the donkey's tail and squirted pepper up his backside. When they arrived at the house the animal was bucking and snorting with energy. The farmer was impressed, the deal was done, and his father made a getaway, limping and laughing all the way home. One day his father hanged a sheepdog from an apple tree. Steven couldn't believe this. His father loved dogs. He saw him many times late at night with a sick puppy in his arms, wrapped in a blanket, and he nursing it back to health with a baby's bottle filled with warm milk. It took Steven a long time to get over his father's death.

He decided to stay a few days to help his mother. His brother, Peter, had to go back to work in the GPO, Brian and Pat had to return to England. It was difficult for his mother with a house full of people, but it was worse when they stopped coming and the house was empty. Marie still made Steven laugh. She followed him everywhere. His home was more run down than he remembered. The kitchen was scraggly and neglected. His bedroom seemed to have shrunk. He met his pals for a drink but they were different. They mocked his accent. He felt uneasy in their company. He had never been interested in alcohol. Now he spent too much time in the pub. Cork had also changed. It was no longer the loquacious playground of his youth. Apathy roamed the streets. Groups of men hung around at corners with their hands in their pockets. The colour and the characters were disappearing. The old lanes were being demolished in the name of progress and families were moving out to faraway estates. He tried to stay at home as much as possible to be with his mother. Behind all the tears she was a tough woman. Early on Thursday she knocked on his bedroom door.

'Steven, I just got a message saying the solicitor wants you to call.'

Steven wondered what the family solicitor wanted with him as he strode down Shandon Street, along the Parade and into the South Mall. He found the brass plate – P J Bolster – and the office on the second floor. Mister Bolster was a small pale-faced man in a pin-striped suit, with half-moon glasses hanging on the tip of his nose. He invited him to sit down as he shuffled through a pile of papers on his desk. He found what he was looking for – an envelope addressed to Steven. It was marked 'personal'.

'My instructions were that you were to receive this envelope on the death of your father.'

He ushered Steven out the door.

As Steven walked up the Mall and past the Coal Quay his mind raced. What was in the envelope? It looked very official. He wondered if it was money. He had to restrain himself from tearing it open. He decided to pay a visit to the *Roundy House* pub on the corner of Castle Street. He ordered a mineral, sat in a corner and carefully opened the letter. It contained one page. He recognised his father's spidery writing. He slowly read it once and had to read it a second time before it sank in.

Dear Steven,
You have always been special to me. I'll be gone when you read this. Anyway I couldn't face you. Please forgive me. I'm not good at writing so I'll come straight to the point. Something is haunting me for years. About two years before you were born I was in Dublin for a match. Cork won and I had too much to drink and Agnes offered me to stay overnight in the Emerald. I don't know how it happened and I don't know how to say this. I'm Molly's father. Agnes went to England and pretended to adopt her but Agnes is her mother. I'm terribly sorry, son. I'll always love you and I'll always be there to protect you and to watch over you.
With all my love forever
Dad

He folded the letter, put it in his pocket, and left the pub. If only he could talk to Peg. She'd know what to do. What about his mother? What would he tell her? He was home before he knew it. His mother was cooking in the kitchen. She was alone.

'What's wrong, son?'

'Nothing, mam. I'm ok.'

'Come on, Steven. What is it?'

Steven handed her the letter. She cleaned her hands on her apron and read it. Steven watched her face as she did so.

'I was going to burn it,' he said.

She sighed and surprised him by taking a bottle of whiskey and two glasses from the cabinet. She filled both glasses and gave one to him. He had never seen his mother drinking.

'I've known about it for years,' she said. 'Agnes was jealous when your dad married me. When he came back from Dublin I knew something had happened. For weeks he hardly spoke to me which was strange for a man who'd talk a rat out of a hole. That was her way of getting back at me, but I'm sure she didn't expect to have a child. Steven, Molly is your sister.'

This was like a punch to his face.

He decided not to tell his mother about her. They sat and talked the way they used to when they were feeding the ducks in the park or up the fair field when he was a small boy. He told her all about Jeff and Susan.

His mother's face lit up

'All that money. I'd be a right glamour-puss.'

His mind was elsewhere.

'Mam, would you mind if I left for Dublin tomorrow?

'You have your own life to live, child. Grab the world by the shirt-tails and don't let go. I always have Marie to look after me in my old age.'

Steven thought he'd never get to Dublin. The train seemed to take forever. He desperately wanted to see Molly. He rushed to her flat, let himself in the street door and hurried up the stairs. The door to her apartment was locked. He could hear music from inside. It was Fats Domino singing 'Blueberry Hill.' He banged on the door. There was no answer. He was worried. He called her name. She might have been having a nap. He banged again. There was still no answer. He stood back and hit the door with his shoulder. It crashed open.

He walked in.

A scream stifled in his throat.

Molly was hanging from a rope tied to one of the varnished beams.

A chair was toppled over on the floor near a torn envelope and a crumpled sheet of paper. He grabbed a knife from the drawer, stood on the chair and managed to cut the rope. She fell into his rms. He put her gently on the bed and removed the rope. He kept calling her name. She looked pale and cold. Her lips were purple. She was dead. He rang the police. He was crying now. While he waited he opened the top button of her blouse. She wore a silver chain with a jagged half-moon pendant. He removed it and compared it with his own, the one his father had given him. It was a perfect match. He also took off her ring and put it in his pocket. The envelope and the crumpled sheet of paper were identical to the one he'd got from the solicitor. He could now hear the sirens in the distance. There was a note in her clenched hand. He prised it open. It was simple:

S - Life wouldn't be worth living without you - M.

He realised that they were the last words he'd spoken to her on Saturday night. He took the envelope, the message, and the note and flushed them down the toilet. The police were outside the door. He sat by Molly's side and held her cold hand.

Steven was two hours at the police station, still dazed, still in shock. He'd told the same story over and over again. He never mentioned the note, the letter from his father or the ring. He felt this would protect Molly. Peg arrived and took him to the Emerald. Agnes had closed it for the night. Donal and John were out but Peg sat on the bed with him talking. She never mentioned Molly's background so he assumed she didn't know. He found it difficult not to confide in her. She gave him a mug of coco and advised him to try and get some sleep. It was impossible.

The next day was worse. People didn't know what to say to him. Donal and John could hardly talk to him and avoided him and he noticed Lillie crying in the corner trying to hide her tears. The police called again to talk to him; the same questions, the same answers.

The funeral was a blessing, a closure on the tragedy. Molly was buried in Glasnevin Cemetery. Steven's mother came up from Cork to attend. She stood by her son at the graveside. He stood there pale and silent in his own thoughts. Grief hung in the air. The cemetery was packed with friends from college and the Gate Theatre. Hilton Edwards and MacLiammoir shook his hand, quietly sympathised with him, and shuffled off into the background. Steven was lost;

Why?

Sweet Jesus, why?

How could a God of love allow this to happen?

Two people he dearly loved dead in just a few days. His father's death was hard to accept. He thought it would never happen. But he had seen some life. It was a hard life but he'd lived seventy years. Molly was so young and full of love. She had so much to live for, her life had barely started.

Agnes was dressed in black. She stood directly across the grave from him. As the prayers were being recited he could see her frowning in his direction. Peg linked her arm. He could hardly keep his eyes off his aunt. He realised that she wasn't aware of what he knew. She didn't know about his father's letter. After all these years was she still jealous of his mother? Did she deliberately set out to seduce his father to get at her sister? Steven couldn't believe what his father did. Yet, he found it difficult to blame him. Steven mind dwelt on Agnes' behaviour. He wondered if the pain of this indiscretion still lingered. Was this the reason why she behaved as she did? Was this why she was so hard on him? Maybe she also had her cross to carry.

When the ceremony was over the family went back to the Emerald. Agnes invited Steven's mother to stay overnight. He could detect a coldness between the two sisters. Desperate to escape, Steven asked his mother if she'd like a short walk. They walked down past Tara Street where they found a quiet pub. Steven looked like someone who had the weight of the world on his shoulders.

His mother knew him so well.

'It helps to get it off your chest. Your ma was there when you fell off a tree or scraped your knee. I was always there to kiss it better.'

He struggled for words.

'This is my fault. I killed Molly.'

'What happened was awful but don't blame yourself.'

Steven felt it was time to confide in his mother.

'We were more than good friends.'

'Your dad told me you were fond of her.'

'Fond of her; we were going to get married. Dad's death changed everything.'

'If he didn't die and if you'd married Molly it would have been a disaster. She was your sister.'

Steven was close to tears.

'Agnes is blaming me for all this. I might go home.'

'There's nothing in Cork, son. What about your American friends'?'

He had completely forgotten about Jeff and Susan.

Steven and his mother left the pub and walked slowly back to the Emerald. The hotel was re-opening in the morning. Steven was on the early shift. When he got to his bedroom Donal and Jim were still up listening to the radio. Steven told them about Jeff and showed them his card. There was a gleam in Donal's eye.

'Los Angeles, wealthy old biddies looking for a young stud like me. I heard they pay you a fortune to do it. What a way to go.'

Jim was very impressed.

'You might even meet Roy Rogers. The only travelling I ever did was to the Aran Islands in a boat when I made my First Communion.

At seven-thirty Steven brought two cups of coffee to Agnes' room. She said nothing. Peg took the tray and thanked him. Steven's mother was up early and had breakfast at a table near the front door. Steven was busy working and had little time to speak to her. Agnes sat at her table for a moment. The animosity between the sisters was still apparent.

'Molly was such a lovely young girl,' said Steven's mother.

'Someone must have driven her to it,' Agnes said.

Steven's mother ignored the innuendo.

'It's a pity you couldn't make Steve's funeral. All Cork was at it. Lots of old neighbours were asking about you.'

'He was very popular,' Agnes said.

Steven's mother looked her sister in the eye.

'Yes. Everybody liked him.'

Eleanor Kennedy waited until her son was finished dealing with some customers. She had one last word before she left.

'Steven, grab a rainbow and don't let go.'

Steven rang the Gresham Hotel. Jeff and Susan were still there. He made an appointment to meet them on his break. They were delighted and looked forward to meeting him again. As he walked to the hotel in the spitting rain he wasn't sure what to say. He was there in ten minutes. They were having coffee in the lounge. He made an instant decision. He sat down next to Susan and told her about the past week. He left nothing out.

'This is a terrible time for you. Our offer still stands. Right now you are the most important person in the world, so look after yourself. Ring us anytime.'

Jeff decided to leave well enough alone. The boy had a lot on his mind. As Steven was leaving the lounge he glanced back. Susan was crying.

Agnes withdrew into herself. She only spoke to Steven when she had to. Peg ran the hotel. One afternoon he was alone in his room. Peg stuck her head in. He was examining Molly's wooden pendant. He showed it to Peg.

'This was Molly's.'

'Your father gave her that when she made her confirmation. It looks as if it's half of something.'

Steven took off his pendant from around his neck. He placed the two together on the table like jig-saw pieces. They made a perfect circle. His head was full of questions about Peg, Agnes and Molly. He told her about Jeff and Susan and asked her for advice.

'It could be a good move for you. Apply for a passport anyway.'

Peg left him with his thoughts. He wondered again about her relationship with Agnes. She always defended her. His mind dwelt on Well Lane, demolished by bureaucratic bulldozers. Shamrock House, once surrounded by a plethora of little houses, now stood erect, sticking out like a phallic symbol, on the edge of a new link road, now surrounded by nothing. The neighbours were scattered, Lizzie Maloney, Dave Cotter, Pat O'Callaghan all gone, his brothers Brian and Pat were in England. Marie was stretching into a proper young lady. He had grown away from Cork. It was not the Cork of his childhood. He felt like a stranger in a town of strangers. What future had he in Dublin? It was impossible to live at the Emerald in the shadow of Agnes, and Molly was gone.

Christmas came and went in a haze. It felt as if everything happened yet nothing was happening. He'd taken Peg's advice and got his passport. He received two letters from Jeff. The new company in New York was up and running. He offered Steven an open invitation to join the family in Los Angeles.

Agnes was back to her old self. He had to be weighed in the kitchen every day. He still attended the Gate Theatre when he could. Hilton Edwards was directing *Three Sisters* by Chekhov. He approached Steven one afternoon and told him that the part of *Andrei* was his if he wanted it. Steven declined. His heart wasn't in it. Every corner of backstage still reminded him of Molly. Hilton felt sorry for him.

'Do you fancy a cup of tea?'

He showed Steven to his office where he boiled a small kettle of water and produced a plate of biscuits.

'Molly wouldn't want you to be moping around like a mushy mackerel. I'm sure you think I'm a silly old codger but you have one life. Follow your heart.'

Steven had always looked up to Hilton.

'I'd appreciate your advice on one thing.'

Steven asked his opinion on the Bradley's offer to go to the U.S.

'I'd seize it with both hands; you could regret it forever. There comes a time when you have to grab life by the testicles.'

'I'll ring them from the GPO on the way home,' Steven said.

Hilton picked up the phone and handed it to him.

'Ring them now. I'll be back in a minute,' he said, and left the office.

Steven slowly dialled the number. He prayed quietly to himself. He was back talking to God again. It seemed to ring forever. Jeff answered.

Steven and his fellow passengers were informed by the pilot that the plane was two hours from New York. He could hardly believe it as he gazed out the window. It was as if they were floating on a magic carpet of candy-floss. It was his first time flying. It was a month since he'd phoned Jeff. The Bradleys were delighted. A week later a registered letter arrived for him with his tickets, flight details, two hundred dollars and a note saying he'd be met at the airport. He gave Agnes his notice. She said nothing. Donal begged him to send for him when he made his first million. Jim shyly shook his hand.

'If you bump into him tell John Wayne I love him.'

When Steven rang his mother to tell her she insisted on travelling to Shannon to see him off. She brought Marie with her. It was a cold wet day. Steven realised how much she'd aged and how unselfishly she'd raised seven children. Marie looked so grown up. She didn't cry. One final wave and he was gone.

Chapter Six

Steven sat by the pool sipping a cool mineral. His legs dangled in the water. He wore baggy shorts and a straw hat to protect himself from the sun. He watched Louise and Mary playing tennis on the court at the side of the house. The two sisters were arguing over some point. It reminded him of watching out his bedroom window at his brothers fighting over a football match in the summer dust of the mangel field. It was the same but different. Charlie Grainger was lost in his own world, singing to himself, as he watered the flowers on the lawn. Steven could hardly believe it. His three years in California had flown by. From the start Charlie had taken him under his wing. From the moment they met they hit it off. Charlie shook his hand, stood back, had a good look at him, and laughed.

'Steven, I'm from Texas, born and bred, cattle country. I can see you are a wet-behind-the-ears little dogie. My job is to Americanize you. The U S of A is two countries. One has forty-nine states and then there's California. Once you accept that you're half-way there. Come on and I'll gently break you in; a quick trip to whet your appetite.'

Charlie jumped in to his nearby jeep.

Steven was excited, seeing places he'd read about or seen in the cinema: Long Beach, Beverly Hills, film stars' homes and the big Hollywood sign. They visited a smoky strip joint where they played pool. Another, even smokier, shook to the rhythm of a jazz band tucked away in a corner. Everybody seemed to know Charlie and he had great fun in introducing the boy as his 'distant cousin from Ireland.' He also realised that Charlie had a serious side to him with some fatherly advice.

'Son, I'd like to talk to you man to man.'

'A bit of honesty never hurt anybody,' Steven said.

'I saw one or two local ladies give you the once over, and why not? But some women I know would have you for breakfast. Remember, he who dips his wick must pay for the oil.'

Charlie winked at him and handed him a small package,

'Here's some Durex. Make sure you wear double glazing on every conceivable occasion.'

On weekends he taught Steven to drive. He took him out early to the nearby race track when there was no racing and they had the car park to themselves. Charlie's idea of driving instructions was simple:

'Take it easy and don't hit nothing.'

When Steven had arrived in New York Jeff took him on a quick tour. As he emerged from Grand Central Station he was stunned by the razzmataz that was New York. He stood next to Madison Square Garden and remembered all the nights his father was glued to the crackling radio listening to Joe Louis, Sugar Ray Robinson and Rocky Marciano boxing at this venue. He could see his father ducking and diving, giving his expert opinion on every punch thrown and his mother quietly knitting, throwing her eyes to heaven, behind his back.

New York was a long way from Well Lane. An elderly lady went flying by on roller-skates pushing herself with ski sticks. Nobody batted an eyelid. He wondered what the reaction would be if she came down Fair Hill like that. Jeff paid a flying visit to the company offices and then they grabbed a yellow cab to Fifth Avenue. Steven watched the bubbling mass of people. It was so different from the quietness of his home where he could sit by a stream and watch the grass grow. He felt as if there were more people here than in all of Ireland. The buildings seemed to touch the sky.

After staying the night in Jeff's apartment they caught an early flight to Los Angeles. Steven was nervous on the journey to Jeff's home but everyone went out of their way to help him. It took him a while to get used to the bathroom and shower and his own bed. After the initial shock Louise and Mary liked Steven. Although they both looked alike they had different personalities. Louise was taller and more easy-going. She had her own apartment downtown and worked for a law firm. Mary still lived at home and worked as a script writer in Hollywood. She was opinionated and impatient and spoke from the hip. At first Steven thought she was being rude to him but he learned to appreciate her honesty. Jeff joked that she had her mother's Irish temper.

As Steven sat by the pool he realised how lucky he'd been. The lowest point was when he got a phone call to say that his mother had suffered a stroke and she was dying. Jeff arranged everything so he could fly home. Steven went straight to the hospital. It broke his heart to see his mother propped up in the bed. The look on her face haunted him; the torment in her eyes and her twisted mouth fighting a losing battle to speak. The words refused to come; just a series of frustrated groans. How terrible it must have been for her, a woman who was so full of talk, now restricted to incoherent spasms. She held his hand as he told her all about California and the sun and Charlie. Her eyes lit up and her grip tightened as he rambled on. He kissed her cheek and told her he loved her. She smiled, sighed, and slowly closed her eyes. She was gone. He didn't cry; there were no tantrums, no tears. He castigated himself and the stupidity of his inhibited Irishness. He had to wait until his mother was on her death-bed to tell her for the first time that he loved her. What kind of a son would do that? She was buried, re-united with her husband, in the family plot in Curraghkippane, the rocky old cemetery looking over the Lee valley. A calm peace hung over that timeless graveyard. Agnes didn't make it, but all the old neighbours from Well Lane were there. Some felt that she died of a broken heart. She was never the same after her husband passed away. Jeff Bradley was as good as his word. Every week a cheque for fifty dollars had been lodged in the bank for her. Typically, she gave most of it away.

Steven stayed a week in Shamrock House. The cluster of little houses which were scattered at its feet were gone but their back gardens remained, each one a reminder of Steven's youth where they once lived out their sporting dreams, winning the high jump at the Olympics, playing for Cork in the All-Ireland final or scoring the winning goal against England in Wembley; always in the dying minutes; always with a diving header. None of them ever really made it. To Steven these old gardens were like headstones, inescapable reminders of a time long gone. The well and the stream and pigeon lofts were also levelled by a fleet of bulldozers and the new road was like a concrete scar across a scattered community. It was strange being back home without his parents. The old house felt empty, no heart, no soul. Yet it was good to have all the family together again. Story followed story; some grew legs with each telling. A few days later Steven found himself alone in his parents' bedroom. He went through an old suitcase overflowing with photographs, mostly yellow with age, in town holding his mother's hand, his curly-headed mop looking down at his feet, sitting under the apple tree, freckle-faced, short pants, his father diving off a rock at Robert's Cove; an infant Marie tottering on Steven's shoulders picking blackberries on Strawberry Hill. His mother's sayings came flooding back; *children should be seen and not heard; it's a long road that has no turning.* He could see her in his mind's eye reprimanding his father with, *never bolt your door with a boiled carrot.* She loved being boss in her kitchen like a proud mother hen surrounded by her clutch of chicks. Part of him was gone with the deaths of his parents. He had no reason to come home; there was no home. On the Saturday he left he stopped at the front gate and looked back and wondered if he'd ever see Shamrock House again.

Jeff was eager to improve Steven's formal education. The Loyola Marymount University had just introduced a two-year business administration course. Run by the Jesuits and Catholic nuns it was a college with a good reputation. Jeff was a friend of the president. Steven was welcomed with open arms. Jeff wanted to make sure he was familiar with the terminology of the advertising world so he invited a retired ad man to give Steven a three-hour grind once a week. The two years seemed to fly. Steven was so caught up in the land of academia he hardly had time for anything else. At first he was embarrassed when a girl asked him out on a date but he soon got used to this custom. He never slept with any girl and there were whispers that he was more interested in boys. Molly's shadow still hung over him. He still wore her Claddagh ring. He enjoyed college but he was getting more caught up in Bradley Advertising. Jeff sat contented in the background like a puppeteer pulling the strings.

Whenever Steven attended the agency he also tried to get in a good workout in the company gym. There was a small pool and the gym was laid out with all kinds of equipment and he loved to go there alone and work on his fitness for an hour or two. But the highlight of the gymnasium was a steam room. He had never seen one before, only in gangster movies. It had tiered wooden seating and was very hot. It was mixed and all a member was allowed wear in the steam room was a large white towel. Men and women were well wrapped up. Late one afternoon he was sitting on the top tier enjoying a chat with a friendly woman in her late thirties. Doris was her name. He'd met her once or twice in the office. They were alone as this was usually a quiet time. He was wondering what Donal would think about this. Steven was very slim and the towel was wrapped around him twice as he sat there in a bog of sweat. Doris now had her hand on his knee as she was telling him all about how they often bump into the film stars around Los Angeles. The feel of her warm hand on his knee caused him to get a lazy erection. He felt self-conscious and moved away a little but this movement caused his towel to open and slip down. He quickly pulled it back up but Doris had got a brief glimpse of his half-awake manhood. She moved down a seat, eased back his towel, put a restraining hand against his chest, took his penis in her other hand, placed it in her mouth and gently caressed it with her tongue. He sat there mortified, red face swamped in perspiration, stiff with mixed emotions; disbelief, pleasure and guilt. Nothing was said. She ran her fingers through his hair, kissed him on the cheek, and left without saying a word. He waited to make sure she was gone, ashamed to face her. It was his last time going near the steam room but any time their paths crossed Doris gave him a quiet wink.

Chapter Seven

Steven's twenty-first birthday was an eventful day. Charlie had orders to take him off for a spin in the jeep and when they returned to the house there was a surprise party for him. He was swamped by friends and neighbours. It was an emotional moment, a milestone in his life. Susan grabbed him, steered him out the hall to the front door, and asked him to close his eyes. She held his hand and guided him to the front of the house. He opened his eyes to see a blue Chevrolet convertible with a red ribbon wrapped around it.

'Your chariot awaits you.'

She handed him the keys. It was his first car. He sat in and repeatedly revved the engine to a round of applause.

By now Steven had taken California in his stride yet he couldn't understand the behaviour of Jeff's daughters. They never seemed to get on. Louise and Mary were still arguing as they walked towards the pool. Steven, lost in his own thoughts, never heard them. Mary sneaked up behind him and pushed him in. His straw hat went flying as he hit the water face first and struggled to grab the nearby bar. Mary didn't realise that he couldn't swim; he'd told no one. He gasped and coughed as she helped him out. She got in to a fit of laughter at the sight of him spluttering.

'You nearly drowned me. I can't swim.'

'I didn't know. Sorry.'

'Mary, that's not one bit funny. I'm going for a shower,' Louise said storming off to the house.

Mary dived expertly in and swam underwater to the far end of the pool and back before emerging at Steven's feet.

'Steven, you must be the only man in California who can't swim. Come on, I'll teach you. It's like riding a bike. Once you learn you'll never forget.'

Steven was still reluctant.

'Come on,' she pleaded. 'We'll practice in three feet of water.'

He made his way to the shallow end. Her white top was soaked. He could see her black bra through it. She told him to lie flat on the water while she held his chin. As he kicked awkwardly he moved across the pool from side to side. He lost his balance and grabbed her to save himself. He could feel her softness against him. When the lesson was over Mary took off her wet T-shirt and dried herself. She knew she was having an effect on him

'Now, Steven, that wasn't too bad.'

'I'd like another lesson sometime.'

She picked up her tennis gear and stood close to him.

'Anytime, if you feel up for it,' she teased and walked away.

She knew his eyes followed her all the way to the house. Louise sat on the bed dressing herself. She was angry with her sister when she entered the room.

'Mary, you're some little vixen, throwing yourself at Steven like that after all he's been through. I saw you out the window, up to your tricks as usual.'

Mary's face was full of mock innocence.

'I was just teaching him how to breast-stroke. He was so eager to learn. What can a girl do? You're jealous because he fancies me. I bet you often wondered what it would be like to do it with him.'

Louise felt Mary was spoiled. She had her father wrapped around her little finger always acting up to him and getting what she wanted.

'This isn't Hollywood and one of your plastic scripts. This is real life and real people. Steven is vulnerable,' Louise said and went off in a huff.

Mary laughed and called after her sister.

'But I'm only trying to help poor Stevie to integrate into the California way of life.'

Susan and Jeff had just finished Sunday lunch. Susan poured a glass of his favourite red wine. He knew she had something on her mind.

'What are your plans for Steven? Where is he going?'

'From tomorrow he'll have to earn his bread and butter. If he doesn't he'll get his ass kicked like everyone else.'

Susan was worried.

'He won't let you down.'

'Tomorrow the umbilical cord will be cut.'

Jeff decided to phone Richard. He felt that Steven could be used best as an initial contact getting new business because he had a certain charm and the older female businesswomen would trust him. Steven was writing a letter to Marie when Jeff called to his bedroom.

'Steven, the time has come to let you loose on L A. You'll be the agency's face, a spoon of honey, mister nice guy. Richard will be talking to you in the morning.'

As he was about to leave he stopped as if he'd remembered something. He took a packet of condoms from his pocket.

'This is a bit personal. Always keep them with you. You never know.'

Steven took the package Charlie had given him from his pocket.

'Thanks but Charlie has already been advising me.'

Richard Steinman showed Steven his office and introduced him to Cathy, his secretary.

'Last year fifteen thousand million dollars was poured into United States advertising. For each man, woman and child this year roughly sixty dollars was spent to persuade him or her to buy certain products. We don't sell merchandise. We buy customers. The average person has five times more money in his pocket than he did twelve years ago. I want no bullshit, no false promises. Step into the customers' shoes. Please them and tease them but make sure you hook them. When you do don't let them fucking go. The customer is as slippery as a rainbow trout. Your first assignment is Holbrook Construction. The boss is Cara Holbrook. She's one tough cookie. Dine her. Wine her. Charm her; but get the job done.'

`Holbrook Construction was just off Baldwin Street. He found Cara Holbrook's office upstairs at the back of the building. She was looking out the window observing the hustle and bustle below in the yard. She was an attractive woman in her early forties.

'Hello, Miss Holbrook. I'm Steven Kennedy from...,'

She shook his hand and interrupted him.

'Jeff Bradley is sending me someone straight from kindergarten. What have you got to offer me?'

'I'm sure you know that Jeff has retired and Mister Steinman is in charge now.'

Cara smiled to herself.

'I know everything about everyone in LA. I like Jeff but that old fart Steinman was always a moneybags. He still has his lollypop money.'

Steven took some brochures from his brief-case and placed them on the table.

'Let's get down to business,' he said. 'What exactly do you want?'

'That's the best offer I've had all day.'

Cara opened a cabinet, took out a bottle of Glenmorangie Malt and filled two glasses.

'Whiskey has been around since the Middle Ages; mothers' milk, seventeen years old; almost as old as yourself.'

She emptied her glass. He tried to do the same. His throat was on fire. She refilled the glasses. He remembered the advice to wine and dine her.

'I think we should discuss what I have in mind for you,' he said.

'Convince me.'

'Miss Holbrook, your problem is Los Angela's problem. You're both expanding but short of room. Space is the buzz word. President Kennedy is forever on about it. Every time he mentions space people will think of Holbrooks. Every home in the United States has a television. Bombard them with the concept: Holbrook Construction – Pioneers of Inner Space. The two key words are space and pioneers.'

'Well, you're different from the usual ass-holes I deal with. Come on. I'll show you around,' she said

She took him to an adjoining room. She often stays here when they're busy. It had office equipment, a drinks cabinet, a double bed and a bathroom. She dimmed the lights and flicked a button. Soft music filled the room - 'I can't stop loving you' by Ray Charles.'

He was still anxious to impress her.

'It will be the best move you ever made,' he said

She put her finger across his lips.

'Steven, will you forget business for a moment. Relax. Whiskey makes me feel like dancing.'

She took off his coat and tie and opened the top buttons of his shirt. He just stood there, his head a little dizzy from the drink. She moved in close against him, put one arm around him and placed his right hand on her breast. He followed her lead as they shuffled around the room while the music still played. He could smell her perfume and feel her breath on his neck. She kissed him on the lips pushing her tongue into his mouth. It was strange and exciting. He was nervous but aroused. She took his hand and led him to the bed, removed his shirt and opened his trouser top. It fell to the ground near the bed. She quickly undressed. They both stood there naked in the semi-darkness. She pulled back the sheets. He lay on the bed. She joined him and picked up the nearby phone.

'Joan, no calls, I'm busy with a client.'

He had never done this. He reached for his trouser pocket for a Durex and struggled in the darkness to put it on. She took over and helped him. She put her arms around him and rolled him over on top of her.

'Come to mama,' she whispered in his ear.

He fumbled at the start but she guided him patiently until he got into a rhythm. His body was now like a coiled spring. She groaned with every thrust and ran her nails down his back. She gripped him tightly, let out a loud moan and lay beside him on the bed breathing heavily. She reached for the malt whiskey and emptied the contents all over his body. She rolled back on top of him and ran her fingers through his hair and started to kiss him and slowly lick him all over his body making animal-like noises. Again, she explored his mouth with her tongue. He lay beside her, drained, his body tingling with excitement.

'Sorry, Cara, it's my first time.'

'I can't believe it's your first time. You must have been locked away in a monastery..

'I grew up in fear of mortal sin and burning in hell.'

'Don't tell me you're still burdened by the guilt of the Irish catholic; all pleasure is a sin; suffering is good for your soul; bollocks. What did we do wrong? Two adults having a bit of fun. No god worth his salt would condemn that.'

They showered together. He couldn't believe how easy he'd taken this in his stride. When they dressed she wanted to get back to business.

'Right, what are you offering?' she asked

'Go for the jugular, our full package. Holbrook Construction will be the name on everyone's lips, a company who build modern factories and dream homes,' he said

Cara Holbrook looked on silently. Steven cleared his throat.

'Cara, it does not come cheaply; a fifty thousand dollar package; six months of intense advertising, star treatment.'

She looked out the window and shook her head.

'I have a great bunch of people working for me,' she said 'one big happy family. Jesus, fifty thousand dollars is a lot of bread.'

'Bradley's also have a fine bunch of workers; two great teams pulling together. We can't go wrong. Our normal fee is fifteen percent but, to you, ten percent. It will save you two and a half thousand dollars. Cara, we'll not sell you bricks. We'll buy you customers.'

She looked across the office at him. He looked so young and innocent.

'I must be mad. I'll take it,' she said.

'You won't regret it. I'll look after the paperwork.'

'All I want is your handshake on it,' she said. 'My lawyers will meet Dicky Steinman's people later and look after the contracts. By the way, how long are you at this game?'

He paused for a moment and looked down at the floor.

'You're my first customer,' he said

'Steven Kennedy, you've got some fucking balls,' she said.

When he passed through the outer office two girls smiled to themselves. They couldn't help but notice Steven's wet hair. On his journey back to work he felt elated but guilty and longed to go to confession. He wondered what Pat O'Callaghan or Davie Cotter would think. Donal O'Reilly would have begged to hear every detail over and over again.

When Steven reached the office Richard Steinman wanted to see him.

'I don't know what you did to Cara Holbrook. That's the biggest deal we've ever done with them. Other firms will be watching us. Our creative team are already working on the layout.'

Steven decided to try his luck.

'Could I be involved in the creative aspect of this project?'

'You're not part of that team. Why do you ask?' Richard said.

'I made a lot of promises to Mrs Holbrook.'

'One question, Steven, how did you come up with your ten percent?'

'It was a spur of the moment decision. She was wriggling off the hook so I put some honey on the bait. She took it and I reeled her in.'

'Two and a half thousand dollars buys a lot of honey. I'm not Father fucking Christmas,' Richard said.

When Steven arrived at the Bradley home Mary was sitting by the pool writing. He decided to join her. He changed down to his shorts, jumped in and struggled through a length of the pool keeping close to the side.

'You'll make the Olympic team yet.'

'I will when you'll get an Oscar for best screenplay. Where's Susan?'

'She's gone to the grave with flowers.'

He sat next to her.

'It's a pity I never met Jeffrey,' he said.

'Every time you look in the mirror you meet him. Mum practically calls you son.'

Steven had noticed.

'I'd like to contribute to my keep, Mary It's not fair.'

'You'll only insult her. Just treat her like a sheepdog; pat her on the back and give her a hug now and then.'

'That's terrible, comparing your mother to Lassie.'

'Steven, will you ever lighten up? I'm only joking.'

He picked up her copy book and glanced at it.

'What are you writing anyway?'

She explained that it was a drama set in the fifties, a feud between Irish and Italian mobsters in Boston. An Italian diplomat has been kidnapped by an Irish gangster and he must get across the city but there are roadblocks everywhere. Steven read the script for a moment.

'Why not drug the diplomat, place him in the boot of his car and have the gangster dress as a priest late for mass or a funeral. In Boston a priest would be waved through every roadblock.'

Mary jumped up and kissed him.

'That's it. A small boat can get him out at night. They'll hardly be noticed.'

She started to write furiously.

'The diplomat wakes up, kicks the boot, they're nearly caught but he kills the security guard and gets away with the help of his priest's outfit, the Italians chase them, there's a shoot-out between the two boats, a priest with a scar and a machine gun, the Italian boat sinks, blood and bodies in the water.'

By now Steven was crouched under the table with his white top in his hand waving it as if in surrender.

'Help, is it safe to come up?'

Susan pulled in to the side of the house. Steven wanted see her. Mary noticed the scrawls on his back as he walked away.

'What happened to your back, Steven?' she asked.

'Oh, I was...messing with the lads in the gym,' he replied.

'Tell her she'd want to cut her nails,' she called after him

Susan was in the kitchen making coffee. She sat down near him. He reached out to rest his hand on hers and squeezed it gently.

'Susan, I love you dearly but I'm not your son. You are not my mother.'

He knew instantly that he shouldn't have said it.

'I'm sorry,' she said. 'I've spent two hours by his grave today telling him all about you. I'm just a silly old woman clinging to the past.'

'The next time you're visiting Jeffrey can I come with you? I'd love to tell him all about his incredible mother.'

Steven couldn't get Cara Holbrook out of his head. Every time his back twinged with pain he thought of her. He couldn't wait to tell Jeff everything about his success at Holbrook's; well, almost everything. Later that evening when he appeared Steven told him about the deal he'd done with Holbrook's including Richard's reaction to the ten percent.

'Don't mind that old moneybags. Right now he's crying into his wallet. That was a carrot. Cara will be back for more,' he said.

Louise Bradley was in the kitchen of her apartment researching old cases. Her door-bell rang. It was Emma, her flat-mate.

'I'm sorry, Lou. I forgot my key this morning.'

She breezed into the kitchen and kissed Louise. They were living together now for almost two years. When Louise turned fifteen she finally accepted that she was a lesbian. She couldn't tell her parents especially her mother. Meeting Emma changed her life. It was love at first sight. Louise was kept busy in her law firm while Emma had a small real estate business.

'Put away those books. All work and no play makes Lou a dull girl.'

'No work and all play leaves Lou with no job,' Louise said.

Emma filled two glasses of wine and rummaged through her bag for a parcel.

'This was sitting in Jacque's window winking at me and begging me to buy it. Try it on. It's you,' Emma said.

It was a knee-length black dress. Louise held it against herself and twirled around in front of the mirror.

'What did I do to deserve this?'

'It suits you. You're disgustingly slim and pretty. Today I turned on the magic and sold three houses.'

'Throw on your glad-rags woman and we'll stroll down to Alberto's,' Louise said.

Richard Steinman kept his word. The creative team welcomed Steven with open minds. Their office was called the 'maternity wing' because they constantly churned out new-born ideas. They agreed that future comfort was the most important theme of the Holbrook campaign. First they swamped California with posters of American astronauts on the moon in their comfortable Holbrook homes. Key words like *success, tranquil* and *atmosphere* were highlighted with the heading – *The Shape of Things to Come*. A film set and actors were prepared and a series of thirty-second television slots were produced showing astronaut parents enjoying a blissful life in their spacious Holbrook home on the moon. Cara was invited to watch the ads being filmed. Holbrook Construction couldn't build houses fast enough for the demand. For Steven success followed success. In a media orientated state like California he was becoming big news. One journalist labelled Steven 'Son of Midas.' This embarrassed him but Richard Steinman encouraged it; it was good for business. His colleagues regularly played pranks on him telling him that John F Kennedy wanted him on the phone but they knew he was making money for them with a string of successful ads. The largest paint manufacturers in LA specifically asked for him. Their sales doubled in a month. He saturated the cities in California with posters.

The home in your life – The life in your home.

He suggested changes in the way they presented their product. Many companies sold all their paint in a white can. Steven had the can the same colour as the paint. It was popular with impatient customers. He introduced paints aimed at the female customer; Paris blue, Gemstone green, Amsterdam red, passionate purple. Women found it attractive. Holbrook wanted to discuss the possibility of another campaign. Cara rang Richard Steinman and stressed that she wanted Steven. He looked forward to doing business with Cara again. She didn't disappoint him. This time he refused the whiskey. He wanted a clear head. They ignored the preliminaries. He gladly accepted and ended up in her bed. This time he skipped the dancing. He made love twice. He poured whiskey all over Cara's naked body and licked it off lingering on her eager breasts. This time he had no remorse.

'The boy has now become a man,' she said.

He was anxious to get down to business.

'At the moment you are doing well,' he said.

'Doing well? We've had to add two more buildings at the back of the compound and I've taken on twenty extra men. What do you suggest?'

'I can give you a three-month package. It will cost forty thousand dollars but it will keep you busy for the next twelve months.'

'Sounds interesting; the usual ten percent?'

Steven shook his head.

'It has to be fifteen percent. I got my wrists slapped the last time. I'm sorry, Cara.'

'The boy has definitely become a man. What have you got in mind?'

'Many Californians still wallow in their past history of cowboys and Indians with brave families in covered wagons overcoming all kinds of danger. We could depict a little girl, pony-tail and freckles, happily playing with her rag doll in her modern Holbrook home; a tug of the heart-strings can loosen the purse-strings.'

'Steven Kennedy, you are some fucking son-of-a-gun. Behind all your angelic innocence lies the string of a scorpion. I'll take it. Tell old Steinman to ring me.'

On the drive back to Bradley's he was surprised that he felt no guilt and looked forward to seeing Cara Holbrook again.

Steven was tidying his bedroom. In one drawer he kept photographs, his passport and bits and pieces. He was looking at old pictures of himself; one with Molly in the Gate. They looked so happy together. He picked up the small box at the back of the drawer and opened it. It was Molly's engagement ring. A knock on his door interrupted his thoughts. Mary opened the door and came in.

'I just want to thank you for your help with the script. Some bigwigs read it and there's talk of it being made into a movie.'

'You might get that Oscar after all.'

'The almighty dollar talks. The problem is financial backing.'

'If you're stuck for the IRA man dressed as a priest keep me in mind. I have the saintly look of a Catholic priest and I can do a great Irish accent.

'I called to tell you the good news and offer you a beer in *Giovani's*. It's the nearest watering hole.'

'I'd like that.'

He showed her the ring.

'Was that Molly's?'

'I'll tell you all the gory details over that beer.'

They were at *Giovani's* in ten minutes. It was an old-fashioned bar with photos of Hollywood stars sprinkled around the walls. He told her all about Well Lane and Molly. She could hardly believe that he'd slept in a bed with two brothers with three more in another bed in the same room; that the nine of them shared one outside toilet; how one wet night he was so hungry that he followed a man, who was eating an apple, all the way up to the top of Fair Hill so he could grab the core when the man threw it away.

'There's a difference between your Ireland and my California.'

'You could say that.'

'It's a way of life here; the old cowpokes against all the odds; a goldmine around the next corner; you might call it bull-shit but it's expected here in Hollywood. We have no time for hard luck stories. This is fairyland. Nothing is impossible.'

'It's a long way from Agoo Murphy and the mangel field,' he said. 'When I was young at home I often slept with the pigs.'

She shook her head in disbelief.

'You slept with a pig?'

'When the sow had a litter of piglets I'd have to lie down next to her all night to stop her from rolling over on the little baby pigs, just for a night or two until they were strong enough to look after themselves.'

'Steven, I don't know what to make of you; no crap; no tantrums. Dad says you are raking in money for the agency. Please promise me one thing; don't ever change.'

Steven shrugged his shoulders.

'I don't understand one thing. Louise is so quiet and you give her a terrible time.'

'But we're sisters. We get on great.'

'You have a funny way of showing it.'

'There's something I should tell you but you must keep it to yourself,'

'You can depend on me.'

'Louise is a lesbian.'

'Are you sure?'

'Come on, I'm her sister.'

'Is that a problem?'

'Jesus, no. Where I work every second person is gay but one night I was in this café and I saw her holding hands and kissing this girl.'

'I like Louise.'

'Everyone loves Lou. I'm the bad egg in the family; motor-mouth, naughty but nice.'

'At least I know where I stand with you.'

'Come on. I'll drive you home. It's way past your bed-time. I think the beer is gone to your head.'

He hardly spoke on the short journey back to her home. She glanced at him a few times but he was miles away. She was beginning to like him more and more.

As the year slipped by Steven could do no wrong. The staff almost doubled. Three extra men were brought in as client advisers under Steven. They did the spade-work and he stepped in to tie up the loose ends. He traded in his Chevrolet for a new Buick Investa. The poor boy from Cork was suddenly somebody. Mary invited him to a showcase of their upcoming films. He wore a tuxedo for the first time. She dragged him out dancing but he spent the night pointing out different celebrities and stepping on her toes. She introduced him to everyone. Burt Lancaster, Peter O'Toole and Mickey Rooney were there and he spoke to Lee Remick. She was dancing with Jack Lemmon. He couldn't find John Wayne to pass on the message from his friend, Jim O'Reilly, from Cong. It was too late to go home so they booked into a hotel for the night. He knew they were going to end up in bed.

Next morning he had a cold shower. The pounding water eased his aching head. His colleagues were surprised when he arrived at the agency in a tuxedo. Richard Steinman waited for him in his office.

'Mister Elcott wants to talk to you about his car project. You know well that first impressions are vital; an early smile, a warm handshake and then, and only then, you grab the client by the balls and don't let go. Steven, there's a smell of fucking alcohol off you. For fuck sake, that sends out all the wrong messages.'

Steven looked sheepishly at him.

'I'm sorry. It'll never happen again.'

'Are you on happy mushrooms?' Richard said. 'Some of your concepts will have people laughing at us; a car designed for the modern woman, using male models in skimpy briefs posing on little pink cars?'

Steven stood up and faced Richard Steinman.

'Let them laugh. Bradley Advertising will be laughing all the way to the bank if we tie up this contract. There's a huge void in the market for a car specifically for women. Why not have a smaller and more economical car geared for women, easier to park, lighter colours? Why not magnolia interior; thrills and frills, a large flip-down mirror to help with make-up? Bathing beauties are used by men to sell cars. Why not the male equivalent for women? Mister Elcott said he'd give my proposals some thought. He must consult the board of directors; two of them are women,' Steven said.

'You cannot change this world overnight. Play safe. You know the house rules. Stick to them and for Christ sake take off that monkey suit.'

Richard Steinman's marriage had been in a mess now for some time. His wife accused him of being married to his job. She was right. He was certain she was having an affair. To make matters worse he was concerned about the agency's New York branch. Something was wrong. He accepted that Steven had been like a breath of fresh air but he was behaving like a spoiled brat trying to get his own way. Richard picked up the phone and dialled a number.

'Hi Jeff...Well, someone has to work. Do you feel like a coffee and a natter? I'd like your advice... Great, I'll see you in *Oscar's* at ten.'

Mister Elcott's office was more like an old boardroom than an office. The tables and chairs were dark oak and a tall glass cabinet looked down on them. Maurice Elcott, was in his sixties. He was a heavy man with a shock of grey hair and a pleasant face. He took out two glasses and a bottle of wine. The chair groaned as he sat down and gestured to Steven.

'It's a bit early, maybe later,' Steven said.

'We had an interesting chat last week. I liked your style. We're very ambitious. Tell me again exactly what we'd get.'

'I think I'd like that drink now,' Steven said.

Richard was already at *Oscar's* at their usual table when Jeff got there at five minutes to ten. Jeff thought he looked serious. That was nothing new. Richard always looked serious.

'How's Sofie?' Jeff said.

'I think she's having an affair. She's acting strange recently, mysterious phone-calls, whispered conversations.'

'I thought your marriage was set in granite,' Jeff said.

'She's dressing like a teenager and going to the beauty parlour once a week. She uses crimson lipstick and her freakin face is covered with make-up. She wears a mini-skirt that barely covers her ass, and she goes to the gym with a personal trainer. Maybe he's banging her. She's a forty-seven year old grandmother. What the hell is she trying to prove?'

'Maybe she's realised she's getting old like the rest of us and this could be one last effort to cling on to her youth.'

Jeff wanted to change the subject

'I hear that New York is not doing well. What's the story?'

'For the past three months profits have been falling.'

'Leave it with me. If some gobshite is trying it on it will be the biggest mistake he's ever made.'

Richard went silent again. He looked even more serious.

'Jeff, tell me one thing; am I being too hard on Steven?'

'I thought he was your golden boy.'

'Clients love him but lately he wants to run the place.'

Jeff burst out laughing.

'He reminds me of a student I took on many years ago. He was a raw, opinionated, young man with stars in his eyes. You had long hair half-way down your back then and you kept telling me how you were going to make your first million. I listened then and I'm still listening now.'

Richard's face was still dour and worried.

'He's taking too many risks. I had to restrain him again this morning.'

'I can see that same flame in his eyes. You'll have to get him a ball and chain.'

'Look in on New York. I smell a rat,' Richard said.

'Take it easy and look after Sophie,' Jeff said.

Both men left with their own thoughts and went their separate ways. Jeff drove back home; he was going golfing with Charlie. Richard walked back to work and anxiously waited for Steven.

Mary Bradley knew that something was up. The studio boss called twice. After lunch she was called in to the director's office. He made the big decisions. A small well-dressed man in a pin-striped suit stood by the window. He was smoking a cigar.

'You wanted me, Mister Grey?'

He took one last long puff on his cigar and waved the smoke away.

'Sit down, young lady.'

He picked up a script and thumbed through it.

'My colleagues have dug up some backers who are willing to take a chance with your film. The principal roles are cast but we're still sussing out people. The main body of the film can be shot in the studio and we could be on location in a month. Certain lines may need rewriting. Actors are bitches. The director is God.'

'Who's playing the godfather or the cardinal and what..,' Mary said.

'That's all for later; first, see your lawyer.'

When Steven arrived at the house Jeff's car was already there. It had been a bad day at the agency. Richard was in a foul mood. He'd just finished a shouting match and slammed down the phone when Steven entered his office. His meeting with Mister Elcott's colleagues had not gone well. They weren't as enthusiastic about the campaign. They wanted definite promises. Steven did what he was told and played safe. He had another row with Richard about this. Eventually Steven stormed out the door.

'Well, Richard, you didn't lose any money. That should keep you happy.'

Jeff was busy in the kitchen cleaning one of his clubs. Charlie had given him another lesson.

'Richard rang,' Jeff smiled.

'I had a feeling he would.'

'Don't take it to heart. The agency is like a marriage, full of ups and downs. It's par for the course.'

'I accept that, Jeff, but I feel as if my hands are tied.'

'He has a lot on his mind. There are problems in New York. Richard's a good man. We all make mistakes,' Jeff said.

'That's the problem. I don't feel I made a mistake,' Steven said.

'Oh, Mary rang; there's a number by the phone you're to ring.'

Jeff sauntered off as Steven dialled the number. Mary was all excited; he could hardly get a word in. She asked him to meet her at the Blue Stove. He wasn't in the mood but her enthusiasm changed his mind. She had something to tell him. He also had something to tell her.

Mary sat near the bar drinking a cocktail. She'd had a few. He had a mineral. Richard was on his mind. Her face was full of passion.

'I want you to be the first to know. My script, your script, is being made into a film. There's a whisper that Gregory Peck and Katharine Hepburn are to star in it and George Stevens is directing.'

'George Stevens directed *Shane*. I'm delighted for you. I could be looking for a job. You're on the way up and I'm on the way down.'

Mary was surprised.

'Dad tells everyone that you're his pride and joy. Don't tell me you're leaving?

Mary called for another cocktail but Steven caught the waiter's eye and changed it to two coffees.

'I have no intention of leaving,' he said.

'Steven, at times I don't know you.'

'There's not much to know. I was nearly always on my own.'

HONOUR THE HOLY GROUND

'You're not on your own now. When you arrived in our home I didn't know what to think. You'd just lost your father and your girlfriend. Molly must have been special.'

She could see the sadness in Steven's eyes.

'Molly was the love of my life but she was also my sister. I can't get her out of my head, the way her eyes danced with happiness, her flaming red hair. How could any God let this happen?'

'Never forget Molly, but she wouldn't like to see you throwing in the towel. She'd like nothing better than to see you kick some California ass.'

Mary slammed the counter. Steven smiled at her.. He felt the cocktails were talking.

'This is your night and I'm spoiling it,' he said.

'I want to know everything about you,' she said.

'Come on, home sweet home, I'll call a cab,' he said.

He rambled on about everything from Railway Cottages and Peg to Lizzie Maloney and the *Lido*. The lights were out in the house as they pulled into the drive. They went to his room; it was furthest from her parents' bedroom.

'I'm sorry. I've been going on a bit too much about Molly?' he said.

'She's a hard act to follow.'

He turned on the bedside lamp and took off his Claddagh ring.

'There was no one like Molly but, in all this world, there is nobody quite like you. Molly gave me this. I would like you to have it, a special ring to a special person on this special night.'

Susan was cleaning the house. Louise had rung to say she was calling. She wanted to talk to her. Susan was worried. Jeff was outside struggling through a game of tennis with Charlie. Susan had just finished tidying Steven's room and was surprised to find Mary's earring in his bed. She felt this was going too far; in their own home. She'd left a scribbled note on the kitchen table telling her parents the news about her film. Louise's car pulled up outside. Her arrival was an excuse for Jeff to escape from his tennis lesson. Charlie went back to the peace and quiet of his garden. Susan had two cups of coffee poured as Louise entered the kitchen.

'Milk, no sugar,' Susan said.

'Some things never change,' Louise said.

'Well, Louise, how are you? You look great.'

'I have something to say but I don't know how to say it.'

Susan sat next to her daughter.

'Are you ill?' she said.

'I'm fine but you know Emma; you've met her once. She's my best friend.'

'Yes. She's a nice girl.'

'Mum, there's no other way to say this. I'm a lesbian. Emma is my partner.'

The colour drained from Susan's face. She stood up and walked across the kitchen. .

'I don't believe this.'

''Mum, it's not the end of the world. I hoped you'd understand. Where's dad?'

'I'll get him.'

Susan left quickly. Louise could hear a muffled conversation. She was crying when Jeff entered the kitchen. He was drying his hair with a towel.

'Hey, love, Come on, your old man is here. What's the problem? It can't be that bad?'

'It's worse.'

Jeff put his arm around her shoulder.

'Have I that effect on women? My wife is crying in the bedroom and my daughter is crying in the kitchen.'

'You know Emma and I share an apartment. She's my girlfriend. Dad, I'm gay.'

Jeff laughed. He looked relieved.

'Is that all? I thought Emma was ill or dying or something like that. Good God, you're gay. So what.'

'I don't think mum is so keen. I just thought that it would be better that you heard it from me rather than somebody else.'

'Your mum loves you; you know that. She's a staunch catholic, the worse kind. It's your life; you live it your way.'

'Emma is the best thing that ever happened to me. I better go.'

'I'll walk you to your car. And there I was looking forward to escorting my beautiful daughter down the aisle.'

'That might happen yet.'

She smiled and kissed him. He watched her disappear down the drive. He found his wife lying on the bed in the darkness.

'Come on, Susan, it's no big deal.'

'Where did I go wrong? My little girl.'

'You did nothing wrong. It's what she wants. I heard Emma is lovely.'

'That girl will never set foot in my house. I have no time for that sort of thing.'

'We'll just have to wait for our star daughter, Mary, for our grandchildren.'

Susan took the earring from her pocket.

'The way she's going that will be sooner rather than later. I found her earring under Steven's pillow,' she said.

HONOUR THE HOLY GROUND

Marie Kennedy was twenty-one. She sat in her room upstairs reading the birthday card from Steven over and over again. The PS at the bottom jumped out at her: *I miss you, princess. Why don't you come over and join me? I'll look after you. XXX Steven.* He also sent a cheque for a thousand dollars. Her brother, Paul, had organised a surprise party. The noise from the music below in the front room shook Shamrock House. She wondered what her future held. She had a job in an office in Cork and she did some part-time modelling at night. There was a knock on the door and Paul stuck his head in.

'Marie, there's a couple of fellas below looking for a dance,'

Paul was the one remaining brother, the youngest in the family. They shared the old house. The orchestra, ensconced in the kitchen, consisted of an elderly neighbour on his fiddle and Pat O'Callaghan's brother, Christy, on a gadget. There was a mighty cheer when Marie appeared. She cut the cake, slices were passed around, cameras clicked and there was a rush for a refill from the barrel of Guinness stashed in the corner. Paul banged the table and called for order. The room went quiet. He put down his drink and took out a crumpled sheet of paper.

'I'd just like to say,' he read, 'that there's another box of boiled crubeens under the table, and when the Guinness is gone there's a few bottles of Paddy in the kitchen. So will you please raise your glasses to the girl of, sorry, to the woman of the house. I have it on very good authority that Marie is now on the look-out for a man, any man; in fact she's desperate.'

Everyone sang 'happy birthday' with gusto. When they finished Marie spoke.

'Thanks for this surprise party organised by my baby brother. This party must have been the worse kept secret in Fair Hill. For the past week everybody is wishing me well with my surprise party. How could I miss the cupboard full of whiskey bottles hidden behind the porridge and the barrel of Guinness covered with a blanket in the shed? There is no truth in the rumour that I'm looking for a husband. Who'd look after Paul, cook for him, do his ironing, mend his socks?'

The music played up again and Marie was asked out for every dance. The barrel didn't last long and the whiskey followed quickly. Eventually the party petered out. A good time was had by all. People started drifting away at midnight. Paul walked a girl home. Marie sat in her room in the empty house and read the card again: *why don't you come over and join me?* As she drifted off to sleep she wondered about California.

It was late Sunday night. Jeff relaxed with a drink on his flight back from New York. It had been a difficult weekend checking up on old friends. After discreet enquiries he got to the cause of the agency's problems. He was forced to trample on a few egos. On the previous Monday he contacted old friend, Ted Dynan, a retired detective. He had a reputation for not getting things done by the book. After a lot of digging they met and worked out the best way to deal with this. He also arranged for an experienced accountant, to have private access to the company's records for a week. They met on Saturday morning to compare notes. It was noon by the time the accountant and the detective finished telling Jeff what exactly had been going on. The accountant read from a brief-case filled with documents, ticking off each item as he went along, and the detective consulted a note book naming names and places.

'Is that it?' Jeff asked.

Both men nodded.

'It's a nasty business. Thanks, 'he said.

Both men left.

Peter Jordan was waiting in his nearby office. Jeff had phoned him on Friday night and asked to meet him the next morning. He had been with Jeff almost from the start in Los Angeles. Married with three children he'd been a respected member of the team and when the New York branch opened, Jeff put him in charge. All was fine until things started going wrong. Jeff knocked on the door and entered. He shook Peter's hand.

'Hello, Peter, how is Rose and the family?'

'It took us a while but we've settled down in Brooklyn.'

'I'm sure you know why I set up this meeting.'

'Well, no. I was wondering if it was business or pleasure.'

'For the last three months you've been robbing me.'

The expression on Peter's face changed.

'That's a terrible thing to say.'

'Shut the fuck up and listen,' Jeff shouted. 'I'm trying to keep you out of jail. Sit down and tell me everything. I know anyway but I want to hear it from the horse's mouth.'

Peter sat squirming in the chair and covered his face with his hands. Finally he spoke, almost pleading.

'When we came to New York it was great; more money, a new home. Then I started going to the track and the casinos and started chasing losers with more losers. I fell in with the wrong crowd especially a man called Rick Guardino. When I was stuck he loaned me money, a few grand here, a few grand there. Before I knew it I was up shit creek. I couldn't pay. This guy doesn't fool around; he has a reputation as a butcher. Pay him back or he chops off your fucking fingers. He came up with the idea to doctor the books. He provided his man to do it, and he regularly siphoned off a percentage of the profits and made sure the books were balanced. Jeff. I'm truly sorry. I fucked up.'

'Guardino is a nasty piece of work. The Mafia got rid of him. Why didn't you ring me? Peter, I'm letting you go.'

Peter knew he'd taken the wrong options. He should have rung Jeff. He thought he could handle it himself.

'Give me one last chance. Please, Jeff. What will I tell Rose?'

'Here's what you do; resign on Monday morning, walk out that door and you don't come back.'

'What about my debts? These gorillas will kill me.'

Jeff was annoyed but he showed some bit of mercy.

'A cheque will arrive in the post. That should cover it. If Guardino comes near you or the agency he'll end up in the East River.'

Peter sat slumped in the chair.

'I'm sure you'll have no trouble finding a job, a man with your reputation. Call me if you need a reference.'

He walked out. He knew it was the right decision. It had to be done and he also knew that the story behind the story would be all over Manhattan tomorrow.

Jeff was an hour from Los Angeles. He ordered another drink and wondered who he'd send to replace Peter in New York. Harry Martin came to mind; a graduate of Yale, Jeff had given him his first break. He was the right age, he knew the business, and he was ambitious. Yes, Harry was perfect.

Steven was driving slowly through the dockland area of Los Angeles. He looked lost. It was dark and overcast. The dim street lights lit up the wet streets. There was an eerie feeling about the place. He glanced in the mirror again. He felt the car behind was following him. It was a black Dodge. He turned sharp left. The car still followed. He picked up speed but suddenly the Dodge was right behind him. He could see two men coldly looking at him. Trying to lose them he swerved into an ally on his right. It was barely the width of his car. He knew he'd made a mistake. It was isolated but worse it was a dead end. He heard a shot ring out and his rear window smashed in around him. There was another volley of shots. He was hit. There was a searing pain in his left shoulder. He lost control of his car. It skidded and crashed into several parked cars and shuddered to a halt against a brick wall. The bonnet shot up on impact and he was covered in glass from the shattered windscreen. He struggled to get out of the car but the door was jammed. He kicked it open and staggered out trying to get away but, by now, the two men were only feet away with guns drawn. Several shots rang out and echoed in the narrow ally. The bullets thudded into his chest. He stumbled and lay face down, crumpled in a pool of water. There was a stillness in the air and everything seemed to happen in slow motion. At first there was an empty silence. Then he could hear the noise of the car driving off into the night. Suddenly powerful spotlights lit up the ally and the area was a hub of activity; there was a prolonged round of applause and people with head-phones and cameras appeared from all angles some hurrying and scurrying, barking out orders. Two of the film crew helped Steven to his feet and sat him on a chair. He looked a mess. Mary Bradley rushed to his side with a glass of water and a towel to clean his face. She had a script in her hands. Steven smiled. He thought the scene went well. One man stood out from the crowd. It was George Stevens. Everybody listened when he spoke.

'Well done, folks. I've seen it on the monitor. Perfect. It's a wrap. Let's get out of here. See you in the morning.'

Everyone cheered and moved quickly. They knew exactly what to do. The director put his arm around Steven.

'Well done, young man. Mary was right. You were perfect for the part. Go and get cleaned up and take this young lady out of my sight before she drives me nuts.'

He gave Mary a hug and left still calling out instructions before he disappeared in to a caravan.

'It looked great,' she said.

'It would want to; we must have done it twenty times. In the end I could do it in my sleep.'

'It has to be faultless. The slightest mistake will be noticed and magnified,' she said.

She waited while he changed. She wanted to celebrate but he preferred to go home.

'I better drive then,' she said. 'I've seen the way you handle a car.'

They slept in his bedroom again. This time they savoured the occasion. They were both tired but they were content and relaxed and made love quietly. Later as he slept Mary lay there beside him. Wrapped in the comfort of the darkness she was sure of one thing. She was falling in love with Steven Kennedy.

Susan and Jeff sat in the kitchen having breakfast. He took life with a pinch of salt. Susan was a religious woman. After Jeffrey's death she firmly believed that God made up for it by sending Steven her way. Why did they go to Ireland at the precise time that Steven was in the Gate Theatre? It was all laid out before them. It was God's will, God's greater plan. Jeff wasn't overly religious. He just tried to get in as much golf as he could and an odd game of tennis. He watched her as she fussed over the kitchen sink. She was still a beautiful woman. Like many mothers she had a sixth sense about her children. She couldn't help but notice that in recent weeks Mary always seemed to be around when Steven was at home.

'Have you noticed that Steven and Mary are seeing a lot of each other,' she said.

'That's only natural. They live in the same house and they've been working in the film.'

'There's more to it than that. Some nights they stay in and look at the telly together and they have breakfast at the same time and last Sunday I saw them holding hands by the pool.'

Jeff found it funny that Susan still worried and kept a special eye on her grown-up daughter.

'When it came to boys Mary was like a butterfly flitting from flower to flower looking for honey. Maybe Steven would be right for her. It would be practical if they were to marry. It would save us a fortune on wedding invitations,' he said.

'This is serious. God moves in mysterious ways,' she said.

'He better move out of my way. I have a date with Charlie. What are you up to?'

'I'm off playing bridge for the morning.'

'While you're downtown keep an eye out for a new outfit for the wedding,' he said.

Richard Steinman was in the middle of a nasty divorce settlement. Steven still didn't see eye to eye with him, but he had a spectacular success with an ambitious clothes manufacturer who did a line in top of the range suits. Their clothes were selling but they were too faceless and mundane. Steven built a personality for them by introducing a series of ads with a list of famous men dressed in the company's modern suits: the ads featured Shakespeare busy with his quill dressed in a tuxedo, a beautifully dressed Abraham Lincoln giving his Gettysburg address, Henry VIII after battle stepping out of his armour to reveal a snazzy pin-stripe suit and top hat, Leonardo Da Vinci in a white sports coat as he painted the Mona Lisa, an immaculately dressed Moses handing over the ten commandments. `California sat up and took notice. Bradley Advertising got an award for this ad. Richard Steinman called Steven in to his office.

'We may have our differences but you did well. Now everybody knows we have the best team in California. I don't know what you're doing to

Cara Holbrook but she rang looking for more business. She insists that she'll only deal with you, so get over there fast and lick her ass,' he said.

Richard Steinman picked up the phone and tried to ring his wife again.

Holbrook's looked busier than ever. Cara was wearing a tight red skirt and a silk blouse. He couldn't help but notice her breasts were bouncing inside her blouse as she walked. He guessed she was about forty-five but looked thirty.

'I'm disappointed that you didn't ring,' she said.

'I've been up the wall with work and very busy in a film.'

'I've been told you're a second Clark Gable.'

Cara sat down and crossed her long legs.

'Steven, I want more. What can you do for me?'

'How much do you want to spend?'

'I want Holbrook to be the biggest in California. What can you give me for around a hundred thousand dollars?'

Steven paced up and down the office before speaking.

'Your father founded this company sixty years ago. Since you took over the acorn has become an oak. That's the theme. Go for it on television. We'll swamp them with images screaming at the viewer, BUY ME, BUY ME. We can have Noah surrounded by frightened animals, a storm, so he has a Holbrook home constructed on his ark to withstand the floods.'

Cara could listen to him forever. She also loved his young body. She was impatient.

'Look after it for me. I'll phone old cranky-balls later and get the contracts drawn up. Now let's get down to real business.'

She unbuttoned her blouse. She wore no bra. She kissed him passionately on the lips. She was surprised when he stopped her and held her at arm's length.

'I'm really fond of you but I have to go; maybe some other time.'

'Can't you stay for five minutes? I've been looking forward to seeing you all the morning. Surely you won't let a girl down now?'

She stood there both breasts hanging out.

'Cara, I've always been honest with you. I'll be honest with you now. I have a girlfriend who means a lot to me.'

'You never cease to amaze me; an Irish catholic with a conscience.'

'I'd feel terrible,' he said.

'I won't tell if you don't tell. Can't we just have a quick hump and you can go to confession on the way home?' she said.

'Please, Cara, you're making it hard for me.'

'That was the object of the exercise,' she said.

'I'll get right back to you when I see Mister Steinman. That's a promise,' he said and left the office.

She sighed and blew him a kiss.

Mary Bradley was thrilled. The film had finally got the thumbs up. She sat in a room-full of men; most of them in their shirt sleeves and chain-smoking. These were the hard-nosed men, the hidden faces, who made all the decisions from location to distribution. The director, George Stevens, had been explaining that the film was nearly complete. There was a tepid round of applause. Everyone headed for the bar. Mary headed for some fresh air.

Steven rang the agency to tell them the good news; he'd struck gold with Holbrook. He was on his way. Richard ordered the team to prepare for the campaign. They swung in to action and began throwing around ideas and working on the project. Steven drove straight back to the agency. He parked his car and took the steps up to his office two at a time. Richard was waiting for him in his office. Steven was surprised. He looked angry.

'Cara Holbrook just rang. She cancelled the campaign.'

'She was all for it. She was ready to sign the contract.'

Steven couldn't understand this. She seemed to be happy with the deal.

'She's changed her mind' Richard said. 'She rang me five minutes ago and slammed the phone down on me. What happened? What the hell did you do to her?' he shouted.

'I did nothing to her. That's her problem.'

He could see that Richard was unsure of what he meant. He tried hard to remain calm. He was aware of Richard's domestic situation.

'What the fuck do you mean?' Richard said.

'Miss Holbrook asked me to have sex with her. I refused. That's what's wrong with her.'

Richard sat in the chair with his face in his hands.

'Good old Cara. Some things never change. Why the fuck didn't you just close your eyes and think of Ireland, say three Hail Marys, and rattle her bones?' he said quietly.

He sat there deflated, all the anger gone.

'I went to bed with her the first two times I called,' Steven said.

Richard rubbed his eyes and shook his head and laughed; a long colourless laugh.

'Cara didn't get her own way so she threw you out of the cot. You realise that your sudden urge for celibacy has cost us a lot of money and there's a strong possibility that Holbrook Construction will never do business with us again? Unless you want to call on Cara, offer your apologies on bended knee, and then hump the ass off her a few times. That should keep her happy and we'd be back in business again,' he said.

'No, thanks, Mister Steinman.'

Richard walked to the window and looked out.

'Women,' he said to Steven. 'You might as well go home, son. I better call to the maternity wing and give them the good news.'

Steven had fallen in love with California, the way of life, the sunshine, but he'd also fallen in love with Mary. She was different yet similar to Molly; stubborn, argumentative yet, behind all her belligerence, overflowing with generosity.

The film was ready for a first showing. The studio audience was limited and critical. They had seen it all before and were not easily pleased. It was a strange experience for Steven seeing scenes from the camera's viewpoint. It was an education to watch Katharine Hepburn and Gregory Peck perform. They were so natural. When the lights came up George Stevens spoke briefly.

'Another baby conceived and delivered. There will be an opening gala night at the Orpheum so start polishing your shoes and get out your glad-rags.'

There was talk about potential Oscars for different aspects of the film, even a whisper about Mary being nominated for her first-time screenplay. This was Hollywood, the dream factory. Steven was relieved when the film was over and he could get back to real life.

The opening night at the Orpheum arrived. Katharine Hepburn and Gregory Peck arrived in a stretch Limousine. It was a night of glitz and razzle-dazzle. The audience loved the glamour and gave the film a standing ovation. Some critics called it a night of magic while others said it was barely mundane. It was not nominated for any Oscar. The standard that year was high.

Attending the Academy Awards ceremony with Steven was another highlight for Mary. They mingled with the stars. Bob Hope was the host. The drama unfolded as *The Sound of Music* beat the likes of *Doctor Zhivago* and *The Spy Who Came in from the Cold* for best picture and Robert Wise won best director. Lee Marvin was a surprise choice for best actor as the drunk in *Cat Ballou*. Other nominees were Richard Burton, Rod Steiger and Laurence Olivier. Julie Christie pipped Julie Andrews for the best actress award. It was an eventful night but it wasn't over yet. Later, when all the excitement was a distant memory, Mary and Steven sat by the pool talking in the moonlight.

'Mary, I never thought I'd find happiness again. Then you came along. I know this is not very romantic, there's no soft music and I have no flowers or no ring, I can get you a ring tomorrow, any ring you want, but please say you'll be my wife. I haven't much to offer but I'll give you my heart and I'll give you my soul and I promise to make you happy for the rest of your life.'

'Who cares about a ring? I'll marry you right now if you'll have me. I dreamed of this moment. In my dream Clark Gable threw me over his shoulder and ran off with me to a romantic island, a Spanish prince kidnapped me or a Greek Adonis on a white horse swept me off my feet. The three of them together couldn't touch you.'

Steven thought back on his fall from Napoleon's back in to the nettles.

'The last time I rode a horse I fell off and broke my leg.'

'Do you want to know a secret?' she asked.

'I have a feeling you're going to tell me anyway.'

'I fell in love with you the first moment I saw you,' she said.

'You had a funny way of showing it. You nearly drowned me.'

Mary went quiet for a moment

'I'm often uncertain so I go on the attack. This is California. Humble pie is not served here. You crashed into my life and turned it upside down. I really don't care about a ring,' she said.

They didn't notice the curtain on the window of their parents' bedroom move. Susan couldn't sleep. She'd been watching for some time now. She didn't like what she'd seen. Steven and Mary quietly made their way to his bedroom. They sat on his bed. It was almost four a.m.

'Will you do one special thing for me on this special night?' she said.

'Of course I will,' he said.

She took the Claddagh ring from her finger, placed it in the palm of his hand and she tightened his fist around it.

'I'll never be Molly and I'll never take her place. This ring means everything to you. It will always remind you of Molly. I hope she'll always have a special place in your heart.'

He put it in the drawer of the bedside locker. He noticed the little box in the corner of the drawer. He opened it and took out Molly's engagement ring.

'Now will you do something for me?' he said.

'Of course I will,' she said.

He took her hand and placed the ring on her finger.

'This ring means a lot to me,' he said. 'but what good is it hidden away in the back of a drawer? Will you do me the honour of wearing it as an engagement ring? Molly would love that. If you wish, you can wear the

Claddagh ring when we get married. I'm sure she'll watch over both of us.'

'Nothing would make me happier,' she said.

'I wonder what Jeff and Susan will think?' he said.

'That should be interesting. Now she can finally call you son,' she said.

They both went to bed. She lay there beside him too excited to sleep. She didn't know it but her mother was also wide awake in her bed.

Susan had a headache. It was seven-thirty in the morning. Jeff was still sleeping. She went to Steven's bedroom. She knocked and waited and opened the door. The room was empty. She saw a note on the table in the hall. It was from Steven.

Susan and Jeff – Want to talk to you real soon. See you later – Steven.

She called Jeff and showed him the note. They sat in the kitchen in their pyjamas. Jeff yawned and scratched his head. Susan paced up and down.

'First Louise tells me she's a lesbian and she wants to go off living with another woman. Now it's Mary; she must be pregnant. How many times did I warn that girl? I saw them through our window this morning. Why would Steven want to talk to us? Don't tell me he's the father,' she said.

She sat down and blessed herself.

'You were spying on them? Mary is not pregnant. Maybe Steven wants to leave. He's not getting on with Richard but why does he want to talk to both of us?' he said.

'It has to be trouble.'

'He might want some advice. In a way we're his mother and father. He adores you,' he said.

Susan threw the note in the plastic bin.

Business in the New York agency had picked up under the guidance of Harry Martin. Harry was thirty-three; he never married; he was one of the old school. He made the decisions and there was no way he'd run to the hierarchy in Los Angeles with a problem. He was the boss. He'd deal with it. Yet he was concerned. In the last few weeks he'd received anonymous phone calls demanding money. He ignored them. Then unsigned letters began arriving at his apartment. Harry decided to ring Ted Dynan, Jeff's detective friend, for advice.

'Mister Dynan, Jeff Bradley asked me to ring you if there was any trouble at the agency. I'm getting threatening phone calls and demands for money.'

'I know this guy. He's a bad lad. He operates out of bars in Hell's Kitchen in the Westside. Leave him to me,' he told Harry.

Ted told him to take note of the conversations and keep the letters in a safe. A week later the phone calls stopped and there were no more letters.

Marie Kennedy lost her job in Cork. The company closed down. She felt in a rut, twenty-one years old with no future. She now had to depend on part-time modelling. Some weeks she got three days. Other weeks there was nothing. At times she felt lonely. Her brother, Paul, was young and wild. He was usually missing, somewhere else, and Marie spent most of the time alone in the crumbling old home. The isolation didn't help; there were no houses or neighbours nearby. It was barren. She picked up Steven's card and read it again. She missed him and wondered if everyone in California was tall and handsome with sparkling white teeth like they were on television.

At last Steven arrived home from work. Susan was nervous as she watched him through the window walking towards the front door.

'Susan, will you give him a chance to explain,' Jeff said.

Steven entered. He looked a bit uneasy. He asked them both to sit down.

'I'm sorry about the note. I didn't want to wake you. I don't know how to say this. I had a great father in Ireland but thanks Jeff for being a second great father. Susan, you're an angel, my second mother.'

Steven took a deep breath and continued.

'Mister and Mrs Bradley, have I your permission to marry Mary?'

Jeff jumped up and shook Steven's hand. Susan smothered him with kisses.

'I take it that's a yes,' Steven said.

'This is unbelievable,' she said.

'At least now you can officially call me son,' Steven said to Susan.

He made his excuses and went to his bedroom. He wanted to let the good news sink in.

'You were right. God definitely moves in mysterious ways,' Jeff said.

'I hope she's not pregnant?' Susan said.

'It's out of the question. I looked after all that.'

Susan was puzzled.

'What do you mean?'

'I took him aside and advised about women. I warned him to be prepared and gave him a packet of Durex to be on the safe side,' he said.

'You what? You gave the boy a packet of those things, the poor innocent child. Jeff, how could you?' she said.

'I thought it would be better to be safe than sorry. He was a bit green coming over from Ireland. Anyway, there was no need. Charlie got there before me and gave him a few packages just in case,' he said.

'The two of you are two great men, practically inviting the boy to hop in to bed with the first girl he met. Wait until I see Charlie, and you're just as bad,' she said.

With all the excitement they hadn't noticed Mary's arrival. She breezed in to the kitchen closely followed by Steven.

'What do you think of your new son-in-law? Will we hang on to him?' Mary said.

'I have to pinch myself,' Susan said.

'Mum, I'd like a simple wedding, just family with Louise as bridesmaid. I m not sure about the best man,' she said looking at Steven.

'I'd be honoured to be married here in my home, with Charlie as my best man, and I'd love my little sister, Marie, to be there' he said.

'I'm dying to meet her,' Susan said.

'Now will you two get out from under our feet?' Susan said

'Come on, son. I know when we're not wanted,' Jeff said.

Steven and Mary watched as the passengers flowed out the exit gate. At last Steven spotted her. He waved at her and she rushed to him. She hardly knew him, so tanned and well-dressed. When Mary and Marie met it was love at first hug. On the journey home they never stopped talking. For once Mary hardly got a word in. He couldn't believe the change in her. She was so tall and elegant. When Mary pulled up outside her home Marie looked wide-eyed at the house, the tennis court and the pool. Everybody wanted to talk to her.

'I'll show you to your room. You might like a little rest,' Susan said.

'I'm grand, Mrs Bradley. I had a nap on the plane,' Marie said.

'Please, call me Susan.'

Mary grabbed Marie's hand.

'Come on, young lady, there's some shopping to be done,' Mary said.

They were half-way down the drive before anyone knew it. Mary gave her a whirl-wind tour. Marie was fascinated with Los Angele. When she'd left Ireland it was dark and damp. They ended up in the Blue Stove drinking coffee.

'Steven always called you his pet,' Mary said.

'He's in all my childhood memories. I missed him so much. I used to cry when I read his letters from Dublin. Steven is tougher than you think. Now all his dreams have come true; living in the land of make believe and marrying his beautiful princess. I know all about you,' Marie said.

'What do you mean?'

Marie smiled, thinking back.

'Every week he poured out his heart, his hopes, his fears, and then you came along. It was nothing but Mary this and Mary that. Two years ago he told me he loved you. I couldn't wait to get those weekly letters from California.'

'You're so like him, Marie. 'You also have this natural charm. Half the men in California will be chasing you.'

'Thank you for bringing so much happiness into his life,' Marie said.

'Come on, there's a queue at home waiting to spoil you,' Mary said.

Harry Martin walked quickly to the car park. It had been a good day at the agency. As he opened the car door he was struck on the head from behind. He stumbled and fell to the ground. He felt the pain from the kicks in the ribs and he heard the grunts of his assailants. He was grabbed roughly and shoved in to the back seat of a red Chrysler. They were two burly men. One was bald with a scar on his left cheek. The other struck him on the head again. A gun was rammed in to his mouth. Harry could feel the cold steel of the barrel and he heard the click of the hammer being cocked. Then a rag was stuffed in his mouth. He remembered no more. The car drove off and quietly joined the stream of traffic.

When Mary and Marie arrived back at the house laden down with boxes Jeff, Charlie and Steven had gone off for a beer. Susan and Louise were still there waiting patiently. Susan opened a bottle of wine and the four women tried on and swopped around skirts, hats, blouses and suits, dresses and shoes. The second bottle was opened. They finally agreed on who was wearing what and where and how and when. Marie looked stunning in the new clothes. Susan took a notebook from her handbag.

'Mary, are you sure you want a small wedding?'

'It's what we both want.'

'None of Steven's brothers can make it so there are the four of us and the three men; that makes seven,' Susan said.

'Don't forget the pianist and Charlie's girl, Sarah, from the library. There's almost another wedding there, and we have Richard Steinman; he's coming on his own, and Cathy, Steven's secretary; she wants to bring someone too. Then we have our close neighbours; that makes a grand total of sixteen,' Mary said.

Susan kept writing in her notebook.

'Don't forget Emma,' Louise said.

'Emma,' Susan said.

'I nearly forgot Emma; she's part of the family,' Mary said.

There was an awkward silence when Susan put her notebook in her handbag and walked out of the room.

Harry Martin felt sick. He wanted to vomit. The smell from the dirty rag in his mouth didn't help. His body ached with pain. His head was pounding. He found it hard to get his bearings in the dim light. He was tied to a chair in the semi-darkness. The ropes hurt his arms. There was a stench of stale meat and patches of dried blood were spattered on the concrete floor. It was a large draughty building. Some of the windows were smashed and there was broken glass scattered all over the area. He felt it was an abandoned abattoir. The two men's voices echoed as they spoke. The man with the scar pulled the rag from Harry's mouth. Harry got sick down the front of his trousers. The men laughed. The other man, the heavier of the two, spat on the ground.

'Well, Mister Martin, you're not such a big man now. You think you're a smart-ass. We ask you for a few bucks. You'd have that in your back pocket. I'm Rick Guardino. I don't want the word to get out that I'm a soft touch. It's nothing personal but I'll have to make an example of you,' the heavy man said.

The other man picked up a tin and poured petrol all over Harry. His hair was soaked and he spat and spluttered petrol from his mouth. He struggled helplessly in the chair. Rick Guardino took out a cigar and lit it with a lighter. He laughed as he puffed slowly on the cigar and still held the flaming lighter in his hand.

'Goodbye, Harry,' he said.

Harry Martin begged for his life.

'I'll have the money tomorrow. Please, just one last chance,' he said.

Rick Guardino flicked the lighter shut. The two men laughed.

'We can hardly let you go without giving you a reminder of what we'll do to you if you if you don't come up with the goodies,' Rick said.

'You'll get your money, Mister Guardino. Don't worry, you'll have it tomorrow,' Harry pleaded.

'I'm not worried, Harry. You're the one with the worries. Here's a small reminder,' he said.

The bald man dragged Harry across the floor to a rough table covered with blood-stains. A butcher's cleaver hung on a hook. Rick Guardino took it down and ran his finger across the sharp edge of the cleaver. The other man pulled Harry's left hand free and held it out flat with the palms down on the table. Harry screamed as Rick held the cleaver over his head.

'An inch off your fingers will help you remember,' Rick said.

The cleaver thudded into the table barely missing Harry's fingers. He wet himself and his body shook with fear as Rick grunted and lifted the cleaver and drove it into the table again just missing Harry's fingers.

'The eyesight ain't what it used to be,' Rick said.

'Your glasses are in the car, boss. Will I get them?' the other man said.

'Don't bother. I think Mister Martin knows we mean business and something tells me that from now on he'll be a good little boy,' Rick said.

The bald man with the scar man untied Harry. He staggered across the floor, struggled to pull open the large iron gate, and shuffled into the night. He could still hear the hollow laughter echoing from the warehouse.

Louise and Emma were sitting in the kitchen of their apartment. Both had a glass of wine. Louise's eyes were still red.

'Come on, Lou, It will all work out fine in the end.'

'How could my mum behave like that? She doesn't want you at my sister's wedding, and I'm bridesmaid.'

'She's just old-fashioned. A lot of people are,' Emma said.

'If you're not going I'm not going,' Louise said.

A knock on the door interrupted them. It was Mary.

'Hi girls. Don't mind my mother. Dad will talk her around. Emma, I'd be honoured if you'll attend my wedding, and Cathy at the agency is gay and she's bringing her partner. Mum will be surrounded by lesbians.

The girls laughed at this. Mary continued.

'Promise me one thing, Emma, no kissing or cuddling and no sex on the dance floor.'

'I'll do my best,' Emma said.

'Emma, you'll be the life and soul of the wedding. I have a husband-to-be waiting for me. See you soon,' Mary said and quickly left.

Harry Martin didn't know how he made it back to his apartment. He was exhausted. He was scared. He peeled off his wet clothes, they reeked of petrol, and had a long hot shower. There was only one way out. He picked up the phone.

Jeff was just going to bed when the phone rang. He was surprised to find it was Harry Martin.

'Hi, Mister Bradley, sorry for ringing you at home but something has come up. I'd welcome your advice.'

'Harry, you can r4ing me anytime. What's the problem?'

'I have a big favour to ask and you've always been like a father to me. My own father has been ill for the last few weeks in LA. I'm the only one who could look after him. Is there any possibility of a re-location to our LA office? It's a lot to ask but it would mean so much to the family.'

'When do you want to finish in New York?' Jeff asked.

'Would it suit you if I finished tomorrow evening? I'd be back in harness the following morning with Mister Steinman?' Harry said.

'I'll ring Richard and let him know. You look after your father and ring me any time.'

Harry Martin was bruised and battered but he moved as quickly as he could. He dumped his stinking clothes in the waste bin and grabbed the bare essentials. He hobbled out on to the street, waited in the shadows, and hailed a cab. He was still terrified. He wanted to disappear in the hurl-burly of Manhattan. This was his last night in New York.

Jeff briefly spoke with Richard Steinman on the phone. He felt it was only fair to ring him. When he eventually went to bed he woke Susan.

'Sorry, love, but I may have to go to New York for a week. There are a few problems in the agency. Do you want to come with me? You could do with a little holiday,' he said.

'Jeff, are you serious? A little holiday? My daughter is getting married next week and you want me to have a holiday. I have a thousand things to do.'

She turned her back in a huff and went back to sleep.

Most of the staff were already working when Jeff arrived at the New York branch early Monday morning. Cliff Wickham had taken charge. Jeff had always liked Cliff. He was hard-working, dependable and he got on well with everybody. Cliff took great pride in his appearance. He was always immaculately dressed. The agency was pleasantly busy. The books were perfect; they showed a substantial profit and the phone hardly ever stopped ringing. Jeff tried to stay out of everyone's way. He mingled with the creative people and tried to be one of the boys and he even called to some first time clients. Harry Martin had settled back in Los Angeles and everyone was happy.

Steven hated sitting around doing nothing in everyone's way. He decided to work right up to the day before the wedding. He tried to contact Peg. There was no response from the number in Dublin. He remembered the cake shop near the Emerald. He got them on the phone. The line was poor and he had to shout.

'Hello, this is Cummins' cakes,' the voice answered.

'I'm trying to contact the Emerald Hotel. Peg Coogan works there, if you know her,' Steven said.

'I knew Peg well; a lovely girl, but I'm afraid the hotel is gone. They say the owner lost the hotel gambling. That's about three years ago. The two lassies went off to Liverpool; never heard of them since.'

'I used to work there as a boy,' Steven said.

'I remember, you used to have her little dog with you.'

'That was Binky. Is he's still alive?' Steven asked.

'That little fecker bit me a few times. He died of old age.'

Steven hung up. He wondered about Peg.

It was a perfect day for a wedding. The pianist played a slow waltz. All eyes were on the couple dancing, lost in each other's arms. Steven looked handsome in his white tuxedo and Mary was stunning in her long, pink dress. When the music stopped the couple took an exaggerated bow to a round of applause. The pianist tore into a pulsating rendition of 'Rock Around the Clock.' Louise, Emma, Cathy and her girlfriend, Jenny, bounced around to the beat of the music. They waved and clapped their hands and wobbled their backsides. Susan wasn't happy. She worried about everything. Jeff took her hand in his.

'It's the first time I was at a wedding where I'm losing a son and a daughter. The house it will be like a morgue,' he said

Jeff kissed her and excused himself. He mingled a little. Richard Steinman sat by the bar alone.

'Hi, Richard, a penny for your thoughts,' Jeff said.

'I was just thinking about the last wedding I was at when my son, Tony, got married; the love, the optimism. Sophie and I were so happy then. What went wrong? The final divorce papers have been signed. I'm a forty-nine year old bachelor; a single man again,' he said.

'Life is funny,' Jeff said.

Richard shook his head. It wasn't funny for him.

'I can go fishing every weekend now and watch the Lakers when I like.'

'Thanks for your New York suggestion, 'Jeff said.

'I'd do anything to get rid of that young man and let me work in peace,' Richard said.

Both men laughed and clinked their glasses. There were roars of laughter behind them. Emma had grabbed the microphone and began belting out 'That's why the Lady is a Tramp.' Charlie, looking unusually serious, stood up and started tapping his glass with a spoon to get attention. He normally lived in a shorts, T-shirt and sandals but he looked a different man in a blue, three-piece suit and red bow tie.

'Will you lot stay quiet for two minutes? When I first met Steven he looked like a long-lost puppy dog with floppy ears and big blue eyes. He's come a long way since. I'm sure Mary in her own shy way had something to do with that.'

Richard Steinman tapped Steven on the shoulder.

'I have a small present for you, our New York branch. You're young, ambitious and a pig-headed son-of-a-gun; the perfect combination. It's yours and you won't have me to annoy you. It will be a new life for you and for Mary,' Richard said

'I don't know what to think? Steven said.

'He'd be honoured to accept your offer,' Mary said.

Steven looked uncertain.

'But what about your writing career and our honeymoon and Niagra Falls?' he said.

'The studio has a branch in New York and I'm sure Niagra Falls will be still there in a few months. Will Wednesday morning be OK to start, Mister Steinman?' Mary said.

'That's acceptable under the circumstances. What do you think, Jeff?' Richard said winking at him

'Will you guys slow down a little?' Steven said.

'This is just normal Californian speed, honey,' Mary said.

Steven shook his head; an advertising agency for a present? This was America.

'I'd be in complete charge?' he asked.

'Yep,' Jeff and Richard said together.

'I don't have to answer to anybody?' Steven said.

'Nope,' Richard and Jeff said.

'When do we leave?' Steven said.

Richard gestured towards Marie who was in deep conversation with Charlie and his girlfriend, Sarah.

'That's not all. I made some phone calls to the Ford Model Agency in New York and recommended your sister. They'll see her and do some promo shots whenever she feels like calling.'

'I'll tell her myself,' Mary said

Marie was in deep conversation. Mary tapped her on the shoulder.

'Do you want the good news or the very good news?'

'Give me the very good news first,' Marie said.

'The Ford Agency in New York wants to talk to you,' Mary said.'You're joking. What's the good news?' Marie asked.

'You can meet them right away.'

Mary gave Charlie a nudge with her elbow.

'You'd want to get a move on. Sarah, will you give that man a gentle push?' Mary said.

'There's an old Irish proverb that says "there's always a marriage after a wedding", Marie said.

'Could somebody translate that in to English for me?' Charlie said.

'I've proposed to him twice and there's not a budge,' Sarah said.

'There's also an old Texas proverb that says "there's a time and a place for everything",' Charlie said.

The day moved pleasantly by. Susan was in a reflective mood. Two glasses of sherry usually did that to her. She was relieved it went well. She looked at her watch. It was 8.30 pm. The sun was sinking in the background. The pianist was still playing love songs. Charlie and Sarah were embraced in a slow waltz. Marie had joined the girls at Emma's table where they were singing 'Kiss me honey, honey kiss me' to themselves. Jeff and Susan sat reminiscing, holding hands. They were back where they'd started; sixty year old teenagers; nostalgia was rampant. .

Cliff Wickham answered the phone in his office.

'Can I speak to Harry Martin, please? We have some business to discuss,' a rough voice asked.

'Mister Martin has gone back to our Los Angeles office,' Cliff said.

'Are you in charge?'

'I am.'

'I want to meet you about a commercial venture I already arranged with Mister Martin.'

'Maybe it would be better if you waited. Mister Kennedy is taking over tomorrow. Can I take your name, sir?' Cliff asked

'Don't bother.'

Rick Guardino swore and hung up.

Steven Kennedy was fascinated with San Francisco. He'd read all about the city's earthquake in 1906, one of the most significant earthquakes of all time with over 3000 casualties. For two days Mary and Steven resided in the Palace Hotel where a long list of greats had also stayed, from Caruso to Winston Churchill and Bing Crosby to Charlie Chaplin. He felt at home in this beautiful city; with its forty-four hills it reminded him of his home town. As he stood on Nob Hill and looked down on Market Street, Union Square and Fisherman's Wharf, it was as if he was at the top of Fair Hill overlooking Cork city. The Golden Gate Bridge was awesome and across the San Francisco Bay Alcatraz Prison had a sinister look about it. Mary showed him the City Hall where Marilyn Monroe married Joe DiMaggio. On their last night they drank wine and made love. He was worried about Marie. The Bradleys talked her into staying for a week before going to New York. Susan was delighted to have her around the house. They became great pals and Louise was happy to meet her any time. Next stop New York.

Steven sat in his New York office. He wondered if this was the final leg of his journey, his last hurrah, his Ithaka. It started in Cork; easy-going and inquisitive with a village-like intimacy. Then there was the sprawling flatness of Dublin spreading its wings, steeped in Irish history, a city of writers; the vast Los Angeles metropolis he had come to love; the vibrant character of San Francisco. But if you mix them all together they wouldn't touch New York. Manhattan was like an explosion; it doesn't say hello; it doesn't kiss you on the cheek; it smacks you in the face and then picks you up and gives you a big hug. He made a point of being early on his first day. Cliff Wickham was there before him. He liked that. Steven introduced himself to the staff.

'My door is always open. Many of our rivals may be blasé and lukewarm. I don't do lukewarm. We'll give our clients flames and passion. I want to shock them, frighten them. Any questions?

One young man put up his hand. Steven had already spoken to him.

'Yes, Brad Thornton, isn't it?' Steven said.

'Where do you hope we'll be in two years?' Brad said.

Everyone laughed. They all knew he was a bit of a joker.

'Good question, Mister Thornton. In two years you'll all be millionaires.'

Steven nodded at Cliff to follow him to his office. He wanted to pick his brains. He wanted to know what the man in the street was thinking, what he was eating, what he was drinking, what he was buying.

Every chance Steven got for the next few months he explored the concrete Shangri-la that was New York: the magic that was Queens, he sauntered around the Bowery and Little Italy, Lafayette Street and Mulberry Street, spoke to the people in Chinatown, relaxed in Battery Park and watched the nonstop river traffic, paid a visit to Soho, Greenwich Village, strolled through Central Park and on to Harlem. Some nights Mary accompanied him to Staten Island, Brooklyn or the Bronx. He talked to barmen, waiters, policemen, shopkeepers and taxi drivers. They were the life-blood of New York. He was surprised at one aspect of his travels; the amount of Irish in New York, especially in Hell's Kitchen in the West Side. He couldn't help but notice large sums of money changing hands. Although it wasn't far from the agency the sense of danger in this infamous area excited him. He heard whispers of the Westies and mobsters and murders but the countless Irish pubs appealed to him. They were overflowing with potential clients. He talked business with them.

He became friendly with one man, Brendan Doyle from the West of Ireland. He had his own pub, *The Harp,* on 9th Avenue. He was a tall, thin man with tightly cropped hair and prominent teeth which gave the impression that he was always smiling. Occasionally they went to a nearby Italian café where they had a meal with Brendan's friends, some Irish, some Italian. Steven decided to take Richard Steinman at his word. He was about to make changes, big changes. Mary was happy in the three-bed apartment near the corner of 47th Street but she couldn't wait to move to her own home. She didn't like Hell's Kitchen.

Charlie Grainger resisted the temptation to grab the handbrake and pull it.

'Slow down, stop, stop. Young lady, you sure are in one goddamn awful hurry. I'm too young to die,' Charlie said.

'Sorry, I got carried away,' Marie said.

Steven's Buick spluttered to a halt. Marie was driving. It was their third lesson. She was getting there surely but oh so slowly. When Steven left for New York he gave Charlie his car as a present. His old jeep had seen better days. Luckily, there wasn't another car in the deserted car park.

'I give up. I can't manage that clutch,' she said.

'Don't rush. Start her up again and we'll have another go,' he said.

Marie turned the key, slowly moved off and made her way around the car park going up and down through the gears.

'You're only fooling poor old Charlie. That's it for the day,' he said.

She was leaving on Saturday. She'd rung the Ford Agency in New York and made an appointment for Monday morning. Susan asked her to stay a little longer. With her two daughters and Steven gone she was lonely. Saturday arrived before she knew it. Charlie drove her to the airport in his jeep. Just before she left he handed her an envelope.

'It's just a few dollars to keep you going in New York.. I sold Steven's car. I'm comfortable in this old banger. Old friends are best,' he said.

Jeff Bradley walked in to the kitchen. He felt tired but happy. He'd had a good day's golf. The phone rang. It was Steven.

'Well, Steven, how's that daughter of mine treating you?' Jeff said.

'We're still on our honeymoon,' Steven said.

'What can I do for you?'

'I'd like to change our New York name to Shamrock Advertising. We'd retain our regular clientele but there's a huge Irish/American market here ready to be plucked, and half of Boston seems to be Irish,' Steven said.

Steven could hear laughter on the other side of the phone.

'It's an important decision' Jeff said.

'What about Richard?' Steven said.

'We said you could do what you want. It's your baby,' Jeff said.

'You might thank him for me.'

'How's Marie? Susan is lost without her,' Jeff said.

'She's crazy about the apartment.'

Jeff hung up and smiled to himself.

Mary and Marie left early for Ford Model Agency. Eileen Ford herself welcomed Marie in the foyer and showed her in to the back studio. Mary waited outside. There was a photographer ready and set up for action. Marie felt self-conscious but just did what she was told. She changed into several different outfits while the photographer took countless shots of her. The Ford people were kind and patient with her. Eileen Ford reappeared, thanked her, and led er to the foyer.

'You have the figure, good skin and the right face. If the camera doesn't like you we can do nothing about it. I'd just like to remind you that being a model is a tough career,' Eileen said.

Mary was all excited and full of questions.

'How did it go?'

'I'm exhausted from smiling. They'll let me know,' Marie said.

'Jesus, you look gorgeous. They'll have to take you on,' Mary said.

'We'll know soon enough.'

'If they're looking for a small, intelligent, pretty girl will you put in a good word for me? I'm cheap and available,' Mary said.

Mary dropped Marie to the apartment and went to the studio. She had a deadline to make with the first draught of her script.

When Steven told the staff of the name change there was a general reaction of approval. He called Cliff Wickham to his office. There was an urgency in his voice.

'Cliff, circularise every business, anyone with a remote Irish connection in New York and Boston. Remind them of our new name. This is priority. I want results.'

Marie was in her apartment looking at the television when the phone rang. It was Eileen Ford.

'We've studied all your developed shots. The camera adores you. Come in at nine in the morning. Bring your lawyer with you,' Eileen said.

There was a long silence.

'That is if you're interested,' Eileen said.

'Yes, of course I'm interested. I'm sorry. I'll see you in the morning. Thanks, Mrs Ford.'

Marie was in a daze. She put down the phone, then picked it up again and rang Mary and Steven. Mary was thrilled; she couldn't wait to get home. Steven said he'd provide the company lawyer for her.

After a week there was a trickle of Irish interest in the agency. A month later that trickle turned into a flood, an avalanche of phone calls from Irish companies, enquiring about possible business. Shamrock Ads quickly dominated a large section of the Irish market. The Italian, German and Jewish clientele followed suit. They wanted satisfaction. Business flourished from cars to carpets and toys to toothpaste. Steven introduced a slogan;

We'll sell it even if they don't want it.

He was honest.

He was different.

Success brought its own problems; daily phone calls, threats, demanding money or else. Cliff usually dealt with these crank calls. One day a nasty caller got through to Steven saying he was a friend. He wanted to meet him about private business. Steven invited the man to call to his office. He hung up.

By now Steven and Mary were in constant demand for social occasions: the Lord Mayor's Ball and charity events. They were treated like a celebrity couple. Their photographs were in the newspapers. Steven didn't like these nights but they were good for business. He met the right people in the right places. Deal were often struck while sipping champagne. Mary was ideal in this situation, the perfect partner, and her charm often swayed a transaction. Although the apartment was fine they continued to look for a home of their own. Mary had her eye on a house in Long Island.

It was Marie Kennedy's first day at the Ford Agency. She was whisked off to wear a selection of outfits in the shadow of the Empire State Building. She posed for several hours in different suits and dresses while the cameras flashed non-stop. The next day she flew to Boston and spent hours in the Cape Cod sunshine displaying a selection of swimsuits. That was to be the pattern of her new life; constant travel, long hours and hard work, but she revelled in it. She was now an assured young model living from a suitcase; today Miami, tomorrow Chicago, next week the Grand Canyon. She was awarded young face of the year in one magazine and she appeared in Vogue and The Tatler. When she was working in New York a chauffeur-driven car collected her from the apartment and brought her to and from work. Ford Agency insisted she keep in shape and provided membership to a gym where she regularly worked out.

At last Mary got her wish. They moved to Long Island. She loved the house. It hadn't a swimming pool or tennis court; just a small rear and front garden. It was an old-fashioned home with an atmosphere of love. They invited Marie to come with them but the apartment was near everything. Mary threw herself into converting the house into her own special home. Susan and Jeff paid a flying visit and stayed for two days. While Mary gave her mother a guided tour of her new home Jeff called to the agency. Steven asked for Jeff's advice. The premises had become too small and he was thinking about taking over another agency. Jeff advised him not to rush into anything. Susan was amazed how mature Marie had become yet she could see glimpses that she was still a shy Irish girl. Jeff was delighted with Steven; he reminded him of himself, full with the brash confidence of youth. Susan had never seen Mary so happy. She still worried.

Marie had a rare day off. She was determined to relax and spoil herself. She had a long lie-in and wrote a letter to her brother, Paul. She decided to go to the gym for a workout. She had a set ninety-minute routine specially prepared by an instructor hired by the agency. He showed her no mercy and put her through her paces. After a sauna and a shower she felt good. She had a coffee and a chat with some friends. All her model friends met here.

It was dark when she finally left the gym. The apartment wasn't far away so she decided to walk. As she turned off Seventh Avenue a red Chrysler pull in near the kerb. A bald man with a scar on his face jumped out of the car and grabbed her around the throat. She was choking. She couldn't call out. He bundled her into the back seat. The driver, a big heavy man, drove off, turned sharply and shot through Times Square. She scrawled and bit and kicked her attacker but the bald man struck her in the head with a hand gun. She slumped unconscious in his arms. He laid her on the floor of the car and covered her with a blanket. Rick Guardino grunted with satisfaction behind the wheel. He'd been reading all about Marie Kennedy. He'd been stalking her for days, observing every move she made, when she left the apartment, when she returned, when she went to the gym, how she occasionally walked home. It helped when he found out she was now living alone. It was pay-back time for Jeff Bradley.

Marie Kennedy regained consciousness. Her eyes were glazed and her mouth was dry. It took her several minutes to find her bearings. Her body ached and her head was throbbing with pain. There was a gag in her mouth and her hands and feet were tied. She was lying awkwardly on a single bed. She tried to move her body to ease the pain but it made it worse. When her eyes got used to the dark she could make out the surroundings; a shabby room with a bare bulb, a bedside locker, one chair in the corner and a window with the curtain drawn. She could see light seeping under a door. There were muted sounds coming from the next room. She could hear two voices, sometimes she could hear laughter. She couldn't understand. Why? How? Who? Where? She was dozing off to sleep when the door was pushed open. She could make out it was a big man. He stood over her and spoke with a rough voice.

'How is my precious butterfly?'

Marie was scared. He put a bowl on the bedside locker, untied her hands and feet, and removed the gag.

'In case you feel like screaming, honey, we're miles from Fifth Avenue. Here's some soup. We don't want anything to happen to you.'

He left the room and locked the door. Marie found the bowl in the darkness and drank the soup. She was starving. She looked out the barred window. There was nothing; blackness. .

When Marie's regular driver got no answer at her apartment he was surprised. Normally she was waiting at the door. The agency later phoned her but there was no reply. They could do nothing. It had happened before with models. She may have met someone and gone off with them. This was New York.

It was five past three in the afternoon when Steven Kennedy's secretary told him that a man wanted him on the phone. He picked up the phone.

'Yes.'.

He could hear the heavy breathing before the man spoke.

'I'm Rick Guardino. It's nice to talk to you.'

'What do you want?'

'I know everything about you and your pretty little sister, Marie.'

'What the hell has Marie got to do with anything?.

'She's here with me now.'

Steven tried to keep calm.

'I don't believe you. Marie is at work today.'

Steven could hear the phone being put down and voices in the background. He could hear Marie crying.

'Steven, please help me. Get me out of here, please.'

Steven tried to control his anger.

'What do you want? Don't hurt her.'

'Bring me ten thousand dollars in old notes and you'll have your sister back in one piece, and you'll never see me again. One hint of trouble she gets her face slashed. Try anything foolish and her two legs will be chopped off at the ankles.'

Steven took a deep breath.

'I'll take me two hours. How do I hand it over to you?'

'Do you know the church on West 51st Street just around the corner from 10th Avenue?'

'I'll find it.'

The voice still rasped and Marie could be heard crying in the background.

'It's a big, red church with bars along the front. Park your car at the corner and wait at the side of the building, eleven o'clock sharp. Don't fuck-up or you'll get your sister's ankles in the post.'

Rick Guardino hung up. Steven hurried to the company bank He explained to the manager that his request was for an urgent business deal. He was desperate. He rang the *The Harp*. Brendan Doyle was there. Steven begged for his advice. He told him that the caller was Rick Guardino. Brendan warned him not to talk over the phone.

'Call here at nine o'clock. Tell no one.'

Marie quietly prayed as the door creaked open and the light from the next room pierced her eyes. There were two men. One stood over her and laughed a harsh laugh while the other stayed by the door. He untied her legs. It hurt her to move them. He took off his coat and unbuckled his belt. He looked down on her. She could feel her clothes being ripped off. She was crushed by his weight. There was no escape. She was engulfed by the stale smell of his body. She felt so helpless and weak. And then came the pain, the searing pain, and the raucous laughter echoed around the room

Steven found it impossible to work for the rest of the day. He told no one, not even Mary. He left for home early. He couldn't rest. She knew there was something wrong. His mind was miles away. He kept pacing up and down and looking at his watch. When he put on his coat she stopped him.

'Steven, what is it?'

He picked his words carefully before he spoke.

'It's just something I must take care of. I'll tell you later.'

He kissed her and left. She stood there helpless.

Steven looked at his watch again as he entered the door of *The Harp*. It was 8.45pm. The bar was scattered with drinkers. Brendan sat alone at a table. He beckoned to Steven.

'Do exactly as I say. Order two whiskeys, act a little drunk, buy a drink for the guys at the bar. Do it.'

Steven called noisily for his drinks, bought a drink for several customers, and sat down again. Brendan pointed to the toilet door.

'Follow me. There's a door just past the toilet. I'll be waiting there.'

Brendan left the bar. Steven waited and then followed him. He tapped on the door and entered the small room. Brendan locked the door.

'This is not your scene. Everyone hates Guardino. That bastard has killed people for peanuts. He's a butcher.'

Steven pleaded with him.

'If he doesn't get the money he said he'd....'

'Steven, I have friends. They can deal with him.'

'If he smells a rat he'll slash her face.'

Brenan opened a safe on the wall, took out a canvas bag and emptied the contents on the table; a handgun, several bits and pieces and a silver tube. He twisted the tube on to the barrel, then picked out a magazine and pushed it up the handle of the gun. It clicked in perfectly. Brendan handed him the gun.

'Take this. It's a Luger P08, eight rounds up the spout.'

Steven took it.

'I never saw a gun in my life never mind fire one.'

'Then hit him with it, Steven. It's simple; catch it, aim it and pull the trigger. There's a silencer on it so no one will hear anything. It's like firing a peashooter. Put it down the back of your trousers. Make sure you bring it back.'

Steven had been driving around Hell's Kitchen in the light drizzle for what seemed like an eternity. He could feel the gun pressing into his back. He feared for Marie. He'd driven past the church for the third time. It was 10.45pm. He turned on to West 52nd Street and pulled in to the kerb. He was sweating. The briefcase of money lay on the passengers' seat. It was time to go. He turned into 10th Avenue. There was a dark area at the end of the church railings. He parked in the shade of a big tree. It was eleven pm sharp. He put the briefcase in the boot and walked to the corner of the church. His eyes raked through the darkness. It was now raining heavily. He waited. A red Chrysler appeared and stopped behind his car. He could make out two men in the car. There was no sign of Marie. He swore to himself. The men got out and walked towards him. The heavy man spoke.

'We meet at last. I trust you brought the money.'

'I trust you brought my sister.'

The heavy man was annoyed..

'You'll get your sister when I see the money.'

'I don't trust you. I want to talk to Marie.'

The heavy man nodded to his colleague who walked towards the Chrysler. Steven followed him. He opened the car and wound down the rear window. Marie was lying on the back seat wrapped in a blanket. When she saw Steven she struggled to sit up and whispered in his ear.

'He raped me.'

The bald man wound up the window and locked the car.

'You've seen her. Where's the money?'

Steven opened his boot and walked back into the darkness. He handed the briefcase to the heavy man who smiled.

'Marie, is a lovely young girl. It was a pleasure getting to know her. She was like your Virgin Mary.'

The two men laughed.

Steven looked calm but a rage was beginning to well up inside him. Memories flashed through his mind.

Bringing Marie to her first day at school.

She danced with excitement.

Reading stories until she fell asleep.

Sitting on his knee all giggles and mischief.

His father's words haunted him. Now he knew what they meant.

In the face of trouble work the backbone, not the wishbone.

He pulled out the Luger. He'd never forget the blank stare on the faces of the two men. The sound surprised him; zip, zip, zip, zip four times in the chest of the big man. He groaned and crumpled to the ground in a heap. Zip, zip and his colleague tumbled silently next to him. Steven fished in his pocket for the keys of the Chrysler and picked up the briefcase. He stood over the heavy man and pumped the last two bullets into his groin. He had one last look around. The coast was clear. He stuck the gun down the back of his trousers and moved quickly. The briefcase was thrown in the boot. Marie was wrapped in the blanket and carefully placed on his back seat. He locked the Chrysler and dropped the keys down between the bars of a drain. Marie heard nothing; she saw nothing. He drove through the rain and parked near *The Harp*.

He had a quick check on Marie.

'You're safe now.'

'Steven, I thought I was going to die. It was a nightmare.'

'I'll be five minutes. You'll stay in our house tonight,' he said.

The Harp was packed. He could see Brendan through the smoke helping out behind the bar. Steven called for a whiskey.

'I think you've had enough, sir. You must have drunk a bottle of Jack Daniels. Here's one for the road but that's it. I'll call a cab for you,' Brendan said and gave him a drink.

He nodded at Steven, gave him his drink and went in the toilet door. Steven drank his whiskey, waited a moment, and followed him. Brendan was opening the wall safe when Steven entered his office.

'How did it go?'

Steven handed him the gun. Brendan flicked open the magazine and whistled when he saw it was empty.

'What happened?'

'I shot them.'.

'Holy fuck, what do you mean "them"?'

Steven was restless. He explained that he had no other choice.

'Guardino raped my sister. His lapdog was with him. They're both dead. Marie is outside in the car. I'll meet you tomorrow. How much will this cost?'

Brendan shook his head.

Remember, you were here all night. There are a dozen witnesses. Let's just say you owe me.'

Steven left quickly. Brendan smiled his smile as he cleaned and dismantled the gun and put each piece back in the canvas bag and locked the safe. The rain had stopped. Steven was surprised at the way he felt. He'd just murdered two men yet there was no remorse, no guilt, no shame, just the satisfaction at having done the right thing. It was justified. It was necessary.

Mary could hardly believe it when he arrived with Marie in his arms.

'I'll explain later but first run a bath and get her out of these filthy clothes. She's staying with us tonight.'

Mary hesitated, but then disappeared in to the bathroom. Steven put Marie on the sofa. She looked so vulnerable.

'Steven, how did you get me free so easily?'

'You know how persuasive I can be when I'm angry.'

'I feel dirty. I hope that awful man won't bother me again,' she said.

'He won't,' he said.

Mary reappeared and walked Marie to the bathroom. The bath was almost ready. She helped her to undress and left the door open in case she needed anything. Marie soaped herself all over and gently examined her body. She was still sore and bruised.

Steven looked unkempt and tired. Mary's eyes challenged him. He filled a large whiskey. She refused a drink. She wanted an explanation. He begged her to trust him. She helped Marie to her bedroom. She looked so frail and vulnerable. Mary couldn't help but notice the ugly bump on her head. Marie was exhausted and quickly fell into a deep sleep. Mary switched off the light and confronted Steven.

'What the hell is going on,' she asked.

'I have no qualms about what I did. I'd do the same thing tomorrow,' he said.

He told her everything; the brutality of Rick Guardino, the trouble he'd caused her father, how he'd taken Marie the night before, what had happened by the church and where he'd got the gun. Mary poured a whiskey for herself.

'You killed two men.'

'They would have killed me and Marie.'

'We have to call the police.'

'We can't.'

Mary pleaded with him.

'Marie was raped. We have to.'

'Under the circumstances we have to keep our mouths shut.'

'Who knows about this?' she asked.

'You, me and Brendan. I'll get rid of her clothes in the morning and put the ransom money back in the bank. There were no witnesses. I have an alibi. No one will miss those two thugs. It will be a blessing to the police. Put the whole thing out of your head.'

Mary was still upset. She had a second whiskey.

'This is not a scene from a film. This is real life and death.'

'Think of what they did to Marie and how she suffered from those animals. What if it had been you? Would it be ok then?' he said.

He had a quick look at Marie and went to bed. Mary sat there for an hour and drank whiskey. She'd never seen this side of her husband. She was concerned about the Irish and Mafia criminals in Hell's Kitchen but Steven assured her that it was nothing personal; business was business.

Mary couldn't sleep. Her head ached. She got up early. Steven had already left for the agency. Marie's dirty clothes were also gone. Mary took a day off from work. She rang Ford's Agency and told them that Marie was ill. Steven carried a holdall stuffed with Marie's clothes and everything he wore the night before and discreetly buried in the large rubbish bin behind the car park.

Steven sat alone in his office. There was a brief note from Cliff Wickham on his desk.

Steven, Maybe good news, Cliff.

Steven wondered what it meant. He laughed at the idea that he was too busy for comfort. Several of his acquaintances in Hell's Kitchen had put business his way. It surprised him the way so many Italian companies, especially restaurants, took out ads with Shamrock. The company's reputation had spread throughout New York, but their hands were tied; there was no more space in 7th Avenue. An excited Cliff Wickham charged in his office door. He was out of breath.

'Steven, while I was getting measured for a suit next door Mister Roskov hinted that he was selling up and going back to Russia. He's an old-fashioned tailor, but times have changed. It's all flash now with boutiques churning out instant suits at half the price. He showed me the factory at the back where he once had twenty women working. Now it's empty.'

'I bumped into him a few times. He's been here since just after the First World War,' Steven said.

'He's no fool. I'll call about my suit, you can drop by looking for me, and ask about getting measured for one yourself. We can nudge him into selling the building, offer him a carrot, cash into his hand. He'll jump at thirty thousand,' Cliff said.'

Steven agreed to meet him next door in an hour. First he replaced the ten grand in the bank. Cliff was in the back room of the tailor's wearing a semi-stitched blue waistcoat when Steven called. Mister Roskov was shuffling around Cliff like an aged bull-fighter, his mouth filled with pins, caught up in his craft, jabbing a pin here, pinching an inch there until, finally, he stood back, his thin face wrinkled in a smile, and admired his work. He looked Steven up and down.

'What can I do for you?'

'I work with Cliff here next door.'

'I know that. I'm not senile. What do you want?'

Steven ran his fingers over Cliff's waistcoat.

'Could you make a nice mohair two-piece for me?' Steven said.

There was a catalogue on the nearby table. Mister Roskov opened it and pushed it towards Steven.

'I've been making suits for fifty years. You can have any style or any colour you want.'

Cliff removed the waistcoat and folded it over a chair. Steven browsed through the catalogue and pointed at one model.

'I like this.'

Mister Rostov raised his bushy eyebrows.

'Cliff, pop in next door and mind the shop,' Steven said.

When Cliff left Mister Roskov waved his tape measure in the air.

'This is the secret of a good suit; perfect measurement makes a perfect suit. The old days are gone; the impatience of youth. They must have everything yesterday,' he said.

Steven glanced around the building. The interior was old but it was spacious. He could envisage this whole new layout joined as one to the existing premises.

'Mister Roskov, I'm caught for time. Would you mind if I got measured in the morning?'

'That's fine. I'll be here looking at four blank walls.'

'Have you ever thought of selling the place? I might be interested if the price was right.'

'It has crossed my mind, if the price was right.'

'What price had you in mind?' Steven asked.

The old man took off his glasses. He smiled at Steven.

'You can move in tomorrow morning for seventy thousand dollars. You'd be getting a bargain at that.'

'You're not serious,' Steven said.

'When it comes to money I'm always serious.'

'But that's double the market value,' Steven said.

Mister Roskov shrugged his shoulders and put the kettle on.

'I'm just a simple old man from a village in Russia. I know nothing about market value.'.

'I'll see you about that suit in the morning.'

Steven left. He went straight to Cliff's office.

'He wants seventy thousand for his place. I have a feeling he's not bluffing,' Steven said.

'He'd probably buy and sell the lot of us.'

'The old so-and-so has me by the balls. I could beg, steal or borrow twenty grand,' Steven said.

Cliff reminded Steven that if he got his hands on the place next door it would be a goldmine. It would unlock the flood-gates. With an extension of premises and staff Shamrock would dominate the New York advertising scene. In two year he'd be calling seventy thousand dollars chicken feed.

'Did I ever think I'd see the day when success was my biggest problem,' Steven said.

'It's a problem many people would love to have,' Cliff smiled.

Steven was tempted to ring Jeff for his advice but he was determined to solve this problem on his own. Jeff would have loved to help. Steven knew that. He picked up the phone and rang *The Harp*. Brendan Doyle answered.

'Brendan, I'd like your opinion on a money problem.'

'Call me later. I'm here all night.'

Steven had been worried about Marie all day. When he arrived home he found her stretched out on the sofa looking at the television. The bruise on her head was almost gone. Mary showed Steven a newspaper. It gave half a page to the deaths on 10th Avenue with photographs of both bodies and stated that the police were treating it as gang related. He explained about his situation with Mister Roskov and the difficulty in getting the money. His heart was set on it. This could be the last piece in the jig-saw. She wasn't happy when he told her he had to go out again to Hell's Kitchen. He stressed it was important and promised he would be home early. Mary went back to her script.

Brendan Doyle was sitting in his office reading a newspaper.

'You made the headlines,' he said.

'The police didn't come banging down my door yet,' Steven said.

'If the cops found out you killed Guardino they'd give you a medal. You were on about money?' Brendan said.

Steven told him how much he wanted to buy the clothes factory but he couldn't come up with the money. The most he could scratch together was twenty thousand dollars. Mister Roskov was a stubborn old Russian. He couldn't see him budging an inch.

'You can come up with twenty. Have one last go at knocking down the price. I rang some friends. They might step in if the price was right. I'll let you know tomorrow,' Brendan said.

When Steven got home Marie was gone to bed. Mary made sure she had plenty of rest. She was still struggling with her script but when Steven arrived she put it away and opened a bottle of wine. She wanted to talk. He told her how the night had unfolded.

'Please be careful,' she said.

'Of course I will.'

Mary looked drained.

'My script needs rewriting, you're never here, then Marie, that was awful, you shoot two men as if it was nothing, and now you're meeting shady characters in a dodgy pub,' she said.

'It's business. I'm caught for money. They want to invest. If it's not right I'll walk away,' he said.

Next morning Steven called in to Mister Roskov to be measured. The old man was shaky on his feet, he hardly said a word, and he had difficulty in breathing. The measuring didn't take long.

'I'll come straight to the point,' Steven said. 'How much?'

'My final price is forty thousand dollars. I won't budge another inch no matter what you do.

Steven didn't know what the old man meant.

'I'll draw up the contract at once and I'll have the papers here tomorrow,' he said.

'Who needs papers? Have the money here and I can go back home where I am safe. I hope you are happy now?' the old man.

'I don't understand. Is there something wrong?' Steven said.

There was anger in the old man's eyes.

'Keep your friends away from me. Go and leave me in peace. I have a suit to make,' he said.

Steven went straight to Cliff's office.

'He'll sell for forty grand. I'll make it with company funds and help from some people I'm meeting later. We could be up and running yet.'

Cliff was a rock of sense.

'Steven, don't rush. Don't open with a big bang when you're only half-ready or you'll close with a bigger bang. Why did he drop his price?'

'I don't know. That surprised me as well.'

'There's something I don't like about this,' Cliff said.

Steven also thought along those lines.

'Maybe someone had a word in his ear and advised him to drop the price.'

'Maybe someone had a size twelve boot in his ear and forced him to drop the price,' Cliff said.

Steven agreed that Mister Roskov looked shaken and there was a veiled innuendo in his voice but he asked the man for a price and he was given a price. What more could he do?

'I did nothing wrong,' Steven said.

'Forty grand was his price. So be it,' Cliff said

At 4.45pm Brendan rang.

'I'll see you in *La Dolce Vita* at six pm. It's on 9th Avenue just around the corner from West 52nd. I have three gentlemen looking forward to meeting you. We'll have a nice meal and maybe we'll do business.'

Steven was delighted. When he got home Mary was engulfed in her script. She'd changed the storyline, rewrote the ending, but it wasn't right. She was worried about her husband. He had time for everything but hadn't time to make love. She missed Louise, and her friends in Los Angeles. Steven lived for his job. She just wanted her husband back.

La Dolce Vita had a relaxed ambience candle-lit tables enhanced the atmosphere. Brendan sat with his three friends drinking wine. He introduced them to Steven. Pat McCoy had his own construction company in Brooklyn, Bill O'Donovan ran a pub, *Paddy's Bar*, in South Boston and the third man was Dino Moretti, the owner of the restaurant and he was also a film producer in New York. Pat and Bill were casually dressed but

Dino was gleaming in a white suit. He had one gold tooth. Brendan suggested that they eat first and talk later. The three of them were aware of how successful Steven had been in such a short time.

'I hear your wife, Mary, is a screenplay writer,' Dino said.

'Yes. She had a bit of success with a film called *Malice,* Steven said.

'I saw it. Is she working on anything at the moment?' he asked.

'Yes, a political thriller set in Washington. It's about a US senator who has an affair with a young Irish immigrant,' Steven said.

There was a burst of laughter from the four men. It broke the ice.

'Excuse me,' Dino said, 'but I have many friends who are senators.'

'Let's get down to business. We are interested in is making money. What's the asking price? How much do you need?' Brendan said.

'He wants forty thousand for it. I'm short twenty,' Steven said.

Brendan looked at his three friends. They nodded their heads.

'We can provide the twenty grand. It's a three-year deal. After that time you pay us back interest free. But, for the next three years, we get 25% of the company profit,' Brendan said.

'With the extra money generated by the extension that will be a lot of money,' Steven said.

'That's the offer. Take it or leave it,' Brendan said.

'Give me a day or two,' Steven said.

'If word gets out about that property it'll be gone,' Brendan said.

Dino put up his hand for silence. He spoke with a calm authority.

'Steven, we are four wealthy men. We have contacts, we have power, we have friends in high places. We can point them in your direction. If you join the team, you hear nothing, see nothing and say nothing. We're here to help you. You're here to help us. Forgive me but we want an answer now, yes or no.'

All eyes were on Steven.

'I'm in,' he said.

'Order a bottle of champagne. It's on me,' Dino said and left.

Pat and Bill gave Steven their cards.

'Call me if you have a problem with construction,' Pat McCoy said.

'Give me a shout if you're in Boston,' Bill O'Donovan said.

Brendan didn't say much through all this. He observed and smiled his smile. Dino reappeared with a brown paper package.

'Here's your money. On the last day of every month put a quarter of your profit in to this account in your bank,' he said.

Dino gave Steven a piece of paper.

'In a case like this we have the books checked but with you that's not needed. You are one of us. For you to do anything silly would be unthinkable,' Bill said.

'The last guy who tried that is still in hospital,' Pat said.

No one laughed.

'Welcome to the club,' Dino said.

'I'll let you know what's happening' Steven said.

They shook hands. Steven decided not to tell Cliff and not to tell Mary. It would be the first time he lied to his wife. On the way home he bought her a bunch of red roses, her favourite.

The next morning Steven spent several hours getting his own twenty thousand together. He made up eighteen thousand and he was forced to borrow just two thousand from the bank. That amount didn't bother him. He called in next door. His briefcase was bulging. Mister Roskov was putting the final touches on his suit. He put the briefcase on the table.

'Forty thousand as agreed. I'll have my lawyer call later with the contract. You just sign on the dotted line and all will be well.'

'You finally got your way,' the old man said.

'Lucky I was able to persuade you to sell,' Steven said.

Mister Roskov got a fit of coughing. He found it hard to breathe.

'You had a funny way of persuading me,' he said.

'What do you mean?' Steven said.

'I didn't find it funny getting my ribs kicked in,' the old man said.

He opened his shirt to show the side of his body black and blue and bruised. Steven was horrified.

'Who did this?'

'Two nasty individuals. They were friends of yours.'

'They were no friends of mine.'

'What's done is done. Let me finish my work.'

'Can I help in any way? Will I call a doctor?' Steven said.

Mister Roskov bent over caught for breath. He got another fit of coughing.

'Don't make me laugh. It really hurts when I laugh. God has a sense of humour. Here I am making my last suit for the man who bought my factory, the man who caused me to be beaten up. You go ahead and send your lawyer. Bring your papers. I will sign them and be gone. Your suit will be ready in one hour. Get out of my sight. Forgive me if I don't shake your hand.'

Chapter Eight

Steven Kennedy was furious at the way Mister Roskov had been treated and annoyed at himself that he'd done nothing about it. He was tempted to ring Brendan and cancel the whole deal but this would be cutting his own throat. He wondered what he was getting himself into. To Mister Roskov the old factory was full of ghosts and happy memories. He'd cried as he locked the door and handed over the key.

Steven rang Pat McCoy. As renovation began he was filled with optimism. There would be more work, more staff, more room and better things to come. Jeff was surprised at how quickly things were happening. He couldn't make the opening but he wished him luck. Steven didn't tell him the full story. Jeff and Susan knew nothing about Marie's ordeal. He felt guilty about this. It took Pat McCoy five weeks to finish the project. Shamrock Ads was now one big building. It had a futuristic look about it. It was a gala opening. His four friends were there with their friends. Steven took Brendan Doyle aside and questioned him about the way Mister Roskov had been treated. He said he knew nothing about it. Dino Moretti spent quite some time in a long discussion with Mary. He was very interested in her work. Champagne flowed. They mingled with politicians, film celebrities and a large media coverage as the Mayor of New York cut the tape. Cliff Wickham was in his element, like a best man at a wedding, always hovering, helping, refilling glasses and handing out company cards. The media were anxious to cover Steven and Mary's background, the mysterious couple who'd conquered New York. Steven was flanked by Marie and Mary. Both looked beautiful. Mary was the perfect wife; by his side, smiling, saying all the right things. Marie was dazzling. The cameras followed her everywhere. Dino Moretti was the last to leave.

'See you at the end of the month,' he smiled.

Steven was hoping the first month would go well. He was surprised; the company was flooded with clients from every corner of New York but he could hardly believe the volume of interest from the Irish community in South Boston. At the end of the month he lodged the cheque in the agreed account. He smiled at the irony that the more money he made the more they made. He realised they had important contacts everywhere and he intended to use those contacts. The Rick Guardino incident was gone from the newspapers and nobody spoke about it anymore. Mary still couldn't get that night out of her mind. She was haunted by the thought that he'd got away with murder. No matter how repulsive they were, and the degrading way they'd treated Marie, the fact remained that her husband killed two men. She completed a final rewrite of her script. The next step was the finance to get the film made. Big-hearted producers were slow to part with their money.

Mary was still in bed when the phone rang. It was Marie.
    'Do you fancy a cuppa? I'm off today,' Marie said.
    'I'm on my way. Throw on the Eggs Benedict.'
    'I need your opinion. It's important,' Marie said.
    'No problem; see you soon.'
    She wondered what Marie wanted as she drove to her apartment. Why ring so early? When she arrived he first thing she noticed was how pale she looked.
    'Are you ok?' Mary asked.
    Marie came straight to the point.
    'I'm pregnant.'
    Are you sure? Mary asked.
    'I've missed two months. I didn't know who to tell.'
    She looked distraught. Mary put her arm around her and sat her down.
    'I'm here for you. We're all here for you,' Mary said.
    'I've been trying to blot that awful night out of my mind and but now this. What am I going to do?' Marie said.
    Mary's heart went out to her as she cried like a little girl in her arms.
    'First we'll make sure you're pregnant. If so, you have several options. It will come down to one thing; do you want to keep the child or do you want to terminate the pregnancy, a difficult choice?' Mary said.
    'There's no choice. I could not kill the baby.'
    'This is Rick Guardino's baby. He raped you.'
    Marie couldn't be consoled.

'I know that but, in the name of God, there's no way I could kill an innocent little child.

Mary reminded her that this child would turn her life upside down. It won't conveniently go away. They agreed that she had to tell Steven but first they had to go to a doctor friend of hers. He'd know what was best for her.

Steven was angry when he heard the news about Marie. He felt that Rick Guardino was having the last laugh. The tests were positive. The doctor discussed all options available to her. Marie was adamant. She was keeping the baby.

'You have to tell mum and dad,' Mary said.

'I can't tell them about the shooting,' Steven said.

'At least tell dad. He'll understand,' Mary said.

She picked up the phone, handed it to Steven, and left the kitchen.

'Hi, Jeff, just a quick update from the big smoke. Mary sends her love. How's Susan?' Steven said.

'She's fine. I hear you've made your first million,' Jeff said.

'We're getting there,' Steven said.

There was an ominous silence before Steven spoke again.

'Jeff, a lot has happened in the last few months. I foolishly thought it might go away. I was wrong. I should have told you, I thought I could deal with it myself. I'm sorry.'

'What's the problem? Just tell me the truth.'

Steven held nothing back. He stressed that he was happy with the arrangement with Brendan's friends. It was working well.

'I don't know how I'm going to face Susan,' he said.

'I'll handle Susan. Guardino finally met his match. Good riddance to that bastard,' Jeff said.

'I had to do it. I had no other choice.'

'Poor Marie. Welcome to America,' Jeff said.

Mary sat writing in her office. The phone rang again. It was her boss. He wanted to speak to her.

Mister Brooke was sitting behind his desk in deep conversation with two men. He was a small, bald man with a pencil-slim moustache and a pale face that seemed to have no chin. He introduced her to the men.

'Mary, this is Mister Tardelli and this is Mister Crochetti. They are both film producers. They want to talk to you about your script.'

He left the office.

Mister Tardelli, the older of the two, spoke first.

'We've read your script many times. It has good pace, a gripping story-line, and the twist at the end is excellent. It doesn't need a costly set and it should not be too much of a financial risk. We would like to do business with you. We feel it would make an excellent low budget movie. We'd prefer if the female lead was Italian. That might give it a broader appeal. Silvio Amadio, that fine Italian director, is interested in coming on board. That will help but anything could happen yet,' he said

'This is all a bit sudden,' Mary said.

'We aim is to shoot the film in Washington and have it shown in every cinema in the United States. It could be big in Italy where they like their movies. Could you and your solicitor meet us here at ten o'clock in the morning?'

Both men shook her hand and left. Mary stood there alone and wondered if this was a dream. Mister Brookes reappeared.

'They rang me an hour ago and turned up at the doorstep looking for you,' he said.

The next two months were hectic for Mary. Karl Malden was roped in to play the senator. She enjoyed watching him perform and bring her words to life. They worked hard and finished the film ahead of time. Mary was offered an unusual deal and, with Steven's advice, she accepted it. The producers asked if she'd prefer a small percentage of the box-office takings or a single fixed sum of ten thousand dollars. Mary took the money.

Marie was five months pregnant. The agency assured her that her job would be there for her. She moved in with Mary but she was involved in her film and Steven was missing twelve hours a day. One morning he got a call from Brendan Doyle to meet him after work in his bar. Brendan didn't beat about the bush.

'The monthly payments are getting bigger. Dino sends his regards. Bill O'Donovan wants to meet you. He has an interesting offer.'

Steven didn't like being told what to do.

'What exactly is this proposition?'

'He'd prefer to tell you himself,' Brendan said.

Chapter Nine

Steven and Brendan landed in Logan Airport on Friday night. Bill was waiting in his jeep and drove them to *Paddy's Bar.* The bar was like a city-centre bar in Dublin with a band on stage playing an Irish waltz and couples out dancing. The walls were plastered with photographs of rebel leaders like Patrick Pearse and Michael Collins and images of burned-out Dublin during the Troubles. Steven wondered what the hell was he doing here. He was busy. He was tired. What did Bill want that was so urgent? It had been a long day. He wanted to retire for the night. Before he left Bill took him aside.

'Tomorrow I want to introduce you to friends of mine in Southie and I want to show you something you'll like. Good night.'

Steven woke at nine the next morning. Bill and Brendan were having breakfast. Dino Moretti had joined them. After breakfast they called to one bar after another where Steven met the owners. Handshakes were warm. Promises seemed genuine. It was similar with all the shops and cafes. He was welcomed with open arms. Dino insisted that they stop for lunch at an Italian hotel. His money was refused everywhere.

'They will be insulted. You are with friends,' Dino said.

'This is embarrassing,' Steven said.

'Two more stops. We've kept the best wine till last,' Bill said.

They drove down Flaherty Way and on to Gold Street where Bill pulled in by an antique shop which was next door to another Irish pub. Dino introduced Steven to the shop owner, Luigi, his brother. Luigi exported antiques all over the world including a thriving market in Ireland. He did steady trade with wealthy Irishmen who could afford his merchandise. Bill took Steven aside and invited him across the street. It was a closed-down shoe factory. Bill showed Steven in. It had a fine ground floor with several offices. Upstairs was equally spacious. The building was empty except for a few scattered chairs and a lone table. He took out sheets of paper and handed them to Steven. He read through the long list.

'These are names and contact numbers of clients who want to do business with you, and that list will grow,' Bill said.

'I can't thank you enough,' Steven said.

The smile disappeared from Bill's face.

'You can thank me in two simple ways. Luigi sends antiques to friends in Ireland. It can be an ordeal going through the official channels, the authorities checking papers and invoices, customs clearance and charges, etc. We're all friends now. Luigi wants to send three boxes of antiques to a customer in Ireland. It would be much more practical if they went by boat with your name as the sender. Shamrock Ads is a respected company and the goods would attract no attention,' Bill said.

'Surely they could easily be discovered. I would be in serious trouble with the authorities,' Steven said.

Bill explained that he'd be doing nothing wrong, just taking a short cut. If they were discovered he can plead innocence and at most he might get a slap on the wrist but he assured him there is no chance of that. The boat was timed to arrive in Kinsale to coincide with an international yachting festival. The harbour will be festooned with boats. Ours will be just another one,

'I want to help but I don't like it,' Steven said.

'You are one of us now. You owe Pat. You owe me. You owe Brendan and you owe Dino. It's payback time,' Bill said.

Steven felt he was trapped.

'We're a team now. We're not asking for much in return for what we've done for you,' Bill said.

'I appreciate that but we just had a business deal,' Steven said.

'Are you forgetting the work Pat did for you? When you were in trouble with Guardino who gave you the gun and when you shot two men Brendan looked after you. I've just given you twelve months work and more to come, and are you forgetting what Dino did for you?' Bill said.

Steven was puzzled.

'What did he do?'

'How do you think that old Russian guy dropped thirty grand from his asking price? You don't think it was from the good of his heart? Two of Dino's nephews had a chat with him.'

'There was no need for that,' Steven said.

'While I'm at it, who the fuck do you think got your wife's film off the ground? It was Dino's associates doing him a favour; well, he did use a little friendly persuasion. Get off your high fucking horse. Say the word and he'll stop the movie and cancel Mary's ten grand. Would you like that? You should be down on your two fucking knees thanking Dino,' Bill said.

Steven never suspected. There was no way he could tell her now. It would break her heart. Bill leaned over and put out his hand. As he did Steven got a glimpse of a handgun strapped to his chest.

'You don't know how lucky you are. Shake on it,' he said.

After a brief pause Steven swore to himself and shook Bill's hand.

'I don't like it but it's a deal,' he said.

'I'll arrange everything. Dino will be delighted with you.'

Bill smiled and walked towards the door. Steven stopped him.

'You said I could thank you in two ways,' he said.

'This building is mine. It could be yours. It has everything needed for a new branch of Shamrock Ads in Boston. Think about it,' Bill said.

He locked up and they walked across the street to the antique shop. A little bell rang when they entered the door. Dino and Brendan were laughing as Luigi was showing them an impressive looking brass harp. Brendan looked up. Bill just nodded his head. Brendan smiled. Dino broke away from his friends and shook hands with Steven.

'Southie could be an untapped gold mine for you. You're happy with Bill's little venture?' Dino asked.

Steven paused for a moment carefully picking his words.

'Yes, with certain reservations.'

'That's a wise decision, You give a little, you get a lot,' Dino said.

Steven decided it would be wiser not to bring up his part in Mary's script at this time. Yet he was determined not to let some things go.

'Why did you get Mister Roskov beaten up?' Steven said.

Dino shrugged his shoulders and smiled. His gold tooth glistened in the light.

'The boys got a bit carried away. Young people can get so enthusiastic these days. They try too hard to impress.'

Luigi was dealing with some customers. Bill and Brendan joined Steven and Dino.

'We can see more of Southie tomorrow if you wish,' Bill said.

'I'll take you up on that some time. My sister is not well,' he said.

We understand Leave it with me,' Bill said as they left the shop.

The Moretti brothers stood by the front door and waved at the jeep as it took off. Bill waved back and honked on the horn as they disappeared around the corner.

Marie was over seven months pregnant. Susan insisted that she would be better off moving to LA. Accompanied by Jeff she flew to New York to bring her back. Jeff looked forward to meeting Mary and seeing the agency. .

'You poor thing; how are you?' Susan said to Marie.

'They won't let me on the catwalk. They're afraid I'll fall off and flatten someone,' Marie said.

Steven was stuck in work so Mary dropped her father to the agency and carried on to Long Island. Jeff arrived upstairs unnoticed. Steven was giving a pep-talk to his staff. Jeff stayed at the back of the room.

'Never be afraid to make a mistake; mistakes were made in bed. Be honest. Get noticed. If you have to grab them by the family jewels, get noticed and, finally, are you listening Brad? Don't be shy,' Steven smiled.

Everybody laughed, especially Brad..

'I am impressed. You certainly seem to run a happy ship,' Jeff said.

'That's my weekly war-cry,' Steven said.

'You have plenty of room and there's a good spirit about the place,' Jeff said.

Cliff Wickham passed with a handful of papers, shook Jeff's hand, and hurried off again.

'I'd be lost without Cliff. He has an assistant now. They keep the cogs in the machine well oiled. Where are the ladies?' Steven asked.

'They're gone to your house to freshen up but, if I know Susan, they won't be there very long,' Jeff said.

'Come on, we'll have the house to ourselves,' Steven said.

When they arrived at Long Island, Steven picked up the note on the table; *Steven – Gone shopping. Don't wait up - Love Mary.*

'Mary's film is coming out in a few weeks. It will be another big night for her,' Jeff said.

Marie's situation hit her badly,' Steven said.

'Guardino was a bad lad. You were lucky to get away with it.'

'I'd do the same again,' Steven said.

Jeff was quietly studying Steven; how much he'd matured, how he now spoke calmly man to man with him. There was an uneasy silence. Steven was the first to speak.

'I'm sorry I didn't fill you in on the way things panned out. It was foolish of me to think I could handle it on my own,' Steven said..

'I owe you an apology. I was afraid you weren't aware of how dangerous your friends in West Manhattan and South Boston were. I got them checked out,' Jeff said.

'What do you mean?'

'I had a word with my old friend, Ted Dynan. He made some enquiries and came back with some interesting facts,' Jeff said.

Steven was clearly annoyed.

'You had me checked out? Jesus, you had me followed.'

'I was worried about you. Susan was worried about you.'

'Susan knows all about my business?' Steven said.

'She lost one son and she doesn't want to lose another.'

'The thought of somebody spying on me annoys me. Aren't you being paranoid? What did your secret surveillance come up with?' Steven said.

'There are nasty individuals out there. You'd be looked on as a soft payday, a quick ransom and a bullet in the back of the head. In South Boston the fighting is between two Irish families. Dino Moretti is as cute as a fox, a wealthy businessman, mainly films and property. There are whispers that he is a drug dealer but he's never been caught. Pat McCoy has his own construction business in the Bronx. Nobody knows how he got the money to start. Brendan Doyle once broke a man's jaw over an unpaid loan. Bill O'Donovan is a dangerous individual. *Paddy's Bar* is a drugs haven. The O'Donovans' and the Cannings' have been at each other's throats for years. Bill got away with murder. He shot a courier over drug money. Witnesses were afraid to testify. He also has connections with the IRA. Locals treat him as if he was Santa Claus. He has a reputation for helping the poor,' Jeff said.

Steven decided to tell Jeff about the recent trip to South Boston, the amount of work that was put his way, and the offer of Bill's empty building. He didn't tell him about Dino's brother and the antiques.

'So far he's been like Santa Claus to me,' Steven said.

'I wonder what they want in return,' Jeff said. 'Ted Dynan was a great undercover cop. He tells me your name came up in a few times in Dan Canning's pub and he's overheard whispers about taking you out. Ted suggested that you think about getting a gun or hiring a bodyguard.'

Steven laughed at this.

'You're taking the piss.'

'This is not Well Lane in Cork. This is South Boston, bandit country. Think about it,' Jeff said.

'I will. How are Louise and Charlie?' Steven said.

'Louise calls now and then with Emma. Susan still hasn't accepted them. Marie is like a new daughter to her. Charlie is still Charlie; he could beat me with his left hand tied behind his back. He got a rush of blood last week and proposed to Sarah,' Jeff said.

Steven wondered if he'd expand again in Boston, Philadelphia or Detroit? What had Bill O'Donovan up his sleeve? Jeff just listened. Mary and Marie arrived laden down with new outfits. Marie was looking forward to going back to Los Angeles and meeting Charlie and Louise. Jeff sneaked off to the tranquillity of the back garden with a bottle of whiskey.

Steven went to bed. The idea of a bodyguard amused him. It would have to be someone he liked and looked up to.

It was 8am. It would be 1pm in Ireland. Steven picked up the phone and spoke to the operator.

'Could you try that number again, please?'

He could hear the clicking sounds followed by a ringing tone. A man answered.

'This is the Spiddal garda barracks; Sergeant Crowley here; what can I do for you?'

'I'm phoning from America. Would you have an address for a Donal Purcell?'.

'He's only ten minutes away down the Barna road. I have a phone number for him. Have you a pencil handy?'

He read out Donal's number. Steven thanked him and asked the operator to ring the number. An elderly woman's voice answered.

'Hello, I'm looking for Donal. Is he in?' Steven asked.

'He's in bed. He was out all night. I'll call him for you,' she said.

Steven could hear the woman's voice calling Donal's name several times in the distance and a man's voice arguing with her. Eventually he could hear a long stifled yawn as the phone was picked up.

'What is it? This is Donal Purcell.'

Steven was delighted to hear his voice again. He felt like a bit of fun and spoke with a strong American accent.

'How ya doin'? Can you help me, sir? I'm calling from the U S of A. I'm looking for a man they call the Spiddal stallion, a Mister Purcell. I heard truly great things about him.'

'You're calling from America? Who am I talking to?'

'I'm here in New York. There are so many stories about you. Are you really the greatest stud in County Galway?'

There was a long silence. Donal spoke again.

'Who the fuck is this? Is that you, Pakie Lynch, doing the bollocks again?'

Steven couldn't keep it up and spoke in his own voice.

'Hi, Donal, my old pal. Do you remember me? Steven Kennedy from Cork; we worked in the Emerald with Jim and Lillie.'

'You're one thundering fucker. Are you really calling from New York? What are you doing there?' Donal said.

'I have a proposition for you.'

'What's this about a proposition?'

'First, are you interested in a job in New York? Second, are you married?' Steven asked.

'Why should I get married and make one woman happy when I can stay single and make a hundred women happy? I thought you went to Los Angeles. What are you doing in New York?'

'It's a long story. This is serious. I want someone to watch my back. You'll have your own apartment, a car and you'll be armed at all times. Can you drive?' Steven asked.

'I have an old Volkswagen Beetle in the back yard. Did you say I'll be armed?'

'Yes, you'll have a gun and bullets.'

'Real fucking bullets. When do I start?' Donal said.

'Will Barna Road, Spiddal, find you?'

'Donal Purcell, Galway, will do. Everyone knows me,' Donal said.

Steven told him he'd get his tickets by registered mail in about a week, from Shannon and he'd meet you at La Guardia in New York. He enquired about Agnes.

'She's gone. One Sunday they were playing cards in the bottom room, all fur coats and red wine. It got out of hand. There was a heap of money on the table. Agnes lost the hotel playing fucking poker. They went off to England somewhere; no one knows,' Donal said.

'Donal, don't let me down. I'm depending on you.'

There was a long pause as if all this was sinking in for Donal.

'Steven, what kind are the women?'

'Donal, they'll love you,' Steven said and hung up.

At last Mary got news that the film was finished. She was excited when she got a special invite to a private showing in the New York studio. Then it was on to the Taormina Film Fest in Sicily followed by a general Italian release. The next step was distribution to cinemas in major US cities. That was the plan. She looked forward to her first visit to Italy and she was delighted when Steven wanted to go with her. He decided that Cliff and his team could handle everything while he was away and with Marie in Los Angeles it would be a break for both of them. They flew to Fiumicino Airport in Rome. Steven longed to see the Eternal City with its great sense of history. The Vatican was first stop. He felt dwarfed by the size of St Peter's Square. Mary was anxious to see the Colosseum. The ancient building took her breath away. She tried to visualise the gladiators fighting for their lives in front of fifty thousand spectators baying for blood.

Steven stood by the River Tiber. Julius Caesar had swum in that river all those years ago. They climbed the Spanish Steps, dominated by the Trinita dei Monti Church, and called to the Keats/Shelley Museum, the house where English poet John Keats had lived and died. After a short walk they came upon the Trevi Fountain, a monument to days gone by. They sat in a coffee shop and watched the spectacle unfold, thousands of different people from different countries united in happiness in the shadow of this unique work of art. They scrambled to throw a coin in the fountain and make a wish. Mary reminded Steven that the award-winning film, *Three Coins in the Fountain,* was set here. She closed her eyes and made a wish and threw a cent in the water. They walked back to their hotel immersed in their own thoughts. Steven couldn't get Donal Purcell out of his mind.

Next morning he decided to drive the rest of the journey to Sicily. Italian drivers seemed to solve every traffic problem by screaming, gesticulating and non-stop hooting on the car horn. He escaped the insanity to the peace of the main highway down the Italian coast, a two-hour drive to Naples. He drove up Vomero Hill to visit the lofty Certosa di San Martino Museum perched on top of the rocky headland. Naples sprawled below them; the ruins of Pompeii beneath Mount Vesuvius, the Bay of Naples and the stunning Amalfi Coast. As they walked the streets of Naples, around every corner was a museum, an art gallery, or a plaque recalling centuries of glorious events. They meandered along the Via Chiaia and lingered for coffee at Gran Caffe Gambrinus, the oldest café in the city. Mary longed to see the Isle of Capri. Steven drove down the coast to Sorrento where they caught the ferry across the bay. They made their way to the Blue Grotto and marvelled as the sun pierced the cavity and shone through the water creating a reflection that illuminated the cavern. The heart of Capri was Piazza Umberto Primo which was surrounded by a maze of narrow lanes winding between white-washed buildings. They got a ferry back to Sorrento, an intimate town spattered with high hills and deep dales; it, too, reminded him of Cork. They found a little cafe at the corner of Tasso Square where they ordered scampi gratinati washed down by a bottle of house wine. Later they walked hand in hand along the Marina Grande beach and watched the flickering lights of Capri across the sea. Mary took Steven's hand and led him into the shadows behind a congregation of rocks where they made passionate love in the moonlight.

The final leg to their destination took forty minutes; down through the picturesque Roccalumera and along the coast to Taormina, the old hilltop town perched high above the sea. The first thing to hit them was Mount Etna which looked like a giant dragon sleeping in the far-off mist. Taormina had been the playground many eminent individuals: Goethe, Dickens, Dumas, Brahms, Wagner, Steinbeck and Greta Garbo. Mary knew she was here on serious business. Her film was being shown to the film world. It was her big night. They were staying at the Villa Sant' Andrea. Steven was surprised when they bumped in to Karl Malden and director

Silvo Amadio who were having a drink in the garden with Dino Moretti, Mister Tardelli and Mister Crochetti. Steven was delighted to meet Karl Malden but on the way to his room he got a bigger shock. Mary stopped him and pointed out a man and a woman sitting by the window drinking coffee.

'There's two old friends of mine. Do you want to say hello?' she said.

'Maybe later. We better get dressed. We'll be late,' he said.

Mary laughed. Steven stopped and had another look at the couple and shook his head.

'They're not who I think they are?' he said.

'Right first time; Elizabeth Taylor and Richard Burton. They're both in *The Taming of the Shrew*. It's being shown later,' she said.

She almost had to drag him up the stairs to their room. A Limousine ferried them to the Teatro Greco, an amphitheatre which, at one time, could seat 30,000 people. The Taormina Fest was Italy's equivalent of the US Oscars. After a brief interval Mary's film was shown. Karl Malden was excellent in the role of the self-centred senator who took advantage of his young secretary. The audience gave it a prolonged round of applause but it won nothing. Carlo Ponti won best foreign producer for *Doctor Zhivago* and Elizabeth Taylor and Richard Burton won the Donatello Awards for best foreign actors in *The Taming of the Shrew*. They both received a standing ovation.

Steven and Mary returned to the hotel where a party was in full swing. Dino Moretti was standing at the bar in deep conversation with his fellow producers. Steven joined them.

'Well, gentlemen, what's the verdict?' Steven said.

'We couldn't ask for more. We are confident it will do well,' Dino said.

The other two nodded their heads in agreement. Steven still felt irritated about the way Dino had influenced the acceptance and production of Mary's script with a touch of arrogance. He would have welcomed some consultation.

'Could I have a quick word in private, Mister Moretti?' Steven said.

They both left their drinks on the counter and sat down in the corner.

'Can I be frank with you?' Steven said.

'I always like to know exactly where I stand,' Dino said flashing his golden smile.

'I should have spoken up much sooner. I didn't like the way Mister Roskov was treated and I didn't like you producing my wife's film because I'm one of the boys. Don't make a fool of her,' he said.

Dino's face turned very serious. His smile disappeared.

'You hang me without trial. What exactly do you mean?' he said.

'Bill O'Donovan filled me in. You scratch my back and I'll scratch yours,' Steven said.

'I did want to help Mary but do you think I'd throw away that much money on a whim if the script wasn't good? I'm taking a chance and I could lose out big-time. So could those two gentlemen. All this is just business,' Dino said looking at his two friends.

'Don't patronise me and don't insult my wife,' Steven said.

'I wouldn't dream of it,' Dino said as they rejoined his friends.

Unaware of what had happened a smiling Mary arrived and kissed Steven on the cheek and spoke to Dino.

'Well, Mister Moretti, two down and more to go. I want to thank you gentlemen for having faith in me. I hope you make a million,' she said.

'The film will be all over Italy next week and next stop is America,' Mister Tardelli said.

'It's our first visit to Italy. It's such a beautiful country,' Mary said.

'Did you get the chance to see Palermo? Dino said to her.

'No, we couldn't fit it in,' Mary said.

'Maybe some other time. It is a very special place for me. I was born there,' Dino said.

'That's Mafia country, isn't it?' Steven said.

Chapter Ten

The sea was rough around the south coast of Ireland. There were yachts of all shapes and sizes struggling through the gale as they approached the safety of Kinsale Harbour. Locals called it sailors' weather. They said it separated the men from the boys. The yachts shuddered and the sails were buffeted by the strong winds while dozens of spectators berthed on the nearby hills observed the spectacle with interest. The onlookers were wrapped up from the cold as the armada unfolded below them. One man in particular, Shaun Dunne, who stood on his own away from the crowd, was more interested than the rest. Looking through his binoculars he smiled as he picked out the *Colleen Bán* battling the waves in the middle of the fleet of yachts. He could barely make out two men on board working at keeping the yacht on its course through the wind.

The sun was sinking in the grey sky as he watched until the Colleen Bán reached the pier and was secured by a rope. Safely berthed it took its place in a queue of yachts. Shaun shivered, pulled his jacket tighter around him and walked the short distance to his black Ford truck parked on a dirt track behind a wall. He turned on the engine trying to get some heat into his body and waited until he was alone in the dark before taking a walky-talky from the glove compartment. He played with the controls. It hissed and spluttered to life.

'The white lady has arrived,' he said.

Shaun pulled out from behind the wall and made his way down the hill and through the town to the now deserted pier. There was no one about as he reversed the truck in as near as he could to the Colleen Bán. He waited in the darkness before flashing his torch three times in the direction of the yacht. Three flashes were returned from the yacht. He opened the back doors as two men struggled with a box and placed it in the truck. Two more boxes quickly followed. One of the men handed Shaun some papers and they shook hands. The men returned to the yacht and the truck disappeared into the night. Shaun left the villages of Belgooly and Riverstick in his wake and passed the airport. He drove carefully conscious of attracting any unwanted attention. He could see the city lights spread out in the valley below. In fifteen minutes he was crossing the bridges over both channels of the river Lee on the verge of Cork's city centre and heading east towards the village of Carrigtuohill. Traffic was quiet as he turned left off the main road at Glounthaune and the truck crept deep into the heart of the countryside. He was certain he wasn't being followed. A 38 Special was tucked under the driver's seat just in case. The roads were now narrow with no lighting but he felt comfortable. He knew where he was going. He saw it; the grey farmhouse almost hidden behind a clump of trees. There was a dull light showing in one downstairs window. He passed the gate and drove on for a mile before turning at a crossroads to return. The coast was clear. There was one car parked at the side of the house. Shaun drove in around the back yard and parked in the corner by a concrete outhouse. He got out, locked the truck, and tapped on the back door of the house. It was opened by an elderly farmer who ushered him in and locked the door.

'You're late, Shaun. I thought something had gone wrong,' he said.

'The *Colleen Bán* was way behind schedule. The weather changed. They could do nothing about it,' Shaun said.

'Will you have a drink?' he said.

'We better put the cargo away first. Have you the key?' Shaun said.

He went out to the yard followed by the old man who opened the door of the outhouse. They carried in the three heavy boxes and lit a lamp. Shaun took an iron bar from the shelf and prised open the top of one box. The contents were carefully wrapped and packed. One by one he laid them on the ground: Browning pistols, hand-guns, AR-18 Armalites, AK-47 Kalashnikovs and several boxes of ammunition. They gleamed in the lamp-light. Shaun picked up an Armalite and kissed it.

'God bless you, Uncle Sam; you're going to make an awful lot of widows.'

The men quickly replaced the weapons and shoved the boxes into the darkness of the back corner and covered them with straw and a heavy canvas. The old man locked up and they returned to the house. He burned the papers Shaun gave him.

'Now do you fancy a drink?'

The old man took a bottle of Paddy from the cabinet and filled two large whiskeys

'First I must make one quick phone call.'

He picked up the phone and dialled.

'It's green for go,' he said.

Both men lifted their glasses high.

'To health and happiness.'

Steven waited in the crowd at the arrivals lounge in La Guardia Airport. The last of the passengers were straggling by. He wondered if Donal had missed his flight. Just when he was giving up hope he spotted him sauntering along in deep conversation with a middle-aged blonde. At first he didn't recognise him. He was wearing jeans, boots, a white jacket and a cowboy hat. As the woman went her own way he called after her.

'Give me a call any time, honey. Have a good day.'

'Donal, where did you park your horse?' Steven said.

'I got talking to yer one. She's a widow from Nantucket,' Donal said.

'You're like Buffalo Bill. This is Manhattan, not Montana,' Steven said as they made their way to the car park.

Steven explained more about the job. Donal hardly changed in ten years. He still had that charmer's smile. When they arrived at the apartment he showed Donal around and gave him a key. With Marie missing he had the place to himself. Steven made a phone call and had a quick conversation with Ted Dynan.

'Donal, I must go back to work. People are waiting for me. A friend is calling here in an hour, Ted Dynan, an ex-cop. He'll take you for some shooting practice. Here's a hundred dollars out of your wages to tide you over. Welcome to America,' Steven said and was gone.

Donal opened the balcony window and he was frightened by the view of New York's skyline and the droves of people like ants way below.

Ted Dynan duly arrived. The two men became instant friends. Ted was in his early sixties, broad-shouldered, with cropped grey hair and sharp blue eyes. He'd been retired for eight years. As he drove Donal through the Manhattan traffic he filled him in on Steven's situation. Having an armed minder watching his back would be protection in itself. Ted reminded him that he was taking on a dangerous job. He pulled in and parked by a gun store and walked in to the shop with Donal in his wake. The man behind the counter saluted Ted and looked Donal up and down.

'Howdy, Ted, so this is Deadwood Dick. I have what you were talking about. That thirty-eight would be easy to handle and light,' he said.

He took out a box and placed it on the counter. Ted picked up a silver gun with a brown handle and admired it while Donal looked on fascinated.

'The double action, six-round cylinder, Smith and Wesson. She's a beauty. I carry one myself,' Ted said.

'This is your new best friend; love her, never let her out of your sight. You're going to spend the rest of the day getting to know everything about her,' he said handing the gun to him.

Donal took it and gave it a twirl, aimed it at an imaginary target, and gave it back to Ted. Ted got a shoulder holster, several boxes of ammunition, signed some papers, and gave the man a cheque.

Ted made his way on to Sixth Avenue and turned in to West Twentieth Street. This was his favourite gun range, one of the most modern in Manhattan. He came here once a month to keep his eye in. He booked a two-hour slot and prepared Donal with special glasses and ear-plugs. Then he had him load and unload the gun a dozen times until he could do it blindfold.

'Watch me, to give you an idea of what I want you to do,' Ted said.

He fired six rounds at the target twenty yards away. Donal's head was dizzy from the noise. Ted scored three bulls.

'The main thing is to relax. Off you go in your own time,' he said.

When Donal fired the gun his hand jerked up and he missed the target. He was annoyed. Ted had him repeat it until his hand was sore. There was a slight improvement. He was an eager pupil. Another session was booked in for the following day.

'Wear the holster and the gun to get used to it and adjust the strap so you can draw it quickly. Make sure your safety catch is on at all times or the gun might go off in your holster. I don't want you singing like a soprano,' Ted said.

Back in his apartment Donal stood in front of the full-length mirror and practised drawing his gun over and over again. He felt like an All-American gunslinger.

The weather in LA was beautiful. Charlie made the most of it. He was singing to himself as he trimmed the hedge at the side of the house. Marie was flopped in a deckchair reading a magazine. She knew her time wasn't far away; her back ached and she'd been getting contraction pains since that morning but in the last hour they'd become more frequent. Susan was in the pool swimming. Marie called out to her.

'Susan, I think it's time to go.'

Susan scrambled up the pool ladder and quickly dried and dressed herself. She called to Charlie to get the car ready. He dropped the clippers and ran. Susan held her hand in the back seat as Charlie skimmed through the traffic. In no time he was pulling in alongside the Cedars Sinai Centre. He ran and grabbed a trolley, placed Marie on it, and hurried to reception where the nurses took over. Marie was whisked away in seconds. Susan sat in silence and waited with Charlie. Two hours went slowly by when a nurse appeared with a big smile on her face.

'The delivery was excellent. Mother and baby are doing fine,' she said.

Charlie wanted to give her a high five. Susan was just relieved. Marie was sitting up in bed, several pillows behind her back, with the baby in her arms. She looked exhausted. She handed the baby to Susan.

She smiled a tired smile.

'It's a beautiful eight and a half pound baby boy.'

Susan moved back the white blanket from his face. He looked so fragile and innocent; blue eyes and a head of black hair. She started to cry. The last time she was here was when her son Jeffry was born. She handed the baby to Charlie.

'Hey, little fella, You're gonna be my best buddy. I'll teach you to play golf and drink beer and chat up women. You and me are gonna have some fun.'

Susan took the baby from him.

'Charlie, stay far away from that child; drink and women how are you? I have it on good authority you may well be having your own little Charlie Grainger any day.'

'You'll be the first to know,' he said.

Susan handed the baby back to Marie.

'Did you think about what you'll call him?' she asked her.

'I made up my mind months ago. If it was going to be a girl it was Susan and if it was a boy it was Steven, so say hello to Steven Kennedy mark two,' she said.

'You were going to call the baby Susan? That would have been special,' she said.

'You're very special. I'd have been lost without you,' Marie said.

Susan went to the corridor where she phoned everyone. Steven was relieved at the good news. He wondered if the world was ready for a second Steven Kennedy. Behind all his joy he felt a smouldering anger. He couldn't get Rick Guardino out of his mind.

Donal's accuracy had improved beyond all recognition. Ted enjoyed Donal. He'd never seen anyone so determined to improve. Mary was besotted with him. She took him shopping and got him a new outfit. He bought a second-hand Rambler. It took him a while to get used to driving on the 'wrong' side of the road. He accompanied Steven to and from work and he joined him for lunch. He got on well with everybody but he never felt at home in the helter-skelter atmosphere.

Marie missed her work but young Steven was a full-time job. Susan offered to look after him in LA if she wanted to return to modelling in

New York. Mary offered to help but she was still caught up with the film and she was busy writing another screenplay. 'Seduction' was a huge success in Italy and ran its course in America. She was writing at home one night when the phone rang. It was Dino Moretti inviting her and Steven to dinner at La Dolce Vita. Steven declined but suggested that Donal go with her. Donal jumped at the idea. With Mary's help he found Dino's restaurant. Dino showed them to a quiet table. A lone candle lit the surroundings. He didn't know what to make of Donal. Donal, in turn, didn't know what to make of him. Dino suggested crab soup followed by roast beef and a bottle of Italian red wine. Donal enjoyed it but he didn't drink. Mary wondered what was behind all this. She was never comfortable in West Manhattan.

'Here's to you, Mary,' Dino said. 'Thank you for your creativity and hard work. My fellow producers couldn't make it tonight.'

'I'm glad it all turned out well for everyone in the end,' she said.

'Now I have a very pleasant duty to perform.'

He handed Mary an envelope.

'I'm sorry for the delay but it was well earned.'

It was a cheque for ten thousand dollars.

'Now will you do me a favour?' she asked.

'Anything; you know that; anything; just ask and it's yours,' he said.

She handed him back the cheque. Now he was even more surprised.

'Steven owes you money and has an agreement to repay you within three years. Please deduct this cheque from your loan. He hates to owe anything to anyone. It must be the Irish in him.'

She smiled.

'I'll never understand your husband. I'd much rather owe someone money than be owed money. It must be the Italian in me,' he said.

Donal hardly spoke for the night. He concentrated on the beef.

'By the way, Mister Moretti, I'm working on a new script. It's early days but I like the way it's turning out,' she said.

'Brains as well as beauty; a rare combination. We must do this again. Feel free to call me any time.'

He kissed her on both cheeks and shook hands with Donal.

Donal was afraid that he was going to kiss him as well.

'Buona notte, ragazzo; it was interesting to meet you,' Dino said.

Chapter Eleven

Steven knew he'd have to make a decision soon. Against all advice he set up a meeting with Bill O'Donovan in Southie Boston. He knew this could be a millstone around his neck but the original twenty thousand had now been repaid in half the time thanks to Mary, so he felt he was only starting again. He was confident that the revenue generated by new business in the Boston agency would soon cover any debts. He owed his wife big-time. She just wanted to help her husband. Steven decided to bring Donal with him. They flew up to Logan. Bill still drove the big jeep. Steven wanted another look at the old building. Bill decided to introduce Steven to the Cannings, his sworn enemy. He parked the jeep in East Fifth Street and invited them in to the *Green Bough* owned by Dan Canning. The Cannings were not his favourite people, but sometimes he enjoyed fraternising with the enemy just to annoy them. It was a quiet bar. A dozen customers were drowning their sorrows, bored and bleary-eyed. Dan was behind the bar. He was a broad-shouldered grizzly bear of a man with an untidy beard barely covering a long scar on his left cheek. He wouldn't have been out of place in the Rocky Mountains. He stopped in his tracks when he saw Bill. He noticed he was carrying a gun; the bulge in his jacket was obvious. Donal could feel the tension. Dan broke the ice. He slammed the counter and laughed out loud. Everybody in the bar stopped what they were doing and looked at him.

'Well, the virtuous Bill O'Donovan, the man himself. This is like a visit from Queen Elizabeth. To what do I owe this great honour?' he said.

'Take it easy, Dan,' Bill said. 'We just want a peaceful pint of Guinness and we'll be on our way. Let me introduce you to two friends of mine from Ireland. This is Donal Purcell, a Galway man, and this is...'

Dan interrupted him looking Steven up and down.

'We all know who this is. Open the paper any night and there he is looking back out at you, Steven Kennedy, the advertising supremo; so he's your friend? How are you, young man? You're not very particular who you drink with. I wonder what brings you to this part of the world? I smell a rat. What has Bill O'Donovan up his sleeve?' Dan said.

'I just called to have a drink, sir. I've heard so much about you. Could you ever be kind enough to fill two pints of the black stuff and a mineral, please? And have something yourself,' Steven said calmly.

Dan smiled and pointed to a nearby table.

'You sit down there I'll bring them over to you in a minute,' Dan said.

They sat down. Customers went back to watching the television. Dan arrived with the drinks in his huge hands and placed them on the table.

'Two Guinness and a bottle of orange for the boy,' he said.

The chair buckled as he sat down next to Donal who watched in silence as Dan held up his large whiskey and demolished it in one gulp.

'As my dead father used to say; here's to the past and here's to the future. May they never meet,' Dan said.

'You have a nice bar, Mister Canning. How's business?' Steven said.

'I get by. Maybe I should have a word with Shamrock Ads. You seem to have the magic touch,' Dan said.

Steven took a card from his inside pocket and gave it to Dan who picked it up and read it

'I'd be delighted to help,' Steven said.

'I might just do that; that is if you have any time to talk to me. I believe you are doing serious business with Bill and his friends. I'm not a fool; you're not here in Southie for the good of your health,' Dan said.

Steven got a glimpse that Dan was carrying a gun strapped to his shoulder. So was Bill and he knew Donal was also armed. Donal watched in silence, fascinated, frightened. It was like a scene from a gangster movie. He was waiting for Humphry Bogart to kick down the front door any minute and spray the bar with bullets. They finished their drinks and decided to go. As Bill got up he offered to shake Dan's hand. Dan looked at him coldly.

'Take your hand away or I'll spit on it,' he said.

Bill's face flushed with anger. He turned to Dan.

'If that's the way you want it, Canning, so be it, but I strongly advise you to stay out of my way,' he said and left.

Dan called Steven back. Steven did so and showed no fear of him as he stood alone looking up at him.

'Anyone who's a friend of Bill O'Donovan is no friend of mine. Consider that a fair warning,' Dan said.

'I'm sorry that's the way you feel. I'm here if you want to do business but don't threaten me. Bullies never scared me, sir,' Steven said.

He turned his back and walked calmly out the door. Bill and Donal were already in the jeep.

'Jesus, I could do with a drink. He's one big fucker,' Donal said.

'Welcome to Southie, Donal, it's a big change from Spiddal,' Bill said.

They were back in *Paddy's Bar* a short time later. Now Steven realised that Ted Dynan knew what he was talking about. The pub was packed with noisy drinkers. Steven wanted to talk to Bill alone. He tempted Donal with a small bottle of scotch if he vanished upstairs for the night. Bill showed Steven to the room behind the bar. The sparring began

'Bill, how about calling a spade a spade. I'd appreciate a little bit of fucking honesty. What's happening with that building? I don't even know if it's your fucking building. Maybe Dan Canning was right and you have something up your sleeve?' Steven said.

'It's mine alright. I hear you're doing so well in Manhattan that you can't handle it. The word is that Boston would be a perfect outlet for your ever-growing clientele; all those homesick Paddies crying in their Guinness and hankering after the oul sod and longing to be associated with Shamrock Ads. That building could be a goldmine to you and you know it so how about a bit of honesty from you,' Bill said.

Steven smiled. At least now he knew where he stood.

'The building would suit me, so is all the 'I'll scratch your back and you'll scratch mine' bollocks gone out the window or is that all another load of bullshit?' Steven said.

'You want honesty so you'll get fucking honesty. That building is no good to me lying idle. There have been many enquiries but I refused. I'm going to make you an offer you can't refuse,' Bill said.

'Convince me.'

'For a once-off payment of five thousand dollars it's yours, lock, stock and barrel but...'

Steven interrupted.

'I had a feeling there was going to be a 'but'.'

Bill ignored him.

'You lodge the five grand in to my account which is conveniently in your bank, Marina Midland. This is all above board, legal, taxes paid, etc. Here comes the 'but'; but you will also lodge small, legitimate sums of money regularly in an account held by our builder friend, Pat McCoy,' Bill said.

'But why should I be caught to pay money for Pat?' Steven said.

'You pay nothing. I'll give you the money. You just lodge it as payment from your company. If needed, Pat will provide the necessary receipts for work done and wages paid. It's simple,' Bill said.

'It sounds dodgy,' Steven said.

'The minute you lodge the five grand, Pat will renovate the building. It will be like printing your own money. Boston will be yours,' Bill said.

Bill could see the hesitation in his eyes.

'You asked for honesty; now you're getting it. The money I give you to lodge will be transferred to the National Bank in London and then to their branch in Dublin. The bar is doing really well. It's my nest egg for my old age. I'm just trying to avoid the taxman. You're doing nothing wrong. Even if there was any kind of inquiry you are completely innocent. Make up your mind. I won't wait forever,' Bill said.

The bar was packed to the rafters. Three barmen struggled to keep the onslaught of demanding drinkers happy. Steven shook Bill's hand.

'When do you want the five grand?'

'Sooner rather than later.'

Donal was snoring when Steven reached the bedroom. The empty bottle of scotch was beside him on the bed. The television was still on. Donal was still wearing his gun in the holster strapped to his shoulder.

Shaun Dunne yawned and stretched. He was tired. He'd been on the road now for five hours. He'd left the farm near Carrigtuohill in darkness at eight am and stopped for a bite to eat on the outskirts of Dublin before continuing north on the long journey to Derry. He drove carefully, the trailer hitched to the truck curtailed his speed. A greyhound was the sole occupant of the trailer on his way to a race in Derry. Shaun passed through Dundalk. There were few people about. It had been this way since the troubles began. Dundalk was one of the biggest towns in Ireland but being close to the border had brought its own troubles. Approaching Northern Ireland Shaun was excited but tense. He could see the roadblock ahead. He was stopped and questioned by an RUC officer while a colleague kept a close eye on him and wrote down his registration number in a notebook.

'Where are you off to, sir?' he asked.

'I'm going to the greyhound track at the Brandywell in Derry. My dog is running there in the big race tonight,' Shaun said.

Could I see your licence, please?'

Shaun gave him the licence and some papers. The policeman read them.

'You're coming a long way to be running a dog in Londonderry. Get out of the vehicle please and stand back,' the RUC man said.

Shaun did so, praying quietly to himself, and stood away from his truck. He had suffered through this ordeal so many times and he still wasn't used to it. The fear of being caught hung over him like a guillotine. The RUC man rummaged around the inside and under the back of the seats before having a quick look in the trailer. The officer waved him on.

'Has that dog of yours got any chance?' he asked.

Green for Go at four to one. He'll go close,' Shaun said.

He was into Newry in fifteen minutes. The Union Jack flag reminded him he was now in British territory. Shaun headed on towards Omagh and swung off the main road to Dungannon and parked behind a bungalow. A young couple approached him and welcomed him to their home.

'Any trouble?' the young woman said.

'No, but we have to move fast. I don't trust the bastards,' Shaun said.

'The two of you get rid of the merchandise. I'll get a quick snack ready for you,' she said and hurried in the back door.

Shaun crawled under the trailer; a section of it came away to reveal half a dozen weapons and several boxes of ammunition. They rushed them inside and hid them in the attic. Shaun reconnected the undercarriage and hooked on the trailer. He grabbed a sandwich and some food for the dog and was back on the road to Strabane and finally across Foyle Bridge and in to Derry. He knew he was almost there when he saw the signs on the outskirts of the town saying, 'Welcome to Londonderry'. He parked near the Brandywell track. The officials took the dog from him, checked it in and put it in his kennel ready for the race. Shaun was staying overnight. He met some friends and they celebrated on another successful mission. There was only one hitch. He'd put ten pounds on the dog. *Green for Go* finished last.

Steven had been in deep conversation with Cliff Wickham for more than an hour. He picked his brain about the Boston project but he didn't tell him the full story. Cliff had a great head for business and gave Steven his objective opinion.

'It's perfect. On one hand it will remove a bit of pressure from this branch by taking the Boston Irish off our backs but it could also cast its net from Rhode Island, greater Massachusetts, Vermont and right up to Maine. Frankly, I'd go for it,' he said.

'I'll get moving at once. I'll promote some of our experienced staff here as a backbone for Boston and recruit the remainder locally. It'll take a month or so to get that together. Will you see to that?' Steven said.

He picked up the phone and lodged the 5,000 in the bank. The transfer was done in minutes. He rang Bill in *Paddy's Bar* to tell him. He made another instant decision. Cliff would be the boss of the Boston branch. Steven smiled as a thought crossed his mind. The new agency was across the street from Luigi Moretti's antique shop.

Mary Kennedy was sitting in *Henry's* café on 7th Avenue where they sometimes met for coffee. She'd been in the area so she rang him to know if he could join her. She was reading a magazine when he appeared.

'Sorry I'm late. We're going ahead with the Boston branch. I'll tell you about it later. What's happening with you?' he said.

'Oh, nothing really, except that I'm pregnant,' she said.

She enjoyed the look on his face.

'Did you just say what I thought you said?' he asked.

'You heard right the first time. In about six months and two weeks, if all goes well, you'll be a dad,' she said.

'Are you sure?'

He felt stupid when he'd said it.

'Being pregnant is not something a girl fools around with,' she said.

'Sorry, that's really great.'

'I got the news an hour ago. I was bursting to tell someone, anyone. You had to be the first to know but I might keep it to myself and wait awhile before telling everyone else,' she said.

'I want to tell the world. This is brilliant,' he said.

'I was afraid of how you might take it,' she said.

'I couldn't be happier. It must have been all that pasta,' he said.

'Do you remember when I threw the coin in the Trevi Fountain. Well, wishes do come true, but maybe the pasta helped,' she smiled.

Bill O'Donovan gave Dino Moretti a small bag of money and shook his hand. He opened a bottle of Jack Daniels and filled four glasses. Luigi offered Bill a cigarette from his silver cigarette case although he knew he didn't smoke. It was the same thing every week. The same four men did the same business in the same back room of *Paddy's Bar*. Nobody noticed them coming or going. Bill and his brother, Liam, handed over the money. Dino and his brother, Luigi, handed over the package of heroin.

'There is no need to count it?' Luigi suggested.

'I would be insulted,' Bill replied.

They said the same thing every week. It was part of the ritual. The Italians drank their drink and left. They didn't like to hang around. It had been a long night. Liam held the heroin in the palm of his hand as if he was weighing it.

'I can't understand. Why don't you double or treble the amount? The demand is there. It's good stuff. This goes quickly and when it's gone it's the same thing every week. Everybody is looking for more,' he said.

'Let them go elsewhere if they want more. If we make it bigger it can attract unwanted attention. Desperate people screaming for a fix will do anything, even murder. The cops would be all over us like a rash. The police accept the limited bit of business we do. It keeps the natives peaceful, everybody is happy, and there's no trouble. Why spoil a good thing?' Bill said.

Liam didn't agree with his older brother. Liam was eight years younger, restless and ambitious. He felt Bill was too set in his ways. If there was money to be made why not grab it. Manhattan was overflowing with wealthy users determined to part with their money, slaves to the habit, heroin was their utopia. Liam was thinking about going into business on his own. He was a fanatical republican, a fierce believer in the Irish cause, thirty-two counties or nothing. He blamed Britain for a long list of Ireland's woes and for years he'd been sending money to the IRA in Dublin and Belfast.

Unknown to Bill O'Donovan the Moretti brothers were on their way to the nearby *Green Bough* to do business with the enemy. He'd heard whispers to that effect. Dino had both Irishmen in his Italian pocket. He played one against the other. He knew that by dealing with both they were afraid he might drop them if they stepped out of line. He wasn't a violent man but he always got what he wanted. Someone else would do his dirty work for him. War-torn Italy was a struggle so he emigrated to New York to pursue the American dream. Life was tough. Manhattan could be a dog-fight. He mingled with the Mafia muscle. His tooth was knocked out in a foolish brawl. Later, he had it replaced with a gold tooth. He would plan a bank robbery but never take part in it. He dabbled in drugs and property and quickly amassed a small fortune. His younger brother, Luigi, joined him in the US and he set him up with an antiques shop in Boston. In recent years Dino became involved in a highly profitable venture. With the escalating troubles in Northern Ireland the IRA were desperate to get their hands on weapons. Dino had no interest in the Irish problem but money talks. He'd provide guns if the price was right. There was a huge community of misguided Irish who'd pay anything for guns to help the Irish cause. Money was no object. Getting the guns to Ireland was the problem. Dino came up with the idea of sending them as antiques from Luigi's shop. They had to avoid customs so he tied in the arrival day with different yachting regattas along the Irish coast. In the event of detection of the cargo there was not connection to him; his name was not on any of the paperwork and he remained a model U S citizen.

Dan and Frank Canning waited in the office of the *Green Bough* for the Moretti brothers. They arrived, as usual, bang on time. The money and drugs were exchanged. They had no drink and indulged in very little small-talk. It was their last visit and Dino was conscious of getting the money safe. They were in dangerous territory and an immaculately dressed man like Dino Moretti would be an obvious target. Big Dan Canning could see they were keen to go.

'See you next week,' he said.

'Same time; same place.'

They were gone quietly into the darkness.

It had been a good night's work for Dino in South Boston. He had called to three Italian restaurants and the *Green Bough* was the seventh and last Irish pub on his list. They drove back to his apartment to celebrate. La vita e stata buona.

Chapter Twelve

Shaun Dunne sat in his Ford truck overlooking the Killybegs pier on the coast of Donegal. He ate a leg of chicken and a sandwich as he watched the incoming cluster of fishing boats and scattered yachts limping home through the waves in Indian file. There was great excitement from the onlookers. As he drove through town earlier there had been a festival atmosphere and the streets had been alive with music and colour. At last he picked out the *Colleen Bán* with the help of his binoculars. It fluttered along in the breeze. This time it carried just one box. The last batch was gone.

Everything had gone smoothly as he'd carried out three more trips, delivering much needed guns to his comrades in Derry. He'd followed the same sequence. All he had to do was tie in his visit with a greyhound meeting in Derry and enter *Green for Go* in a race.

He collected the weapons, hid them in the trailer base, and headed north. The only difference this time was that he didn't use the main route through Dublin and on to Newry. The police had taken note of his name and van registration. It could be one trip too many. Each time he took a different entry point crossing the border.

On the second run he avoided the main roads and made the journey up the midlands and on to the isolated check-point at Castlederg in Tyrone and on the third occasion he chose Ballyconnell in Cavan. Both crossings were uneventful. His battered old truck had seen better days and didn't arouse suspicions. The border between the North and South of Ireland was over two hundred miles long. There had once been a labyrinth of side-roads on both sides where anyone could come and go. The authorities decided to put a stop to this. Much to the frustration of both sides of the community every one of those roads was put out of action. Anyone now crossing the border had to do so at an official checkpoint which was manned twenty-four hours a day.

Shaun waited one more hour. He made a mental note to get a new battery for the truck. The present one was beginning to act up. He rummaged through the glove compartment and dug out his favourite photograph, his wife, Eileen, and two-year-old daughter, Orla. He missed her and couldn't wait to get home. The activity had quietened down around the pier. It was time to go. He blessed himself and said a small prayer. He opened the zip underneath his seat, took out the 38, flicked the safety catch on and off a few times, replaced it, and closed the zip. This trip was different from the previous three; the cargo was much smaller and he was not storing it in Cork and then taking it on the long journey north. Killybegs was only a seventy-mile trip to Derry. It was a simple operation taking it straight from the port to Derry, but if anything went wrong it would be much more dangerous. To be caught with guns in the North was a far more serious crime than in the Republic. Yet he felt safe. The cover of the trailer, the old truck, and the dog going racing looked authentic and he was waved through the barriers every time.

He made his way down to the pier and reversed in to the *Colleen Bán*. A man stepped from the yacht and put a wooden box in the back of the truck. Shaun drove off in the direction of Letterkenny. He turned off the road and found a deserted lane where he hid the contents of the box in the trailer base. He broke the box in to small pieces, tore up the invoices into shreds, scattered them along the countryside, and drove south towards the border. As he approached Strabane he could see the checkpoint ahead. He joined the queue. There were two uniformed RUC at the barrier. One walked towards him.

'Could I see your licence, please?' he asked.

Shaun gave it to him with some papers for the race entry. The officer studied them carefully.

'What business have you in Strabane? It's a long road up from Cork? What were you doing in Donegal?' he asked.

'I was calling to see a friend. I'm going to a greyhound meeting in Derry. My dog is in the trailer. He's running in the first race,' Shaun said. 'Turn off your engine and stand away from the vehicle,' he said.

He took out a notebook and glanced through it before consulting the driving licence again. He told Shaun to stay where he was and he walked into a nearby hut and made a phone-call. His colleague looked tense as he watched. The officer put down the phone and walked back towards Shaun.

'Pull your truck off the road and let the traffic through. We want to check something. There's an officer on his way to talk to you,' he said.

Something was wrong. Shaun could smell trouble. He turned the key in the ignition. The engine coughed into life at the second attempt. Shaun stood on the accelerator and the engine roared loudly. He grabbed the wheel and swerved violently across the road but the truck couldn't make it in one turn. By now the RUC officers were running towards him with their revolvers in their hands. As he rammed the gear lever into reverse the engine whimpered and shuddered and cut out. He tore open the zip under his seat, whipped out the 38, and fired several shots at the nearest officer as he tried to start the engine. The officer tumbled to the ground at the side of the truck. The other officer fired a burst at Shaun. The bullets shattered the windscreen and left him hunched over the steering wheel. The remaining glass was spattered with blood. The officer had a quick look at his fallen colleague and ran to the hut to phone for help. There was an eerie silence as the passengers in the queue of cars looked on in disbelief. The only sound was the nervous barking of *Green for Go*.

Steven and Donal stood and admired the inside of the new branch in Boston. Pat McCoy was as good as his word. He'd met him twice and discussed what could be done with the old building. Steven left it with him. He could hardly believe the end result as he stood there in admiration. The agency had been in operation now for the past two days just to break it in. The official opening was an hour away. The caterers were beginning to arrive and get to work. The complete layout was gleaming and ready for action. They strolled around the building and examined every nook and cranny, the beautiful furniture, each office with its own colour scheme. Donal was star-struck with the surroundings.

'Well, Donal, have they anything like that in Spiddal?' Steven asked.

'It's like something from outer fucking space. You'd want sun-glasses in here,' he said.

At first he thought it was a foolish whim bringing Donal to New York as a minder. It turned out to be an inspired move. Donal took his job seriously. He was always available and willing to help, anywhere, anytime. He showed an eagerness to learn and having him around was a comfort. Everybody liked him especially women. On his regular calls to the agency with Steven the female staff always found some excuse to talk to him. He was a man of mystery. They loved his devil-may-care attitude, his 'quaint' accent and some women, in a strange way, found his constant swearing a fascination. Many of these females were immersed in the synthetic world of advertising, and they were drawn to Donal's blunt honesty of the real world. Donal could also play the charmer. Sometimes he'd deliberately open his jacket button to allow his gun to be seen. Some girls were attracted by this sense of danger. He'd gone on a date with one of the girls in the office. The fact that she asked him out surprised him. Steven was aware of this. One night he asked him how he'd got on with his date. He didn't expect Donal to be so coy about it.

'I'll tell you one thing; them American girls aren't one bit shy. By Jaysus, they don't half let you know what they want,' Donal said.

Steven could see that he didn't want to talk about it so he left it go and never brought the subject up again. Outside of his long hours with Steven he kept busy. He still went to target practice. He was now a better shot than Ted. He also attended judo classes and he was quickly working his way up through the relative belts.

The media trickled in and the caterers were now in full swing. Cliff Wickham appeared and took over like Napoleon marshalling his troops. Steven decided it was definitely time to get out from under his feet.

Luigi and Dino Moretti were in a heated discussion. Luigi was about to finish for the day. Business had been bad. They were the only two in the antique shop.

'It wasn't my fault if something went wrong,' Luigi stressed.

'I just got an angry phone call from a certain IRA officer in Belfast that our cover was blown. These individuals would annihilate your knee-caps just for fun. Their courier was put out of action. What if it's traced back to us?' Dino said.

'There's nothing to tie us in with it. The papers are false. There are no names even if the authorities got their hands on them. The contents were down as being sent by Shamrock Advertising and all documentation was to be destroyed on landing. Bill O'Donovan was looking after that side of the deal,' Luigi said.

Dino waved his arms about. He was angry.

'Bill is a mad Irish bastard. It's not our fault. The money was good but we'd be better off out of that arrangement.'

'We'll sit tight until we hear from Bill. Why should we fear anyone? Our family fears no one. They wouldn't put up with any shit from the IRA.'

Dino turned on his younger brother.

'Luigi, I hope you're not fucking around with the IRA.'

Do you think I'm mad, Dino? I'm not that badly off.'

Dino knew that his brother was strapped for cash with increasing gambling debts.

'The shop isn't doing well and the word is you're losing big time.'

'For fuck sake, it's nothing,' Luigi said.

The brothers were so caught up in their argument they hadn't noticed that Steven and Donal had entered the shop and were standing by the front door. Steven gave an exaggerated cough.

'Please excuse us. We were across the street at the agency. The official opening is in half an hour. We'd be delighted if you drop by and share a glass of wine with us.'

Luigi and Dino regained a little composure.

'Please forgive us. We'd be delighted to call over,' Luigi said.

'Will your charming wife be there?' asked Dino.

'She's expecting a baby,' Steven said.

'It's a night for double celebrations then. Lead the way,' Dino said.

Mary was taking no chances. She knew her time was near. She drove carefully through the Long Island traffic and twenty minutes later she turned on to Community Drive in Manhasset and pulled into the car park at NSUH and checked herself in. Three hours later she gave birth to a baby boy. She called him Jeffry. She had chosen that name from the moment she became pregnant. She knew that it would mean so much to her mother. She phoned Steven. He rang Los Angeles. Charlie answered the phone. He quickly told him the good news and asked for Susan. He could hear Charlie calling her.

'Yes, Susan here,' she said.

'Could I ever speak to Granny Bradley, please?' Steven said.

There was a brief silence.

'Granny ...? Is that you, Steven? Does that mean...?' she said.

'I'm ringing to let you know that your gorgeous daughter had a bouncing baby boy. He weighed in at seven pounds and five ounces. Jeff will be delighted to know that he's a granda,' he said..

'What's the baby's name?' she asked.

'Mary is calling him Jeffrey. She said that from the start.'

He could hear her crying as she hung up.

Tim McGrath and Brian Cogan sat in the upstairs room of the *Croppy Boy* pub just outside Athlone. It was a safe house for the IRA. Over the years deals done, plots were hatched, and vital decisions made in this small out of the way room: bank robberies, assassinations and bombings. Members laid low here when they were on the run. It was an ideal location, safe and secluded. Both men were officers in the IRA. Tim was a school teacher and Brian was a respected auctioneer in the town. Tim, the older of the two, watched in silence as his colleague spoke angrily on the phone.

'Something went wrong. Take care of it. If there's a leak in the system fix it. Let me know how you get on. Ok, Liam, talk to you soon. Slán.'

Brian hung up.

'At least he took one of them with him. If there's a mole he must be exterminated. Liam O'Donovan is a bit hot-headed but he'll sort it out. Surely one of our own wouldn't rat on us?' Tim said.

'It's happened before in the States with a star-spangled Paddy, some lily-livered fucker with a drink problem. Liam has someone in mind.'

'We'll have to look after Eileen and Shaun's little girl.'

'I must get back to work. Keep in touch,' Brian said.

The two men left quietly by the side door.

Mary sat on the step in her garden playing with her little baby. Jeffry gurgled with happiness as he gripped her finger. She picked him up in her arms as she heard the familiar voices by the back door. She was quickly surrounded by Susan and Jeff and Louise. Steven stood back.

'You're looking good, Lou, what's happening?' Mary said.

'I'm hanging in there. Emma sends her love. She couldn't make it. She's selling houses like hotcakes.'

'I miss our tennis matches. It was so much fun kicking your ass,' Mary said.

'I'll let you in on a secret. I deliberately took it easy on you. You kicked up such a rumpus when you lost I felt sorry for you,' Louise said.

Mary gave her dad a hug. He looked well and tanned from all those hours on the golf course.

'Why don't you guys go in and have a drink. Louise and I have a lot of catching up to do,' Mary.

Jeff, Steven and Susan went in to the kitchen.

'Well, how's your love life?' Mary said.

'Emma and I couldn't be happier. She'd have loved to see you but she didn't want to spoil your day,' Louise said.

Louise told her that Susan wanted nothing to do with Emma. They had many arguments about it.

'She hasn't accepted her yet. I can't believe it,' Mary said.

'She's keeps trying to fix me up with blokes. If it's not the postman it's the bank manager,' Louise said.

'How are Marie and young Steven?' Mary said.

'Marie does some part-time modelling. Mum looks after the baby. She'd adopt him if she could. You better keep an eye on Jeffrey or she'll take him back to Los Angeles with her,' Louise said.

'Marie is amazing,' Mary said.

'I hate her. God must have been an Irish woman,' Louise said. 'She'd eat a horse, yet she's wafer thin and gorgeous.'

They went in to the kitchen to join the others. Steven and Jeff were in the corner talking golf.

'You must be scratch with all that practice,' Steven said.

'I'm ten at the moment but I still can't get near Charlie,' Jeff said.

'I saw more of that man when he was working,' Susan said. 'Charlie is getting married so he'll have to change his tune.'

'Did he set a date?' Mary said.

'No, but it's definitely the high jump for him. He had a good innings. He can't be happy all his life,' Jeff said.

'Well, honey, you know where the door is. I have my own little darling man here,' Susan said kissing Jeffry.

'Come on, Jeff, I want your advice,' Steven said.

They made their way outside to the bench.

I'd like your opinion on something,' Steven said.

Steven was surprised when Jeff started laughing and put his arm around his shoulder.

'You're a born Taurus. You ask me for advice. You listen carefully and then you go and do exactly what you want to do.'

'I've been doing some work for John Maloney in Chicago. He worked with my father years ago in the railway. John runs a pub, *The Paddock*, just off Belmont Avenue,' Steven said.

'Don't tell me you're buying a pub,' Jeff said.

'No, well, yes. John's wife died last year. He's offered me the pub for half nothing. It seems that my father once did him a big favour. He'd like to spend his old age in Florida. We're meeting in Bill's bar on Friday to close the deal. Donal is coming with me.'

'Will the premises be big enough?' Jeff said.

'There's a yard behind the pub. It was once a stable. John has given me first refusal,' Steven said.

'Why do I have the feeling that no matter what I say you're going to buy this pub?' Jeff said.

'I want the deal done on Saturday. My mind is made up,' Steven said.

'I rest my case,' Jeff said. 'Come on, they'll spoil that son of yours. Good luck on Saturday. Watch your back.'

Jeff made up his mind. He'd have a word with Ted Dynan later.

Luigi Moretti was tidying up at the back of his shop. It had been another quiet day. He lit another cigarette. He was preparing to close for the day when he heard the bell as the front door opened. It was Liam O'Donovan. Luigi hardly recognised him. He was wearing an overcoat and a hat pulled down over his face. Luigi shook his hand.

'Hello, Liam. Are you interested in antiques?'

'I don't trust the antique business.'

'A little bird told me you might be interested in doing a bit more business with heroin,' Luigi said.

Liam asked Luigi if they could go somewhere to discuss terms. Luigi was delighted; at last his run of bad luck was changing. He had his own supply of heroin stashed away. No one knew about it, not even his brother, Dino. He locked the front door, switched off the shop lights, and showed Liam to a room where items were prepared and packed. Luigi quickly opened the safe. When he turned around Liam was pointing a gun at him. He waved the gun towards a chair. Luigi noticed he was wearing gloves.

'Sit down,' Liam said.

He found a roll of duct tape on a shelf and wrapped it around Luigi's body several times binding him to the chair. He did the same with his legs. Luigi squirmed in the chair.

'There's not much money there, a few hundred dollars. If you're that bad for a fix take the stash. Be my guest.'

'I don't take drugs. They're bad for the health,' Liam said.

'What do you want?' Luigi said.

Liam slowly walked around the chair. He was angry.

'I heard you were a naughty boy. You hung us out to dry. A friend of mine is dead because of you and your big Italian mouth.'

'That's not true.'

Liam smacked Luigi across the face with the gun. Blood spurted from his mouth. He screamed with pain as he slumped back in the chair.

'Fuck you,' Luigi said. 'You're full of patriotic crap, with your bellies full of drink. You must feel like a big boy now with your gun; big brave bullshit. I'm three times your age.'

'Your big mouth will get you into trouble,' Liam said.

'If you had a brain you'd know I'd never tell anyone,' Luigi said.

Liam's face flushed with anger. He struck Luigi again. His head fell forward but he surprised Liam by laughing, a loud high-pitched laugh.

'You brainless fucking idiot. I was getting good money from your people. Why would I squeal and cut my own throat?'

'That's what I want to find out,' Liam said

He punched him full in the face with his free hand. The blow broke his nose. Blood pumped down his clothes. Liam shouted at him.

'Who got to you? Who paid you your twelve pieces of silver, you miserable bastard?'

'No one paid me. I did nothing.'

Liam took a step nearer and held out the gun at arm's length.

Luigi begged for his life.

'Stop and think. You hate the English. I can make them suffer. I can arrange to have a bomb in a crate delivered to London and detonated anywhere you like. Give me the chance to prove myself.'

Liam shot him twice in the chest.

'You can't be trusted. Arrivederci, Judas.'

The force of the bullets caused Luigi's chair to topple back. Liam took the money and the heroin from the safe and knocked over the furniture to make it seem like a robbery. He pulled down his hat and turned up his overcoat collar and calmly walked the few blocks to his parked car.

Dino Moretti knew something was wrong. He'd phoned his brother at home. He wasn't there and he wasn't answering his phone in the shop. He paid a quick call to find out what was happening. When he pulled up outside he was surprised to find the shop in darkness and the front door unlocked. The light was on in the back room. He hurried in and was shocked to see Luigi on the ground. He struggled to lift the chair upright. His brother was alive but his face was covered in blood and bruises. His nose was swelled and out of shape.

'Who did this, the IRA? You're lucky to be alive,' Dino said.

Luigi groped in his breast pocket and took out his silver cigarette holder. The case was warped with two dents in the middle.

'I am lucky to be alive.'

'I'll get you straight to hospital to get that face fixed,' Dino said.

'No hospital, no police,' Luigi said.

Dino knew a friendly doctor. He was angry.

'Who did this?'

'Bill's son, Liam O'Donovan,' Luigi said.

'That arrogant little bastard. Leave this to me,' Dino said.

Liam O'Donovan dialled a number and listened impatiently to the dial tone. At last Brian Cogan picked up the phone. He said nothing.

'I'm ringing to let you know that the job is done. It was nasty but the leak is now fixed,' Liam said.

'I hope it wasn't too much of a problem.'

'It won't give you any more trouble.'

'Can you tell me who you were dealing with?'

'Luigi was in charge but he has now departed the scene.'

'I'll be in touch if I need you again,' Brian said and hung up.

Liam was pleased. He was moving up the ladder.

The christening ceremony was a simple affair. They chose St Mary's Catholic Church on Vernon Boulevard. Mary had called there a few times with Steven and she was impressed. Little Jeffrey was unimpressed and bawled his head off as the water was being pour over his head. It was an intimate gathering. Later they went back to Steven's house for a small celebration.

'It's dinner time for the little fellow,' Steven said.

He took the baby and left the room.

'Mary, you have Steven well trained,' Jeff said.

'He feeds him, changes his diapers, puts him to bed, gets up at all hours if he cries. I'm redundant.'

'We spent years chasing our tails. Then suddenly they're all grown up and gone,' Susan said.

'Time flies when you're having fun,' Jeff said.

'It wasn't all fun,' Susan said.

Mary got up to leave the room.

'I better check to see if he's alright.'

She made her way down the hall to the bedroom. She peeped in through the half-open door to see Steven sitting on the bed feeding the baby.

'Come on, champ, drink up. It's you and me against the world. Some day you might even run for president, that is if you want to. You'll have to visit Ireland. We'll walk up and down the hills of Cork. That's where your old man lived. Did I ever tell you about my dad? He'd have loved you. He'd bring home a sick little puppy and feed him with a baby's milk bottle and he'd tell him bed-time stories until he went to sleep. He'd have loved you.'

The bottle was empty and the child was asleep in his arms. As Mary went back down the hall she realised how much she loved the two men in her life.

Big Dan Canning was a man of few words. He scratched his head as he put down the phone in his pub. He was confused. He was slow to trust anyone. He didn't make friends easily. He'd hardly ever had two words with Dino Moretti, and now Dino rang him and wanted to meet him for his advice. Dan was no fool. Dino happened to be conveniently nearby and wanted a quick word. Dan was suspicious. The bar was quiet so he decided to wait in his office. Dino was as good as his word. Within five minutes he knocked on the office door and entered. Dan looked even more intimidating in the small room.

'Can you recommend someone to do a little job for me, Dan? He'll be well paid but he must keep his mouth shut.'

'What kind of a job?'

'I want someone quietly disposed of,' Dino said.

Dan was irritated.

'Will you come to the fucking point?'

'I want a certain individual dead,' Dino said.

Dan didn't trust him.

'Who?'

'Liam O'Donovan,' Dino said.

Dan became very interested. He hated the O'Donovans.

'Why?'

'That bastard tried to kill my brother. In fact, he thinks he killed him. It's about time this little shit was taught a lesson. Can you find someone to do the job? Dino said.

'If the price is right. I have someone in mind.'

'Can I depend on him?' Dino asked.

'Yes, but he won't come cheap.'

Dino took a wad of money from his pocket and handed it to Dan.

'Five thousand should make it worth his while. Here's two thousand five hundred dollars. He'll get the same when the job is done. My name must not be mentioned. This has nothing to do with me.'

Dan flicked through the bundle of notes. He knew someone who was perfect for the job.

Steven and Donal arrived in Logan Airport at midday on Saturday. Steven was excited about what lay ahead, another branch, another city. Bill O'Donovan and John Maloney were waiting for them. John flew in from Chicago the night before. He'd already had a few Guinness. The pub was smoky and half-full. Bill showed Steven to a table and went to get the drinks. Liam O'Donovan sat at a nearby table involved in a game of cards. John Maloney was enjoying this. He stood up and called for order. The bar went quiet with curiosity.

'Could I have a small bit of hush and buckets of shush. I'd like to sing a song in honour of a good friend of mine.'

After a bout of coughing he blasted out a passionate version of the ballad, *Danny Boy*. When he finished there was a round of applause. Donal patted him on the back.

'That was your father's favourite song. You should have heard him sing it; what a voice,' John said to Steven.

Steven found it strange that he'd never heard his father singing; he hadn't very much to sing about. The bar settled down again to a steady drone of conversation. Suddenly a voice came from the front door. Everybody turned around. Liam O'Donovan froze. Dan Canning stood there smiling, towering over him. He wore a large hat and a long black coat hanging open. There was an eerie silence; a frightening anticipation.

'Hello, Liam, I have a message from Luigi for you but I decided to deliver it myself,' Dan said.

Liam stood up and turned to run. Dan took a HK21 machine gun from inside his coat. Its blackness glinted in the dull light. He fired a short burst at Liam. The impact sent him flying across the bar. Bill stooped behind the counter for his revolver but Dan spotted him and raked him with bullets. Donal jumped up to try and protect Steven by pulling him to the ground under the table. He pulled out his gun but Dan took no chances. He shot him dead. In the screaming confusion no one noticed the elderly man sitting in the corner. Ted Dynan whipped out the gun he had taped to his ankle and fired all in the one movement. Dan was a big target. Two bullets struck him in the chest. His body jerked and he staggered a few steps and stumbled forward. As he fell he let out one final burst before he hit the ground. The bullets crashed across the opposite wall and shattered the mirror where Ted was sitting. Some people became hysterical. They ran out on to the safety of the street. John Maloney sat there pale-faced and numb with shock. Steven stood helpless by the table trying to come to terms with what had happened. His head was dizzy. His ears were pounding. Donal Purcell lay motionless by his feet in a pool of blood. Liam O'Donovan's body was crumpled under a smashed table. Ted Dynan was covered in glass under the window by the far wall. Bill O'Donovan's legs were sticking grotesquely half-out the counter door. Dan Canning lay face down stretched in a lifeless heap by the front door. It was as if a bomb had exploded in the bar; it was a wreck, broken furniture and glass, and injured people calling out for help. Police sirens could be heard in the distance. As Steven stood there spattered with blood, Jeff's words haunted him; *watch your back.*

Chapter Thirteen

Steven Kennedy sat on the bench in the back garden of his home in Long Island. It had been a good day at the agency. Mary had been begging him to take it easy. They didn't need the money. He was on his third whiskey which was unusual for him. He was in a reflective mood. So much had happened in the last twenty years. He couldn't believe it; twenty years. Where did they go? They seemed to have flown by in a flash. He smiled at the thought that he was now almost fifty and going grey. Maybe the whiskey fuelled his nostalgia but for some strange reason he dwelt on his father, his raggy old jumper, the cap perched on his head, the cursed cigarette stuck in his mouth, hobbling down Fair Hill, late for mass to worship God, a God who didn't do him any favours. His father was a man who had few ups and many downs; a man who never had much. Yet he was happy with his lot, laughed at life, and worried about nothing. No matter what his God threw at him he just smiled.

Health is wealth.

Steven wished he had his father's attitude but he was more like his mother, a worrier.

It was a beautiful New York twilight; the sun was sinking in the sky; shadows danced across the garden. He was tempted to move many times but Mary loved her home in Long Island. It was her nest, each twig moulded with her own hands. She had given up writing. Steven laughed at her excuse; to concentrate on raising her family. He should have introduced her to Lizzie Maloney in Well Lane. She had seventeen children, yet she had a part-time job scrubbing the floor of the cathedral seven mornings a week. Lately he longed to return to Cork like a salmon at sea making the long journey back to his spawning ground. As he could barely swim he smiled at this analogy. Recently he'd been feeling full of remorse about the night he shot Rick Guardino and his friend. The memory wouldn't go away. It took him a long time to finally get over that awful night in *Paddy's Bar.* The police finally shut down the bar. The biggest tragedy was Donal Purcell's death. He arranged to have the body flown back to Ireland. He travelled with the coffin to Shannon and drove the rest of the way to Spiddal in the heart of Connemara. Donal was laid to rest alongside his father's grave. His elderly mother was distraught with grief. She had been so excited as she saw him off on his big adventure to America. At last her little boy was going to make something of himself. Now all her dreams were shattered. She stood there hunched in her thoughts, her white hair shuddering in the sea breeze. It helped when Steven explained how her son had saved his life. Everybody missed Donal. He made everyone laugh.

Ted Dynan was another brave man. He'd lived a life fraught with danger. It was still sad to see him go in this manner. Steven wondered if it was all out in front of him, all laid out as part of God's greater plan. He laughed as he remembered another one of his father's sayings; *every dog has his day.* How right he was. Jeff was now dead almost five years. He'd eventually made it down to six handicap. He collapsed on the golf course. He'd have wanted to go that way. Susan was never the same after losing her husband and she died in her sleep twelve months later. The family home was left to Louise. Emma moved in with her and they lived happily together. Richard Steinman remarried and retired and he was replaced by Harry Martin. Harry surprised everyone and the branch went from strength to strength. He'd been given a second chance and he grabbed it with both hands. The biggest surprise was Charlie Grainger. He married his sweetheart, Sarah, and he was now the father of three daughters. He still lived on the Bradley estate. Cliff Wickham was thriving at the Boston branch. The Chicago agency and the newest branch in Detroit were both doing well after slow starts. Steven was especially pleased with this success because there was hardly any Irish influence involved and this proved that the agency had what it takes. Jeff had left Steven the apartments in New York and London and the remaining money was to be divided between Mary and Louise. Marie had moved permanently to New York and lived in the apartment with her son. Young Steven had now turned twenty-one. He was a fine golfer and Jeff had set him up with his own sports shop in Manhattan. He specialised in golf equipment. Marie still had what it takes in the modelling world and the camera still loved her. In New York there was a booming market in clothes for the older woman. She never married.

Steven knew they had more than enough money to last them a lifetime but he was still restless, still chasing rainbows. Mary kept reminding him of this and she hinted that he could easily afford to retire. Their son,

Jeffry, was doing business studies in Harvard and he was caught up in his own life, living with his girlfriend in their own apartment. Steven begged him to join the agency but he wanted to wait until he graduated before he made any decision. Steven hadn't gone near Southie Boston since that awful night. The IRA in Dublin cancelled all gun-running from Boston. They were ruffling too many bureaucratic feathers. The flow of dollars still made its way to help the cause. When Brendan Doyle heard about the shooting he just shrugged his shoulders and said, 'shit happens.' Steven called to the *Harp Bar* one night just to say hello. It was remembered as just another incident in a long line of incidents. Nothing changed. The same old Brendan was still there serving pints of Guinness and doing what he did. That was the last time Steven set foot in Hell's Kitchen. That night left an indelible mark. It was time to stop dicing with the devil.

Steven could hear voices coming from the kitchen. Mary stuck her head out the backdoor.

'Is my workaholic husband learning to relax at last?' she said.

'We had a good day at the office. Is Marie with you?'

'She's having a quick cuppa before she runs.'

'I'll join you,' he said and they went in to the kitchen.

Marie was preparing three cups of coffee.

'I'm thinking of a visit home next weekend,' she said to Steven.

'Any particular reason to see the old sod?' he asked.

'I got a letter from Paul yesterday. I'm worried about him. Steven wants to come with me. It'll be a nice holiday for him,' she said.

'I'd love to visit Ireland,' Mary said.

'We'll go to Cork someday. It's a little bit quieter than New York but you'll like it,' Steven said.

'I'll hold you to that,' Mary said.

The Aer Lingus flight from New York made a perfect landing at Dublin Airport. There was a round of applause from the passengers. As they made their way down the steps Marie and her son, Steven, were greeted by a soft shower of rain. The bus weaved its way through the busy streets of Dublin to Heuston Station and they caught the 10.30 train to Cork. It was a packed train bubbling with noisy students determined to enjoy the bank holiday Monday. Steven had a seat by the window and he was fascinated at the greenness of the landscape and the cattle grazing so close to the tracks. He could see for miles across the flatness of the midlands. In no time they were clipping through the rugged terrain of County Cork. As they approached Buttevant Marie put her arm around Steven's shoulder.

'We're nearly there; home sweet home,' she said.

She didn't know what happened next. It was a blur. Everything was in slow motion. She could hear screams piercing the darkness. Everything went black. She was numb and unable to move as if she was trapped in a nightmare. She tried to reach out to Steven but she was groping at nothing. He wasn't there. Suddenly there was silence, a hollow, strange silence.

Steven Kennedy was at home looking at the television as he finished his breakfast. Mary was still in bed. A news flash interrupted the programme: Words like 'Ireland's worse rail disaster' and 'Dublin to Cork train crash at Buttevant' jumped out at him. The announcer continued: 'the emergency services in the North Cork town say that at the moment there are 18 dead and over 70 people injured.' He gave a number to ring for anyone making enquiries. Steven jotted it down and rang it. It was the police station at the Bridewell Barracks in Cork. He was told it was too early to know anything for definite but if he left his number someone would ring him back. He woke Mary and told her. She dressed and joined him in the kitchen and they waited. After what seemed like an eternity the phone rang. It was from the Bridewell. As he spoke Mary could see the horror in his face. The policeman's voice was sympathetic: 'Marie Kennedy was badly injured. She is currently in the Mercy Hospital but I'm afraid Steven Kennedy was killed in the crash. His body has been removed to the morgue in the South Infirmary. I'm very sorry for your loss.'

Steven replaced the phone and sat down. He looked drained and avoided Mary's eyes.

'Marie is fine but Steven didn't make it. He's dead,' he said.

'Sweet Jesus, how much more does Marie have to suffer? The poor boy; what did she do to deserve this?' she said.

'I'm getting the first plane to Ireland,' he said.

'I'm coming with you. Marie will need all the support she can get,' Mary said.

They landed in Shannon Airport on Tuesday morning. Steven hired a car and drove to Cork. They decided to stop first at his Uncle Con's house in Cattle Market Lane. He'd have all the news. Steven knew Shamrock House would be packed with people. All his life Con worked as a cobbler from his little cottage. He knew everything about everyone. He said the bit of work kept him 'above ground.' Steven learned that the crash was a freak accident. The three carriages at the front of the train were derailed and jack-knifed into each other. Marie and Steven were seated here. His nephew died instantly. Marie was in a coma. Steven drove straight to the

Mercy Hospital. Marie was in a small private ward. She looked frail in the big bed. Her face was ashen and her head was covered in bandages. Mary was heart-broken. The doctor explained that broken bones were generally no problem. They'd heal in time. Head injuries were different, but they were hopeful of a full recovery. He reminded them that rest was essential. Steven decided to head for home. Family and friends would be expecting him. As Steven left the ward he turned back to see Mary holding Marie's hand and quietly talking to her.

Steven was saddened at the condition of Shamrock House. The front gate was broken and covered with rust. The path was overgrown with weeds. The old house looked dilapidated, covered with ivy, and the roof had several missing slates. His brothers had returned from England. They looked well. They all had scattered families now and getting on with their lives. Youngest brother, Paul, was sitting on his own by the window drinking whiskey. He did not look well. Steven was told that Brian and John had made the funeral arrangements. He would have liked to have been consulted.

The removal was from O'Connor's Funeral Home at the bottom of Shandon Street and the burial, after mass at the cathedral, was to be at Curraghkippane Cemetery. The funeral home was packed with mourners, heads bowed, Rosary beads clutched in their hands. Steven felt suffocated. He was angry. He didn't join in the Rosary. He didn't mumble any prayers for the dead. He had one last look at his nephew and left.

Chapter Fourteen

Mass finished at the cathedral. It had been a long mass. Funeral masses usually were. Steven Kennedy and his brothers, Brian, John and Paul shouldered the coffin down the aisle with several priests, family and friends traipsing behind in Indian file. It was a struggle to get through the crowd at the back of the church. Sad organ music could be heard from high up in the gallery. The distant voice of a woman was singing Ave Maria. The window frame still rattled. A strong wind still blustered outside the cathedral as Steven stood under the weather-beaten bust of the old bishop. The coffin was placed in the waiting hearse at the bottom of the stone steps. It was covered with flowers. Many of his old friends had emigrated, but it was good to see Pat O'Callaghan again. Strangers approached Steven, slipped him a mass card, and vanished into the crowd. Steven escaped to his own car and sat in silence watching the unfolding ritual outside. How could a loving God allow this to happen?

What the hell was God up to?

Was God playing tricks?

If anything went wrong his mother used to say 'God is good'. You can say that again, Steven thought. I'd hate to see him if He was bad. Steven was bitter. Was this a delayed punishment by God for his two murders? Was this payback time? Was God laughing at him?

A long line of cars slowly followed the hearse up Cathedral Road, on to Blarney Street, through Clogheen village, and down the narrow road to the Curraghkippane Cemetery. Throughout the journey onlookers stopped and blessed themselves as the funeral passed. The coffin was carried down the rocky path as it twisted and turned to the family grave in the far corner and the boy was united with his grandparents.

Steven stood at the back of the congregation. He had been here many times as a child surrounded by headstones he knew so well. The view of the Lee Valley spreading into the distance still took his breath away; the lazy River Lee winding through the green meadows disappearing into the horizon. He stood there, head bowed, it was over.

There was nothing he could say.

There was nothing he could do.

He felt helpless.

The mourners dispersed; scattered back up the slope. Steven had enough sorrow and sad memories to last him a lifetime. He called to see Mary at the hospital. He couldn't believe it when he saw Marie propped up in bed with Mary spoon-feeding her from a bowl of porridge. He looked at Mary, his eyes full of questions.

'Sorry, does she...?' he asked.

'The doctor told her when she came round. He felt it was better to be honest from the start,' Mary aid.

Marie was numb with drugs. She looked as if she was still in a trance.

'I can't believe my son is dead. We were laughing and joking one minute. Then I don't know what happened. The darkness was frightening, the crunching of metal, the voices crying out for help, someone was lying across me, I think they were dead. I couldn't move, the pain was awful, and then the horrible silence.'

Steven held her hand.

'Will you come back to New York? Our house is your house.'

'My poor boy, I can't leave my son all alone by himself.'

A doctor appeared in the ward to have a look at her. He took them aside and told them she had a nasty head injury, a broken leg and cracked ribs. He stressed that she needed plenty of rest and ushered them out.

Steven's car was parked nearby.

'Shamrock House will have wall to wall mourners. We'll book into a hotel later. Come on, I'll show you the playground of my youth.' He said.

He drove up to Sun Valley Drive where she could see how run-down the family home had become. The car crawled up Fair Hill. As a boy he used to cycle up that hill. He continued on foot past Knockpogue – *the hill of the kisses* – until the road twisted down to the fair field and on to the Blackstone Bridge. They made their way alongside the stream on Killeens Road where they dodged furze bushes, crossed the water on stepping stones, struggled up a steep field and climbed a gate at the top of Nash's Road to the Veranda where spectators could observe the distant drag-hunts. Steven took her hand. He led her up a boreen, through a jungle of foliage, until they emerged back out onto Fair Hill. Mary felt as if she was standing at the top of a mountain. On her right she could see Blarney Castle. Down below, the twin towers of the cathedral and Shandon steeple seemed to pierce the sky, and off to the left was the sprawling harbour. The strangest sight was the city directly below them like a saucer surrounded by water. Mary stood there silently for some time.

'I'm falling in love with this place,' she said.

He called to the old house to show Mary and he wanted a word with Paul. He introduced her to his brothers and showed her around the house. Paul was in bed with a bottle of whiskey.

'It's not the Waldorf but it served its purpose,' Steven said.

'It must have been an exciting place to grow up in,' Mary said.

'Life was different then. We were poor but we survived, mainly because of our parents. They showered us with love,' he said.

'You don't know how lucky you were. All the money in the world can't buy you love,' Mary said.

She joined the mourners in the front room. They were still singing. She loved the way they celebrated death in Ireland. It was so natural; the end of one chapter and moving on to the next. Brian and Paul were having a good-natured argument in the corner. After all these years they still could never agree. Pat, always the shy one, lingered silently on the verge of the conversation. Steven went upstairs and woke Paul. He was groggy and didn't know where he was for a moment.

'Welcome to the land of the living. How are you?' Steven asked.

'I've been better,' Paul said.

'I know the feeling.' Steven said.

'How's Marie? Tough break, poor kid,' Paul said.

'She'll need your help,' Steven said. 'Look after her until she's strong enough to cope. She's pumped up with pain-killers but when the cold light of day arrives she'll need a shoulder to cry on. Paul, be there for her. Ring me every day. There's an envelope downstairs for you. Can I depend on you?' Steven said.

'I'll look after her. I need something to keep me on the straight and narrow,' Paul said.

Steven gave him a hug and told him go back to sleep.

Steven sat in his New York office. It had been two months since the train crash. The memory of the tragic death of his nephew wouldn't go away. He couldn't get Marie out of his mind. It was a dreary existence in an old house with too many ghosts. Paul was as good as his word but he had a job and Marie was by herself most of the day. Her leg was in plaster and she struggled on her crutches. The cemetery was four miles away and full of rocks to make life more difficult. She went every day to tell her son how much she missed him.

Steven looked out the window of his office. It was a hive of activity. They were a great team, each of them delighted to be an important link in

Steven's ever-growing chain. Mary often joked that if he ever went away for a month he wouldn't be missed. Lately he was beginning to realise she was right. He left work earlier than usual. When he got home Mary was on the phone. He filled two glasses of wine and waited for her to finish. She sipped her wine and looked at her watch.

'Is the boss sneaking off before his time? What did a girl do to deserve this? Next thing I'll know you'll be trying to lure me into the bedroom.'

'Sit down,' he said.

'This is serious.'

'It is serious.'

'Is there something wrong?'

'You know how you're always saying the agency could run itself without me.'

'Yes,' she laughed, 'and it would probably make more money.'

He finished his wine and sat down near her.

'Several companies have been trying to buy us out. I wasn't interested. Lately I wonder where I'm going. Maybe young Steven's death triggered this off. Is the great puppeteer in the sky pulling strings again? Is God teasing us? Last month, I was invited to meet the Saatchi and Saatchi people. They made me an offer. I refused. They called to my office this morning. They want to buy out Shamrock Ads for an amazing amount of money. I must give them an answer tomorrow.'

Mary filled another glass of wine.

'I can see that old gleam in your eye,' she said.

'I insisted that I had to see my wife first and if I was to accept their offer every one of my staff would keep his job.'

'What have you in mind? I'm afraid to ask,' she said.

His mind was miles away.

'It's up to you. We could live the rest of our lives in Cork. You can buy a yacht, go back writing. I know you miss it. You can do whatever you want and you'll have me all to yourself.'

She laughed and clicked her fingers.

'Just like that.'

'When we were over for the funeral I noticed an acre of land at the top of Fair Hill. We can build a house there, any kind of house you want. You tell me. I'll start the ball rolling.'

'Four bedrooms, a swimming pool,' she said.

'Whatever you want. We'll fly over for a few days and I'll show you the real Cork. I want to look in on Marie.'

'When do you want to know?'

'Tomorrow will be fine.'

'Give a girl a chance to pack a bag.'

He reminded her that it would be a big change; no sunshine, no Queens, Fifth Avenue or Macys but, against that, the fresh air at the top of Fair Hill was supposed to be a well-known aphrodisiac.

'Where's my suit-case. You've just convinced me,' she said.

The following day, surrounded by solicitors, Steven signed the contracts. The staff was surprised but happy that their jobs were safe. He phoned Cliff Wickham and asked him to oversee the change-over. He felt comfortable with everything in Cliff's capable hands.

Steven and an architect stood in the mud at the top of Fair Hill. They were busy measuring a section of the site with a long tape. Both wore wellington boots. It was raining. The architect was taking notes as he went along.

'That's everything for the time being. I'll be talking to the builder. You'll be facing south, the view is staggering, and griselinia hedge all round to set it off. Ring me if there's anything else,' he said.

Steven drove down the hill to home. Mary and Marie were sitting on the sofa looking at the television. Paul was at work.

'Come on, girls, I'm in the mood for a guided tour,' he said.

Marie refused. She was going to the cemetery later. Steven was like a schoolboy as he set off around the city. He pointed out places of historical interest to Mary. Some of the place-names fascinated her: Peacock Lane, Fish Street, Man's Lane, Cutthroat Alley, Bulldog Lane, Hangdog Road, Sober Lane, Toffee Apple Hill and Elbow Lane.

He then decided to take her on a flying tour of the nearby coastline. First stop was Youghal where he spent half his childhood. Mary loved the winding streets. They had a coffee in the *Nook* pub, snuggled up a lane, off a lane. He once had a drink here, his first and only drink with his father. Redbarn strand stretched for miles. He drove over by the lighthouse to Ballycotton Beach and on past Crosshaven surrounded by a fleet of yachts. He made his way down the twisting road until he pulled into his favourite pub in Ireland – *Bunnyconellen's* – named after the previous owner's three children – Bunny, Con and Ellen. It was tucked into the rocks high on the cliff face overlooking the sea. Across the way stood Cobh, with the spire of the cathedral reaching into the clouds, the last port of call for the tragic Titanic.

He ordered corn beef and cabbage.

Mary loved it.

Later he crawled along the narrow mountain path to Fountainstown and on to Robert's Cove, a gem, hidden away from everywhere, around the corner was the Spanish-looking town of Kinsale surrounded by a labyrinth of lanes, a gourmet paradise, spattered with delightful eating houses. He quickly made his way to Rosscarbery and the rugged Red Strand on the edge of Clonakilty. Mary kissed him on the cheek.

'I give in. You've convinced me,' she said.

'We've only scratched the surface. There will be great days ahead of us,' he said.

After four days an exhausted Mary returned to New York. She now stood back and saw it through different eyes. Marie surprised everyone. She also went back to New York. She said it was time to start living again. She owed it to her son. The past had passed, nothing could be done to change it. The future would look after itself. She wanted to begin living in the now. She loved the buzz of Manhattan. It would help her to forget.

Steven stayed in Shamrock House for another week. He had enjoyed meeting his brothers. Sadly, it took a tragedy to bring them together. He later met the decorators to make sure everyone knew what Mary wanted. She had a long list of what was needed and where to get it.

Saatchi and Saatchi agreed that he could stay on until it suited him to go. After two months he finally got word from Cork that his house was ready. Mary flew over with her list and her plans; the right painting for here, the proper mirror for there, the appropriate figurine for the hall. She walked all over the house and purred with satisfaction. Steven had one more task. He phoned the Cork City Council and told them to demolish his old home before it fell down. He said his goodbyes to friends and staff and left quickly. It took him two days to get his affairs in order and, with mixed feelings, he flew to Ireland. Filled with anticipation he drove up Shandon Street and onto Sun Valley Drive.

It was strange to see the old home gone forever, flattened. He stopped for a while and looked around. He could hear the noise, the prattle of voices, the laughter, always the laughter, his mother with her pot of stew, and waving her big wooden spoon in the air, conducting her orchestra of hungry children, *the fastest man gets the most,* Agoo Murphy, Lizzie Maloney, *your eyes are bigger than your belly*, his father strutting, boasting about his boxing heroes, Joe Louis and Rocky Marciano, puffing on his cigarette as he handed out chocolates on a Friday night, his wife giving out to him, *never bolt your door with a boiled carrot.*

Steven had seen enough. It was time to bury the ghosts. There was a light drizzle as he walked across the green at the top of Fair Hill. He saw it for the first time; a brass plaque on one of the pillars – *Shamrock House*. His heart skipped a beat. He strode up the path. A row of daffodils hugged each other in the corner of the garden. He smiled when he saw the sapling apple tree swaying in the light breeze. The front door was open.

Mary was on the phone. He had never seen her so lovely, her eyes sparkling, on fire, dancing. When she saw him she put her hand over the mouthpiece.

'I'm talking to Louise. Have a look at the master bedroom. We must christen the bed. It's an old Irish custom,' she said and went back to her conversation.

He was amazed when he saw what she'd done; an electrically heated toilet seat, Mozart music in the bathroom. He'd built a house but she'd created a home. When he'd finished his inspection she was still on the phone, giggling like a schoolgirl; two sisters so far apart and yet so near. Steven shrugged his shoulders and went out to the front garden. He sat on the wooden bench and looked down Fair Hill and out over the city. He thought back on that wet night when he was a hungry child following a man up that hill for the remains of his apple. The wheel had turned full circle. At last he'd found true happiness. He reminded himself that this day was the first day of the rest of his life. The rain stopped. A rainbow appeared and lit up the sky. He laughed out loud. He felt like putting his hand up and grabbing the rainbow. Life was good.

Lightning Source UK Ltd.
Milton Keynes UK
UKOW04f1935010614

232645UK00001B/40/P

9 781622 876273